Who Killed Bob Lawson?

Alex M. and Ethel S. Arnett

Revised and completed by
Georgia Arnett Bonds

*For Nora and Jay
with best wishes from
Georgiana Arnett Bonds*

VANTAGE PRESS
New York

This is a work of fiction, although the places and locales mentioned are genuine and historically accurate. Any similarity between the names and characters in this book and any persons, living or dead, is purely coincidental.

Cover design by Susan Thomas

FIRST EDITION

All rights reserved, including the right of
reproduction in whole or in part in any form.

Copyright © 2003 by Georgia Arnett Bonds

Published by Vantage Press, Inc.
516 West 34th Street, New York, New York 10001

Manufactured in the United States of America
ISBN: 0-533-14420-5

Library of Congress Catalog Card No.: 2002093926

0 9 8 7 6 5 4 3 2 1

To Carey George Arnett

Screven County, Georgia

June, 1936

Dear Carey:

Here is our account of *Who Killed Bob Lawson?* which we have so often talked about with you.

You will notice that we have held true to the local geography and general character of the region in the 1930s. But you know, of course, that all the characters are fictitious. While some of them bear resemblances to real people in that locality, it is not intended to represent any actual person, living or dead.

We are deeply indebted to you for all the valuable suggestions that you have made, especially in matters of local color.

—Alex and Ethel

Contents

	Preface	vii
I.	"Welcome to God's Country"	1
II.	All Sorts of People	11
III.	One Side of a Triangle	24
IV.	The Ghost Oak	35
V.	Midnight Talk	54
VI.	Another Side of the Triangle	67
VII.	Other People's Money	74
VIII.	Rendezvous with a Bootlegger	82
IX.	In the Old Lawson Yard	88
X.	At the Hendrix Distillery	101
XI.	Barren Ground	110
XII.	Taft Is Deputized	120
XIII.	Dark Counsels	128
XIV.	He Talked Too Much	139
XV.	The Coroner Presides	146
XVI.	Blood on the Grass	154
XVII.	Dust to Dust	168
XVIII.	An Alibi Upset	178
XIX.	Grapevine Gossip	189
XX.	The Checkered Coat	201
XXI.	Confidences	211
XXII.	In Yamacraw	220
XXIII.	"A Pretty Kettle of Fish"	228
XXIV.	Confessions	237

Preface

Who Killed Bob Lawson? was originally written in the 1930s. The major portion of the novel was written by my parents, Alex M. and Ethel S. Arnett, while I was living at home. They were both natives of Georgia, and the scene is laid near my father's hometown of Sylvania in south Georgia. The book was a major topic of discussion among members of the family for several years. I knew well all the characters and scenes, and even wrote portions of the book. It was left unfinished because of the untimely death of my father.

I found the manuscript when I was settling the estate of my mother some forty years later. It was like finding buried treasure. By that time the book had become both a historical novel and a mystery story. I reread the manuscript and lent it to several friends to read. They agreed with me that it would be exciting reading for people who like fiction. I spent several years editing, making politically necessary changes, and completing the story. However, I was careful to maintain the atmosphere and historical accuracy of the original manuscript.

—Georgia Arnett Bonds

I
"Welcome to God's Country"

Early Friday morning

Nothing was farther from the thoughts of Bob Lawson than death, particularly his own death. He was in the best of health, and no one ever anticipates death by accident. Of course, there were some people who might have preferred him out of the way, but surely no one would dream of killing him. Or so he might have thought, if he had thought of the matter at all. But he had not, and why should he?

Foremost in Bob's mind that morning was the fact that Priscilla was coming. As he walked along the graveled stretch that served as a platform for the train station, he kept looking at his watch with growing impatience. The Central of Georgia train from Atlanta was marked: June 21, 1936–on time. It was already ten minutes late, and there was still no sign of smoke. He returned to the motley group that was milling around the station—tenant farmers in overalls and plantation owners in dress suits, even on a hot day.

"Morning, Bob." It was Dr. Evans, as seedily aristocratic as ever. "Meeting more guests for your house party?"

"Yes, Mr. Evans, the Harveys from Atlanta. And you?"

"Oh, just running down to Savannah for the day. A mere chore, a mere chore." He stroked his white Vandyke beard and fixed his eyes on nowhere.

A rumbling mail truck separated the two, and Bob returned to his thoughts.

Why had he said "the Harveys" when he knew from the telegram in his pocket that only Priscilla was coming at that time? Allen, her husband, had been delayed at the last minute and would drive down in his car the next day. How wonderful! Bob thought. His secret wish would come true; he could have hours and hours alone with Priscilla.

As he turned again toward the little red station, his eyes fell upon the sign in the gable so familiar to him.

DOVER, GEORGIA
Atlanta, 238.4 mi.   Savannah, 57.3 mi.

He went into the white waiting room and looked at the bulletin board. The train was now marked ten minutes late. It was already fifteen minutes overdue.

"Funny how the railroads let us down easy," Bob said and returned to the gravel platform.

He took a deep breath and stopped short alongside Dr. Evans. "I want you to drop in and meet my guests, Doctor."

"More new people—" Dr. Evans nodded his head in approval, "you're really waking us up around here. It's good to have you back home again. I'll be over, surely, surely."

The doctor evaluated Bob at a glance. Here was the puny baby he had brought into the world some thirty-six years ago, now over six feet, bronzed by the summer sun, and as strong as an athlete.

At this little country station in the edge of the Ogeechee River swamp, among Negroes and ill-kept whites, with an occasional proud, but threadbare planter, Bob, dark-haired and handsome in his immaculate white linen suit, appeared quite exotic. And yet it was his native community. About a mile away was the old planter village, Cooperville, in which he was reared and to which he had nostalgically returned after a successful business career in Atlanta. He soon assumed the role of village philosopher and community leader.

As a student at Georgia Tech, Bob had made the greater part of his expense writing life insurance. Three years out of college, he had led the state in volume of business for a New York company. That gave him and some of his business friends an idea: Why not start a life insurance company of their own?

So Georgia Life was launched in Atlanta. Bob was its chief promoter and, though only twenty-six at the time, its first president.

The company prospered. But, office work and city life were not satisfying to Bob. He had always wanted to be a gentleman farmer. So, with arrangements whereby he retained a dominant position in the company as chairman of the board of directors, he had resigned the presidency about three years before and had gone back to his native village to live.

The main reason that Bob had made the move at the time he did was the death of his sister's husband, Wesley Morris. Morris had seemed a promising young lawyer when he had married Prudence Lawson and they had settled down in Sylvania, their county-seat town. But, he had turned out to be a shyster of the worst type. If he had gotten what was coming to him, he would have died in jail. As it was he died "honorable," and left a son in his own image.

Young Lester Morris was a wild one. His mother was too motherly to tame him, and his father had been too hell-and-be-damned. Yet Lester was the only descendant of the Lawson family in the younger generation and apparently would be left to inherit the estate and carry on the tradition. Now that Lester was coming to feel himself a man, Bob had determined to make a man out of him or die in the attempt.

"I'll do it! I'll go back to Cooperville," Bob had said, "and, by God, I'll civilize that young savage!"

So with Prudence and Lester to live with him, Bob had built Linger-long, the new Lawson place.

Whooonk! whonk-whonk! The train was pulling in. And there was good old Charley, smiling as ever, leaning from the steps of the Pullman car as the train was easing toward a stop.

"Hello, Charley, have a passenger for me?" Bob asked.

"Yes, sir, Mister Bob; she's here."

Then from above the bulk that was Charley appeared a radiant blond head. "Hey, Bob!" Priscilla Harvey greeted, exhilaratedly waving her hand.

"Pris! Welcome to God's Country!"

She stepped lightly to the ground, and Bob took both her hands in his. There were glints of gold in her soft blonde hair, and her sea-blue eyes were bluer under the open sky. *God! What a lovely creature,* he thought. "As fresh as if you'd been wrapped in cellophane," he said.

"Wrong, Bob; it's soot."

He looked as her fair skin and trim aquamarine costume. "Wrong yourself, Pris; not a trace of soot."

Priscilla smiled broadly. "So you prefer me wrapped in cellophane?"

"Only in absentia."

She blushed. "You win. How's Prudence?"

"Fine. She sent her regrets for not meeting you; she's busy arranging for breakfast."

"Reason enough, my tummy tells me. Where's the Lincoln?"

"In dry dock; we've had rain. The roadster's over there."

They turned and picked their way across a muddy road toward a huddle of dingy country stores, half surrounded by dirty Model T's, ancient Buicks, and other rattletraps, with here and there a wagon and forlorn team of mules. Beyond was a dense wildwood, from which came a symphony of bird song:

mocking birds, buntings, orioles; and occasionally the deep bass of bullfrogs.

"Listen, Pris, you're welcomed by our native orchestra."

"I've never heard an orchestra that could equal that."

"You're absolutely right. Here's the roadster."

Bob motioned to an antiquated road cart and a drowsy old horse that had long since seen his best days. He was chewing at his bit like an old woman with ill-fitting teeth. "Pris, this is Balaam. Wake up, Balaam; here's Pris!"

Balaam's dejected posture and melancholy eyes were unmoved.

"So!" Priscilla laughed, her voice pitched high with excitement. "Country life begins at the station."

"Well, I thought you ought to meet Balaam right away. He's one of my oldest pals."

Priscilla shook her hankerchief in the horse's face. "Perk up, Balaam! Aren't you glad to see me?" There was no response beyond the blinking of an eye.

"Sorry, he's so ungracious; he's getting old and absent-minded. But he's a good horse. He minds his own business—like the three monkeys."

Bob lifted Priscilla into the cart, unclasped the hitching rein, patted Balaam's drooping head, and got in himself. The horse automatically turned into the road for home.

"Balaam and I were colts together."

"The difference being that he's grown out of it?"

"Yes, I suppose I'm a perennial colt."

They turned eastward across the railroad tracks and entered a wood that was dark and cool. Flowering honeysuckle vines and mimosas lined the roadside. Overspreading oaks were hung with gray festoons of Spanish moss, opalescent in the sunlight, pale and eerie in the shadows.

"Bee-utiful!" Priscilla exclaimed. "It makes me feel sort of creepy. If I were alone, I think I'd be afraid."

"Afraid—of what?"

"Oh," Priscilla shrugged, "afraid I'd see a ghost—or a black witch riding on a broomstick, maybe."

"Don't you want to see?"

"I'm dying to see one But I don't want to be alone when I do."

"You're just like Prude. She's an absolute authority on ghosts around here, but I believe if she saw one she'd die in her tracks."

They ascended a short hillside, steep and miry. A ramshackle Model T tried to pass them, slipping and sliding, but confidently making its way. "Watch out!" Priscilla exclaimed, "That car is going to hit us." She instinctively threw her arms around Bob for protection.

Bob felt the warmth of her arms and wished she would never let go. "Don't worry, Pris," Bob comforted her. "This is known around this area as the Dover Hill. A part of driver's education here is learning to negotiate this hill. When it's wet, it's muddy; and when it's dry, it's sandy." By the time the car had passed, Priscilla had relaxed her grip on Bob.

At the top they came upon a broad expanse of growing cotton and corn. "Ahhh!" said Priscilla, "the planter's paradise."

"And often his paradox," Bob replied knowingly.

For a moment there was silence, except for the grinding of the cart wheels in the sand. Bob was thinking: *Why had Priscilla come on without waiting for Allen?* Was it merely that she was unwilling to miss the extra time in the country? Or was it possible that she was as anxious to be with him as he was to be with her?

And what about Allen? Had he never suspected—as jealousy possessive as he was and hell bent? *But Allen was so absorbed in his business,* Bob thought, *that he could not appreciate such a treasure as Priscilla.* Allen possessed her, and in his business-like manner felt a great proprietary pride in his possession. Bob was sure Allen loved her, too, with the same jealous love that a miser has for his gold. But with Allen, business came first.

But Bob refused to think of this further for the time. After all, he was not sure how Priscilla felt toward Allen, or for that matter toward him. He only knew that he was determined to make the most of his association with her.

"Have the Tylers come?" Priscilla asked.

"Came yesterday."

"I certainly hope they're in a holiday mood. Gordon, especially, can be so much fun when he wants to be. But he's changed so in the last few years, ever since he married Irene. Whatever has come over him? He acts so dignified, so nervous, and . . . preoccupied. He's almost become dull."

"So you've noticed it too? Well, to tell the truth, Pris, Gordon is money mad. He's been getting control of a number of small insurance companies and is building them into a sort of empire, and he's making pretty big money in the process. He's trying now to get his hands on Georgia Life. Understand, that's confidential—"

"Oh, certainly."

"As you know, Gordon and I have been buddies since college days. But friendship is one thing. Business is another. And I'm going to keep his hands off Georgia Life."

"It may be a catty thing to say, Bob, but I wonder if Irene is pushing him. She does like expensive things. But never mind. Who else is coming?"

"Albert Wormser. He and the Tylers came down together."

"Albert Wormser? Who's he?"

"Just a middle-aged bachelor. Rather taciturn. He won't interest you much."

"I know some bachelors that interest me an awful lot," Priscilla replied, her eyes roguishly dancing.

"Some?"

"Oh, not too many."

Bob smiled and directed Balaam northward into an avenue of huge live oaks, forming a moss-hung canopy overhead as far as the eye could reach.

"Entering Cooperville! It's like the end of a dream."

"The end?"

"I mean it's like a dream come true."

"That's better."

Cooperville took great pride in its beauty and quiet dignity. It was a village of half-a-dozen planter families who had handed down their customs and traditions for centuries. At one time it had been one of the proudest and liveliest centers of aristocratic life in that region. And even though farming had been profitless for two generations, it still maintained an air of gentility. The houses, gray and dingy from age and lack of paint, were quaintly serene. They were all set back from the road about a hundred yards and were almost hidden by oaks, sycamores, crepe myrtles, and a variegated assemblage of roses.

"This is the once famous Louisville Road," Bob said as Balaam trudged through the deep, white sand. "Not much of a road now, but it's one of the oldest roads in the state and in its day was one of the most aristocratic. It used to be *the* highway between Savannah and the big plantations of middle Georgia. But now, at least in this region, it has dwindled to little more than a succession of neighborhood roads. Tourist and business travel keep to the main highways and—"

"To the beaten paths," Priscilla said with a sigh, "always the beaten paths. All my life I've been held to the beaten paths. And ever since I've known you, and you've told me about this charming old place, with its delightful seclusion and unspoiled beauty, I've wanted to come here, to see and experience it with you—and with Prudence and the rest. I came on without waiting for Allen, because I was afraid he'd be tied up with business affairs indefinitely and we'd both lose the opportunity, as we did last summer."

"Well, I'm the happiest man alive to have you here. And I'm going to keep you as long as I can."

"And you'll tell me more of the interesting traditions that center around these quaint old homes, won't you?"

"You bet your pretty head I'll tell you all you'll listen to, and I'll see that you have all the thrilling experiences that can be had down here."

"I want especially to see the old swimming hole and the haunted houses you've talked so much about. Stories about ghosts and haunted places have always intrigued me."

"You'll find there are plenty of ghosts around here. There are more of them by the square inch along this road than anywhere else in this hemisphere. And I mean real ghosts, not just the story-book kind. . . . Ghosts," Bob added, maintaining an air of solemnity, "are among our liveliest inhabitants."

"Bob, you almost convince me sometimes that you really believe in ghosts."

"I do; everyone does, consciously or subconsciously."

"Bob Lawson, look me straight in the eyes. Do you mean to tell me that you're superstitious?"

She might as well have put her question to the Sphinx. Bob was that way at times. One could not be sure whether he was quite serious or drolly amusing. "Not superstitious. That word keeps bad company. I'd say that I believe and have always believed in spiritual phenomena."

Balaam turned into a long driveway. Bob pulled him to a stop and pointed through an opening in the trees to the desolated hulk of what had been something of a mansion. "That old place over there is 'Exhibit A' of the haunted houses along the Louisville Road. It's the most authentically haunted place in seven states."

"O-o-oh! That's the old Lawson house!"

"Right you are. I grew up in the shadows of that old place. If I could have had my way I would have reconditioned it, and we'd be living in it now. But Prude was insistent upon a modernized colonial, with all the latest conveniences, like the Tiltons' in Sylvania. She got an architect from Savannah to condemn the old house as beyond repair; so I compromised by letting her have her way."

Bob shook the reins and clucked; Balaam pulled slowly up the moss-hung driveway. "And over here," he said, "is—"

"Linger-long! At long last!" Priscilla exclaimed.

The name of the new Lawson home was well chosen. For, as it turned out, Linger-long was frequently filled with guests who were loath to leave. Friends came whenever they pleased, on specific or general invitations, and were welcomed to stay as long as they would.

Priscilla admired the new colonial—a bit too fresh and white, perhaps, too imposing for its environment, but happily inviting nevertheless. Her gaze was lured back to those ancient ruins, now closer and more discernible. Crumbling facade; sagging roofs; blearing, sightless windows—all overrun with English ivy and Virginia creeper.

"Has anything ever—ever really happened?"

"Yes, plenty, but that was a long time ago; I'll tell you about it sometime. Since then nothing very exciting has happened in this placid community since Sherman's march to the sea."

Could they only have lifted the veil—even to the weekend! But if they could have, it would not have happened. At least not then.

II
All Sorts of People

Friday morning

"I have some business in Sylvania today, so why don't we all go over there this morning? You should see our county seat," Bob Lawson suggested when, after breakfast, he and Prudence and their guests were lolling on the north porch of Linger-long.

All agreed.

"We'll take both cars," Bob said. "Gordon and Irene, Mr. Wormser, and Prude can go in the Lincoln, with Taft to drive, and Pris and I will go in the roadster."

"Do you mean the road cart?" Priscilla countered, her eyes a-twinkle.

"Oh, no, Balaam's done his daily dozen. Dumplin's put him back to bed. We'll take the Plymouth roadster."

"What about the roads?" she inquired impishly.

"There aren't any Dover Hills between here and Sylvania." Only Bob and Priscilla were aware of the significance of his smile.

"Oh, yes?" Priscilla said, and excused herself to powder her nose.

Gordon Tyler was blowing rings from the cigar he was smoking. "While we're waiting for Mrs. Harvey, Bob, let's have one of your latest yarns," he said, knowing that Bob's store of them was inexhaustible.

"Sorry, Gordon, I don't tell yarns; all my stories are entirely authentic. I could document them if necessary." As usual Bob's drollery was masked with an expression of impassive seriousness.

"We'll waive that point," Gordon persisted, smoothing down his well-trimmed mustache.

"I suppose you refer to one of these little incidents that happen around here that people think are funny. I came across one last week—I can't see any particular point to it, but somehow, every time I tell it folks laugh. I don't know why. I don't see anything funny about it, but my saintly sister here usually cackles loudest of all—and gives me a curtain lecture afterwards."

"Bob!" Prudence exclaimed, "that's not fair. You give people the impression that your nickname for me is really fitting."

"*Oh, no, honey,*" Bob replied; "everybody knows I've called you 'Prude' since I was a baby, when I couldn't have had the slightest notion of the word's significance. But, honey, you are a bit conservative. And you do sometimes give me nice, sweet, little curtain lectures." Bob put his arm around Prudence. Their resemblance was remarkable: identical dark brown hair and eyes, identical skin tone, and the unmistakable Lawson features.

"But back to the incident," Bob continued. "I missed a side of bacon from my smokehouse one day—"

"Bob, you are not going to tell that story!" Prudence admonished, drawing away from him.

"And, I had reason to suspect Chunky, one of the negro boys on the place, of having taken the meat," Bob went on in a mock-serious manner.

"Irene, let's go and powder our noses, too," Prudence suggested.

Irene Tyler stood straight and tall. Her black hair was brushed back slick from her face in a way that emphasized the height of her forehead. Her green eyes bore reproachfully toward Bob as she and Prudence turned to go inside.

Bob went on to explain that by quietly observing both direct and circumstantial evidence and by putting two and two together, he had so often discovered petty thievery among the servants on the place that some of them had come to feel that he had an uncanny, if not supernatural, power of seeing through all their actions.

"I called Chunky in to see me. After all the evidence was brought out and the boy was cross-examined, he finally admitted the theft.

" 'Chunky', I asked in solemn tones, 'what did you *do* with that meat?'

" 'I took it to my gal.'

" 'Did she give you anything for it?'

" 'Yes sir!'

" 'How much did she pay you?'

" 'She ain't paid me nothin'.'

" 'Haven't you just told me she gave you something for it?'

" 'Yes, sir; she gimme somethin' for it.'

" 'Well, what did you she give?'

" 'She gimme monkey.'

" 'Do you mean to tell me that girl had a monkey and gave it to you for the meat?'

" 'No sir, Mister Bob. She just gimme monkey.'

" 'Chunky, what do you mean by saying that the girl didn't give you a monkey for the meat and yet she give you monkey for it?'

" 'Now, Mister Bob, you're too smart a man not to know what monkey is.' "

"Had it been your purpose, Bob," Gordon asked, "to collect what the boy got for the meat?"

The ensuing laughter was taken by the ladies as a signal for their return to the porch. Bob excused himself and started toward the back yard to have the cars brought out.

Priscilla turned to go with him. "Mind if I come?" she asked.

"Delighted, my dear," Bob answered and took her arm.

"I'm simply in love with this place, and I don't want to miss anything," she said with colorful enthusiasm.

"Down, Starvation!" Bob sternly commanded and barely saved his spotless flannels from the forepaws of an over affectionate, nondescript dog. He then atoned for the rebuke with a consoling pat. "Good dog, but you mustn't spoil your master's Sunday-go-to-meetin' clothes."

"Starvation!" laughed Priscilla. "Why such a name? He looks to me like he should be counting his calories."

"You ought to have seen him when he took up here. Too pitiful to shoot and too appreciative to turn away. And now, of all God's creatures, he's the most ardently devoted to the master he adopted."

"What kind of dog is he?"

"He'd probably classify as *dawgus plainus;* his family tree would stump any dogologist."

Priscilla smiled and stroked the dog's sleek back. She was rewarded with eyes full of worship and a tail full of glee.

"Dumplin," Bob called to a rotund negro boy who was leaning against the trunk of a sycamore tree. "Get out the roadster. Where's Taft?"

"He's in de smoke house, sir." Dumplin ambled toward the garage.

"Want me, Mister Bob?" A large negro man of respectful and kindly demeanor stepped out of the smokehouse.

"Yes, Taft. Pris, this is Taft Cooper, as fine a fellow as God ever made. Taft, this is Mrs. Harvey, you've heard me speak of her."

"Yes sir, Mister Bob; I sure have." Taft was smiling to the back of his neck, his teeth and eyes shining. "I'm proud to make your acquaintance, Miss Harvey."

"I'm sure that's mutual, Taft," Priscilla smiled.

"Get out the Lincoln," Bob said. "I want you to drive a group to Sylvania. Drop them at the Screven Drug Store and be ready to take any of them wherever they may wish to go."

"Yes sir, Mister Bob." Taft replaced his cap and followed Dumplin to the garage.

Taft was born and raised on the Lawson Plantation and had spent his entire life there. He and Bob had been babies at the same time. Bob's mother was a frail woman and had almost died at his birth, and for weeks it was doubtful whether Bob would live. Taft's mother, a fine, strong woman, was the Lawsons' head cook at the time. She had taken Bob to her own cabin and had fed him along with Taft from her own breasts.

The two boys had grown up together: had fished, hunted, frequented the "old swimmin' hole," and shared each other's joy and sorrows. The bond between them was almost as strong as that of brothers. For some years before Bob's return to Cooperville, Taft had acted as plantation manager. While race, traditions, and differences in contacts and educational opportunities had brought changes in their social relationships, these had not lessened their mutual devotion.

Taft backed the Lincoln out of the garage. A few minutes later Bob and Priscilla waved to the departing group and turned toward a Plymouth coupe. Priscilla's attention was attracted by a large, slatternly negro woman wandering down the driveway, mumbling to herself and occasionally stooping to pick up some scarcely visible object in her path.

"Queer looking creature," Priscilla remarked quietly.

"That's Mom Liza," Bob explained, as he lifted Priscilla into the car, sprang in himself, and drove away. "She is queer, and pitiful, but an interesting old soul. She mumbles to herself all the time, mostly about nothing, and picks up every pin, every piece of string, every discarded scrap of anything, mumbling every time in a drawling monotone, 'Save all things, save all things.' "

"Does she really save all the things she picks up?" Priscilla inquired.

"Everything. Her bedroom is half-full of all sorts of odds and ends, and it never seems to occur to her that rarely is any of it needed. She saves practically all the money she earns and keeps it hidden somewhere. The Lord knows where."

"I wish I could see inside her house. Does she live near Linger-long?"

"Yes, in a two-room cabin, the only remaining one of the quarters back of the old Lawson house. She was born there and has lived there all her life."

"Does she have any family?"

"Not with her. Her husband has long been dead and her children are all grown up and scattered. I take care of her, and give her occasional jobs to earn what little money she has. She's awfully sensitive, often having notions that someone has it in for her. She prowls all over the place, especially at night; she says she has the 'wakin' sickness.' "

"*Wakin' sickness!* That's wonderful!" Priscilla's laughter was reminiscent of a waterfall, so natural and free. "But isn't she afraid at night? Isn't she superstitious?"

"She's superstitious a-plenty, but she's on speaking terms with all the neighborhood spirits; says she walks and talks with ghosts, holds communion with them."

Bob and Priscilla were bumping along a rambling, unpaved road through a succession of broad fields and deep woodlands. This was the Sylvania Highway.

A mile or so out of Cooperville Bob pulled the car aside and stopped in the shade of a large water oak.

"Listen, Pris. . . " Over the surrounding silence there came a distant roaring or bellowing sound.

"You don't have lions down here! Or is that a cow? What on earth is it?"

"That's Sam Holloman, another of the curiosities in our community," Bob said as he drove on. "A sort of recluse and religious crank."

"You mean he's a hermit?"

"Well, he keeps mostly to himself. What you heard, believe it or not, was the old fellow praying. He seems to think God's terribly hard of hearing."

"What does he do for a living?"

"He farms in his own way. He came here about fifteen or twenty years ago and bought a few acres of God-forsaken land on the edge of a frog pond over a mile from his nearest neighbor. Then, he built himself a two-room shack, cleared and drained a few fields, bought an ox, and settled down to subsistence farming. He raises everything that he uses, even his own tobacco."

"I didn't know that tobacco was grown this far south."

"It isn't—except what Holloman raises for his own use."

"And he stays there alone all the time?"

"He goes to Sylvania or Dover occasionally and sells enough produce from his garden and orchard to pay his puny taxes and buy physic and quinine. Otherwise he mostly keeps to himself. Oh, he goes fishing now and then. I've run into him several times at the Old Mill Creek. He can be chatty enough when his mind's off religion."

"Well, how does he amuse himself? Does he have books?"

"Yes and no; he has a book, the Bible—ought almost to know it by heart."

"And you say he was praying?"

"Either praying or preaching. He does both. Always at the top of his deep, bass voice."

"To whom does he preach?"

"To God's great out of doors, to lost humanity in the abstract, to frogs, alligators, and moccasins. A sermon he often preaches is to a snake in his well."

"To a *snake?*" Priscilla's eyes were wide with amusement.

"Yes." Bob chuckled. "That sermon has become a classic in the tradition of this community. Everyone who knows about Sam Holloman, and everyone for miles around knows that he preaches to a snake in his well."

"Do people know what he says?"

"Only vaguely. It's rare that anyone catches much of what he says, and he has come to be taken so much for granted that little attention is given to his supplications and admonitions. But on one occasion, several turpentine men happened to be working near enough to his house to catch the general drift of what he said."

"What was it? Tell it! Don't be so roundabout."

Bob refused to be hurried. "It seems that he went out to his well for water and spied a moccasin, doubtless from the near-by pond, calmly enjoying the cool depths of the well. He was naturally annoyed, and at the same time reminded of how the serpent came to be cursed of God and made the enemy of many. So, in his usual stentorian voice he reminded the snake in his well that its tribe, led astray by the devil, had been responsible for all the sin and sorrow that mankind had suffered since Adam and Eve."

Priscilla interrupted, "But I thought it was Eve's fault. She ate the apple."

"Granted But as Holloman preaches, the snake had formerly been a perfectly good and reputable creature. Wasn't Eve on friendly terms with it? Then, the snake had been weak; it had allowed itself to the beguiled by the devil to play a dirty trick on mankind that led to the original sin. If snakes could only see their folly, throw off the power of the devil, and be reconciled to all God's creatures, they could make their peace with God and mankind. At least that's what Holloman said."

"You're not just making that up as you go, Bob?"

"No, really, that's the way the story goes. It has probably been elaborated a bit in the many retellings, but there's no doubt that he does preach to a snake in his well."

"Do you remember any other of his sermons?"

"Not off hand, I may think of some later. But we have another interesting fellow in the neighborhood. Oh, the woods are full of them, but one in particular: a negro, who is also a preacher but of a very different type. If I've ever seen a rascally charlatan, he's it. He appeared around here about six or eight weeks ago with what turned out to be a triple mission.

"First he was going to build a college for the negroes. A few days after he came, a small pile of bricks which he claimed was the first shipment for the college was unloaded at Dover. That was tangible evidence, you see. A rich Yankee, he said, would contribute half the building costs when the other half was raised, and would endow the institution. He pled eloquently for subscriptions in all the neighboring colored churches and collected several hundred dollars.

"Meanwhile, with the aid of the good brethren, he built a brush arbor meeting place near the Louisville Road about a mile below Cooperville. Here he has a nightly assembly of the more gullible of his race, and preaches what he calls the New Gospel. It seems that he's a saint. His name is Ezra Starkes, but he wants to be called 'Saint Ezra.'

"Physically, he might be called well built. He's a handsome mulatto with a powerful physique and remarkable magnetism, it seems, mostly for the women."

"And he is a saint? What sort of gospel does he preach?"

"It's all very simple, his doctrine is. He says that God does not expect His children to be perfect. He knows they're bound to sin—expects it of most of them—but He wants them frequently to repent and have their sins washed away. In fact there's nothing that pleases Him more than to have them repent. So it's not so bad to sin, just so you give God and the angels the joy of seeing you forgiven. But every chance you get, you must repent and be baptized. And the baptizer, of course, is worthy of his hire."

"I thought that was coming," Priscilla said. "Does he immerse them?"

"Oh, yes! In the Old Mill Creek. Especially the women, he takes a high and low hold on them. Br'er Burke, one of the servants in my place, says the man has baptized his wife so much that he's afraid she'll turn into a mermaid."

"A mermaid!" Priscilla laughed explosively. "That's almost as good as 'wakin' sickness'."

"Not content to be just an educator and a minister, Saint Ezra also claims to be a faith healer, and has started calling himself the 'Divine Healer.' He calls his technique the laying on of hands. It consists in rubbing the limbs and bodies while pronouncing incantations. It seems to work wonders among his patients, nearly all women and girls.

"Br'er Burke says he never knew the women around here could get took with so many ailments and be so powerfully helped and have so many relapses."

"Bob, if I didn't know you to be an honest man, I wouldn't believe you."

Bob's face was aglow as he looked at Priscilla and went on with his story. "In time, numbers of negro men around, mostly men on my place, got the fellow's number, and as affairs have become more and more scandalous, they have determined to be rid of the man. And, to tell the truth, I have backed them up. Br'er Burke called a meeting of the Black Lodge, and the lodge voted to ask the man to leave our community. That's one thing I have to check on in Sylvania this morning."

"Tell me about some others—you said the woods are full of them."

"The rest of them will have to wait. We are almost to Sylvania now and we'll soon be rejoining the rest of our group."

"Speaking of the others, Bob, the Tylers worry me. Of course I don't know them very well, but it seems that Gordon has changed an awful lot. He used to be loads of fun. But now he seems restless and preoccupied.

"Yes, Gordon has changed. Business success has gone to his head, and he's overreaching himself. Remember, I told you this morning that he has been buying in, or gaining control of, a number of small insurance companies, forming a sort of empire of them and in the process has made money for himself. And, confidentially, he's moving heaven and earth right now to buy Georgia Life, but he'll certainly not get it if I can help it. Of course I invited him, but I think he came more for business than for pleasure. And that's what on his mind. Gordon, as you know, has been one of my very closest friends. We were associated in the same office for several years, and were almost inseparable. I'm still fond of him, but I don't approve of some of his business tactics."

"Do you mean to tell me that Gordon is trying to put over a deal like that in spite of your disapproval?" Priscilla asked in surprise.

"I'm afraid so. I thought you might as well know it, as it will come out sooner or later, and you'll better understand how the land lies. As a matter of fact, one reason I wanted to come to Sylvania this morning is to see our bank president, Mr. Underhill, a local member of our board of directors."

"And Mr. Wormser?" Priscilla asked. "I've been wondering about Mr. Wormser—what connection he has with Gordon—or with you?"

"He's helped me in my business, so I invited him down here," Bob said no more.

"Here we are." Bob drove into a parking space beside the Lincoln near the Screven Drug Store, then he and Priscilla joined the rest of the party who had arrived in Sylvania somewhat earlier and were seated at a table, drinking Coca-Cola.

Although Sylvania was the county seat, its main street was one long block with the court house at one end and a church at the other. The north side of the street was separated from the south side by a triangular parking lot for horses, wagons, buggies, and cars. The drug store was on the north side of the street.

Bob hurried his drink and excused himself, leaving his guests with Prudence, with the understanding that all of them would meet there again one hour later. He went at once to the court house, where he met with Sheriff Satterfield in his office.

As soon as Bob left, Gordon suggested, "I think I'll go to that men's store and see if I can get a straw hat. This south Georgia sun is baking my brains."

"I'd go with you," said Wormser, "but see that hardware store across the parking lot? I'm going to see if they have a hunting knife. I've heard you can get some good buys in these out-of-the-way places."

Priscilla was still finishing her Coca-Cola when Irene said to Prudence, "Do you think I could get silk stockings at that ladies' store down the block? My best pair got a run in them this morning."

"I'll go with you and we'll take a look," Prudence replied.

"Wait a minute until I finish this drink, and I'll go, too," Priscilla added.

As they were leaving the drug store a tall, muscular man came in to buy some quinine.

"Will that be all, Mr. Holloman?" asked the druggist.

"All for today," replied Holloman. He took his package and headed for his ox cart. About the same time a tall mulatto drove up in a shiny black Buick.

"Scared hell out of my ox!" Holloman yelled at him.

"You son of a bitch—preaching to a damned snake in your well," the mulatto retorted. "You'd better stay out of my territory. Too many cooks spoil the broth. And too many preachers spoil the take."

Holloman pulled on his ox yoke to quiet the beast. "I don't steal money from nobody."

"Who said anything about stealing money? I'm raising funds for the work of the Lord."

"The work of the Lord is to save the world from sin," Holloman yelled at him.

"You old fool," Ezra snapped back. "You stay out of my business or I'll have Bob Lawson put you into the looney-bin where you belong."

Bob Lawson came out of the court house just in time to hear his name mentioned. But he was in a hurry to get to the Bank of Screven County to meet with Mr. Underhill.

He saw the ox cart driving away, and was stopped by Ezra who came over to him and said with a disarming smile, "Mister Bob, you haven't made your contribution to the negro college yet."

Hollomn looked back to see Ezra talking to Bob.

"Reverend Starkes," Bob replied, "I have just been by to see Sheriff Satterfield, and he and I have agreed that if you cause any more trouble among my colored neighbors, you could be charged with practicing medicine without a license."

"The hell you say. I know my rights," Ezra told him and stomped into the court house. Bob headed for the bank and was closeted in with Mr. Underhill for half an hour.

As Bob walked toward the drug store, he saw Gordon Tyler walking toward the bank. Bob paused for a moment in the shadows and saw Wormser saunter into the bank also.

Bob had his ideas.

III
One Side of a Triangle

Friday afternoon

The group returned to Linger-long for a midday dinner. The conversation at the table was mainly about plantation affairs.

Agriculturally, Bob was unique in his community in that he planted no cotton. He had added to what was left of the ancestral estate, at trifling cost, some ten thousand acres of Ogeechee River swamp land regarded as practically worthless, and was converting it into pasture land for cattle and hogs. Having won blue ribbons at state fairs and cattle shows, and being exceptionally skilled in curing processes, he was able to sell his products well above the market price to high-class restaurants and hotels in various cities, mainly Savannah. That was why he could make money as a planter when others could not. At times, Bob may have appeared boastful with reference to his agricultural achievements, at least some of his neighbors seemed to think so. But their attitudes may well have risen from envy and resentment of his shrewdness.

"Mr. Lawson, how did you ever get onto all this? Did you learn it at Tech?" Wormser bestirred himself to ask. His thin, swarthy countenance, always inscrutable, had seemed to indicate indifference to, or merely a passive interest in, Bob's details.

"Well, to be specific, Mr. Wormser, I learned to fatten hogs partly out of books and partly by the grace of God and the hogs' appetites."

"Quite comprehensive and very illuminating," Wormser threw back.

"You know, Bob, it's still hard for me to think of you as sloppin' hogs," Gordon put in with apparent jocularity. "But you're evidently making a success of it."

"Well, seeing is believing; we'll just take a look over the place," Bob said enthusiastically and rose from the table.

A few minutes later, the group was getting into the cars, naturally falling into the same arrangement as in the morning.

"Taft knows the place as well as I do," Bob called over to the Lincoln. "Prude, you'll see that those in your car don't miss anything."

"Oh, yes," replied Prudence, entering into his mood. "Taft and I are getting to be quite expert tour guides."

The Plymouth started off on a circuitous drive. Bob soon managed to elude the Lincoln by turning onto an unfrequented road. Then, with almost childish enthusiasm, he began pointing out to Priscilla various places of particular interest and charm. Bob was determined to stir in her a depth of interest and delight comparable to his own in this place, its environs, and its life. And he had the gift of being able to sell these as well as other things—including himself—for all they were worth. He pointed out trees and shrubs that he had taken from areas too densely wooded and had planted in eroded places where they were needed. He showed her the grassy meadows he had developed after removing the strangling undergrowth and draining the mudflats. All of this had greatly improved the landscape as well as the soil and pasturage. He drove along hedgerows between fields of corn and hay, through shady, vine-clad lanes, and over all sorts of picturesque byways that seemed scarcely passable with a car. Bob did this partly for the novelty it afforded Priscilla, and partly to reach out-of-the-way pastures where his largest herds of sleek cattle were grazing leisurely. He brought the car to a stop alongside a broad expanse carpeted with clover and lespedesa.

"When I came back here a few years ago," he said, "this was only a swampy bog covered with an almost impenetrable undergrowth. It has been an inspiring adventure to see what can be made of such a place."

"More and more, Bob, I understand why you wanted to come back—" Priscilla suddenly cringed, as if frightened.

"What's the matter, Pris?"

"I heard someone in the bushes over there," she whispered. "He was looking at us. . . . Just ahead there. . . . On my side of the road." Priscilla was not accustomed to such wild growth with peering faces. It reminded her of tense places in Africa in movies that she had seen.

"Where? I don't see anybody." There was no fear in Bob's voice.

"There!" Priscilla motioned to the right of her. "Didn't you see the branches moving?"

At this, Bob was out of the car and walking in long, deliberate strides toward the moving limbs. He had advanced but a few steps when Chunky grinned himself out of the bushes.

"Chunky Williams, what're you doing way over here this time of the day?" Bob's voice was stern.

"What you doin' yourself? Ain't I got a right to be here same as you?"

"None of your sass, young man!"

"My paw sent me here," Chunky said with a note of resentment.

"You're lying, Chunky."

Bob advanced a few steps toward the clump of bushes when suddenly a defiant negro girl stepped out. Bob turned again to Chunky, who faced him wide-eyed but squarely.

"No use for you to lie to me, boy. Don't you know I can read your mind?"

"We were just walkin' along here and seen you all coming and hid so's—"

"You send this girl back to where she belongs and get yourself back to help your paw stack that hay before it rains."

"Yes sir, Mister Bob." Chunky was still sullen.

Back in the car Bob said: "You know, I like Chunky in spite of his pertness. He has personality and will of his own. Does well in school, too. If I can keep him from getting that girl into trouble until he's through school here, I'm going to arrange for him to go to the Tuskegee Institute."

On the way home, Bob purposely took a roundabout way in order to drive through miles of lanes that were flanked with wild flowers.

"I never saw such profusion of color from wild growth!" Priscilla said exuberantly. "I have to pinch myself to be sure I'm not dreaming."

"It's this way the year round," Bob replied. "I wish you could see it in its various seasons. There's not a time in the year when the landscape is not colorful. In spring and early summer the woods are alive with pink honeysuckle, yellow jasmine, purple azalea, white berry blossoms, green bulrushes, and well, too many others to mention."

"It must be a veritable fairyland."

"Before they are gone the late summer flowers are here—water lilies, wild asters, white ghost flowers—"

"I never heard of ghost flowers before. Have the spirits taken to wearing corsages too?"

Bob answered with an appreciative smile, and continued: "But, best of all, are the late fall and winter seasons when the bare woods are brightened with red holly berries, orange bitter sweet, blue clusters of bamboo, and silver-green mistletoe. And always there are the blue-green, long-leafed pines."

"Absolutely idyllic, Bob, and you make it so romantic." Priscilla breathed deeply.

The car was barely creeping along a ribbon of sand. Bob looked at Priscilla's sparkling eyes and her full round lips. His grasp on the steering wheel slackened. Then he thought of Allen and the mores of the community in which he lived. He fixed his eyes upon the road ahead and drove on.

When the two returned to Linger-long at about four o'clock, the others had already arrived and were seated on the north porch, just beginning a game of bridge. Ruby had seen them coming while she was serving Tom Collinses to the others; so she was ready, tray in hand, with tall sparkling glasses for them.

Ruby, a combination of first maid and head cook, was a direct descendant of the negroes that had come to Cooperville with the first Coopers and Lawsons. Like Taft, she was saturated in the traditions of the Lawson household.

Bob took the glasses and handed one to Priscilla, then turned back to Ruby and said in an undertone, "I want you to name your next baby Miss Pris, since your first one is named Mister Bob."

"Mister Bob, you sure are a caution!" Ruby replied with a pleased, but embarrassed, smile and left the porch.

"I'll have to hand it to you, Bob." Gordon ran his fingers through his thin, graying hair and said with some enthusiasm, "I grant you now that there's more to the life of a gentleman farmer than slopping hogs. By the way, how much will you take for your place?"

"Money couldn't buy it," Bob told him.

"Playing bridge!" Priscilla reproved. "You're old sissies! You can play bridge anytime. While we're in the country, let's enjoy the country. Bob, can't we all go fishing?"

"Sure thing," Bob replied.

"Please, you all," Priscilla begged excitedly.

"Not now. We've just got a good game started," Irene condescended. "Besides, who'd want to move from this cool porch," she gestured over the colorful glazed chintz furnishings, "into that blistering sun again?"

"Uncle Spode said just a little while ago that the fish wouldn't be biting this afternoon. They never bite just after a rain like we had yesterday," Wormser argued between puffs from his cigar.

Uncle Spode was one of the family heirlooms. He had been born on the day that a shipment of Spode porcelain had arrived from England to be used by the Lawsons on festive occasions. It had been a day of excitement for the servants and when his mother, one of the Lawsons' maids, referred jestingly to the new baby as "my little Spode" she hardly dreamed that the name would follow her son these eighty years. White kinks now covered his head and the chin of his black face, and added dignity to his air of authority. He was too old for heavy labor, but was wonderfully well suited to do the chores of a fishing expedition. Priscilla turned to her host. "Bob, can't we make them go fishing?"

"Well, Pris," Bob smiled, "this is a free country, and I promised them freedom was theirs. We'll just have to have two parties; one for fishing and one for cards. If there aren't enough left to play bridge, those who stay can play solitaire or setback. I'll have Uncle Spode dig some worms right away and all who want to join the fishing group will leave in half an hour."

When time came for the fishing jaunt only three appeared to make up the party: Priscilla, Bob, and Uncle Spode, who always went along to bait the hooks, take the fish off the line, and look after the boat.

The foot-path to the boat landing stretched almost a mile from the house and was cut through a field and shaded woodlands, dense with underbrush and palmettoes. There was a roundabout way that one could drive, but Priscilla preferred to walk. They had to go single file and Uncle Spode did most of the talking—apparently to himself.

"I done told them dat I'll eat *alive* all de fishes dey catch—fins, and bones, and tails, and all. I never knew no fish to bite after such rains as we done had. Mister Bob act like he don't know no rules for fishin'. . . . Watch out, Miss Harvey, dis here look like quicksand. Better let me set my foot on it first. . . .

"I guess dese worms is a-laughin' at me a-playin' like dey's gonna be et. I said when I was diggin', for dem not to be skeered; I'd fetch dem back safe to sleep in dey own beds. Ain't no fishes gonna bite today."

A bluebird flew across their path and lighted on a dead limb nearby.

"Bob!" Priscilla suddenly stopped. "Look at that bird! It's bluer than the sky above it. Let's make a wish. You know that a wish comes true if made when you see a bluebird."

"All right. I wish—"

"Oh, no, you mustn't tell what it is. Just wait and see if it comes true."

"Well, if yours comes true will you tell me what it was?" Bob asked.

"If you'll tell me yours." Priscilla threw Bob a challenging smile over her shoulder.

"That's a bargain."

"You needn't waste your time makin' no wish for fishes to bite," Uncle Spode added. "You might as well wish dat Gabriel let you blow his trumpet." His chatter temporarily ceased but his thoughts ran on: Mister Bob acts like he ain't in his right mind today anyhow.

As they approached the Lawson boat landing, Uncle Spode caught a glimpse of the river through an opening in the trees. "Well, bless God, look at dat water; its near 'bout clear. It mustn't have rained up de river like it rained aroun' here; you might catch a few little fishes after all."

"Mind, Uncle Spode, you may have to eat your own words besides the fish we catch," Bob bantered.

Once the boat was out on the river, Uncle Spode quieted down and watched the lines with as much eagerness as a cat watches a mouse. He knew he would be the most humiliated one of the group if Bob Lawson had to go home without fish. For he had always boasted that no fish could resist a worm that wiggled from Mister Bob's hook.

Before the afternoon was over, the bottom of the boat was spotted with sizable trout and with an occasional perch or bream.

"Okay, Uncle Spode, you'd better get started if you're going to eat all these fish—'fins' and bones and tails and all," Priscilla teased.

Uncle Spode dropped his eyes and licked his toothless gums and lips. "Now, Miss Harvey, can't you take a little joke?" he grinned.

The boat hit the landing with a thud.

"Fasten the chain, Uncle Spode, and get all the fish into the basket. You can take them to the house and dress them for supper. Tell Ruby to outdo herself frying them. We're going back by the old swimming hole. I want to show Mrs. Harvey that particular spot that played a part bringing me back to Screven. We'll be along before supper time."

"Yes sir, Mister Bob."

The swimming hole was in the Old Mill Creek just above where it emptied into the river. The path to it was so narrow and uncertain in places that Bob had to lead the way, holding the sprawling bushes and limbs aside for Priscilla to pass. It was late afternoon and the frogs' chorus was well underway, occasionlly enlivened by the shrill calls of subtropical birds.

"Well, here we are. I can't see that the old hole has changed much since I was a child." Bob took Priscilla's hand and led her up beside him.

"Heavenly!" Priscilla exclaimed. "It looks so inviting that I just want to plunge right in."

The wild growth, riotous about the pool, was darkly reflected in the water. The air was damp and cool and smelled of green leaves, wet moss, and summer ferns. They stood silently on the bank for an instant.

"Here's the old mound where I used to sit daydreaming." Bob motioned directly ahead of them. "Let's—"

"Look, Bob!" Priscilla cried, "a little duck across on the other side. I believe it's tangled in that old fish net in the edge of the water."

Quickly Priscilla unbuttoned her sandals and the skirt to the three piece sport suit she was wearing, and let them drop to the ground. Before Bob knew what she was about, she had dived into the water and was swimming toward the duck. Holding the wee thing above her, as though afraid it would drown, she swam back across. She reached for Bob's hand to pull her onto the bank, where she lay for a minute to rest from swimming in such an awkward position.

"You little daredevil!" Bob said sternly as he sat down beside her as she shook the water from her hair. "Why did you do that? Haven't I told you that alligators sometimes come up here from the river, and we always look the place over before we go in? We never go in it when it's not clear enough to see the bottom? You might have lost an arm, or a leg."

"Not really?" Priscilla could not be sure whether Bob was serious or teasing. She sat upright, her eyes flashing in momentary alarm, then fixed upon Bob with complete *en rapport*. "Somehow I'm never afraid to do anything when you're around. You're so big and brave and strong. A big man, if he's like you, makes one feel that way, you know—never thinking of danger." Priscilla was looking directly at him.

"But you're all dripping wet now," Bob observed.

"That's okay," Priscilla answered. "I can dry myself with my skirt, and these clothes will dry quickly in this hot air. I guess I didn't think before I jumped into the water, but being with you makes me think that only good things can happen." Priscilla was enjoying the cool feeling of her damp clothes as she dried herself in her shorts and blouse.

"Don't talk to me like that, Pris. No man is so strong but that he weakens in the face of flattery from a woman he loves. Don't look at me like that. I have hardly dared look into your eyes. The sweep of your lashes—but, I suppose all men tell you the same thing."

"No, Bob, and if they did, it wouldn't sound the same. A dewdrop in the sunshine has about as much lustre as that diamond in the ring you are wearing, but as you look at the dewdrop you feel that it won't endure. You—you give me the feeling that there's something about you that's—that's eternal."

"You little daredevil," he whispered and drew her to him, kissing her passionately on the lips.

Priscilla's mind went blank; then she wandered in multicolored fields, or was it a deep, dark perfumed wood? Or was it heaven? Or, where was she? To Bob, nothing else mattered. Neither yesterday, nor today, nor tomorrow had any meaning for him. He was completely lost to everything and everybody, save Priscilla, himself, and the moment.

The sun hung low in the west when the two relaxed, looked at each other, and smiled. A blue jay called wildly from a bare branch overhanging the water.

"I never knew," Priscilla whispered, "that a wish on a bluebird could be fulfilled so promptly."

"So that was your wish. Well, I guess we're even at that," Bob said and kissed her again.

"We must be going," Priscilla said, picking up the little duck that was waddling aimlessly about. Bob stood up and pulled her up beside him. Priscilla handed him the duckling while she buttoned on her skirt, and then they turned and walked in the direction of the house.

Along the way, they emerged from the wood into the fields, just behind the Linger-long grounds. Bob pulled a bunch of daisies and handed them to Priscilla. "There's an old song about these," he said.

Priscilla turned the full light of her eyes upon him. "I remember," she smiled.

As they approached the north porch of Linger-long they saw that Allen Harvey was among the group—a day earlier than he was expected.

IV
The Ghost Oak

Friday evening

Night had fallen over Cooperville. On the south porch of Linger-long, the Lawsons and their guests lounged in the moonlight, sipping mint juleps, as they faced the somber ruins of the old Lawson place. The moonlight played eerily on such patches of the sagging roof as were visible through the trees and glared upon such windowpanes as remained in the house, striking contrast with the black depths of the empty openings.

Prudence had wanted to have the old building torn down and the grounds made into a sort of memorial park. But Bob had refused to yield on this point. To have destroyed the old house would have been, to him, like uprooting his past.

"Bob says that's the most authentically haunted house in seven states," Prudence said, in an almost accusatory tone. "I don't know why he insists on leaving it standing there."

"Well, it *is* haunted!" Bob maintained. "I've never had any doubt about it since my earliest recollections. I was brought up with those ghosts. So was Prude."

"I think Prudence should testify for herself," Irene Tyler said, a muffled dagger in her voice.

Prudence was evasive. "I know that the place has had that reputation for a great many years."

"But you don't take any stock in it?" snapped Irene.

Bob countered: "Your honor, counsel's leading the witness."

"I wouldn't put it that way, Irene," Prudence replied. "I neither accept nor deny the possibility of spiritual phenomena. Some of the most intelligent people believe in them. I've never heard nor seen a ghost or a spirit myself, if that's what you mean. But numbers of our friends are quite convinced that they've seen departed spirits haunting various places around here, especially those old grounds over there. Bob and I were brought up with ghosts."

"My dear Irene," Bob interrupted, "you may deny it as you please, but everyone carries through life strains of what you call superstition."

"Indeed *I* don't," Irene said, sarcastically.

"Oh, we may try to hide it, even from ourselves, as most sophisticated people do," Bob answered. "But as Schopenhauer says, every human being in every age and clime is innately and everlastingly possessed with a sense of being surrounded by supernatural phenomena. Everyone openly or covertly believes in spirits, however he may try to suppress the fact by rationalizations. In a pinch he gives the ghost the benefit of the doubt—if he thinks there is a doubt."

"You are just being facetious, Bob." Irene felt that she had diagnosed Bob's mood.

He refused to be diverted. "As many honest and dependable people, Irene, as have testified positively to having seen spirits, and even communicated with them, how can you account for such a fact? Can you simply brush their testimony aside? Is that fair—or even logical?

"How many people," Bob continued, "would walk through a graveyard alone at night? A few might steel themselves to it, in a spirit of bravado or to achieve some nefarious purpose; but how normal could they keep their nerves and their heart beat? It is said that even ghouls—"

"Bob!" Priscilla chided.

Gordon Tyler rose from the depths of his reclining chair. "I believe it was Charles A. Dana who expressed my sentiment on that subject: 'I don't believe in ghosts, but I've been afraid of them all my life.'"

"Oh, I could name a raft of the most intelligent people who believe in spiritual phenomena—or did in their day—William Butler Yeats, Conan Doyle, Thomas Edison, Sir Oliver Lodge. As to that place over there," Bob nodded toward the Old Lawson Ruins, "very few whites and no negroes, so far as I know—except Mom Liza—would ever enter the grounds at night. They pass it with their eyes straight ahead and whistling to keep their courage up. Even in the daytime, most of them are wary about it."

"As children," Prudence said, "Bob and I always avoided the sight of the Ghost Oak at night. Neither of us would ever sleep in a room with a window facing toward it."

"What's the Ghost Oak?" came a chorus of questions.

Prudence answered: "See the largest, tallest tree up near the old house? That's the Ghost Oak. It's been haunted since time out of mind. I remember when the very sight of that tree at night sent shivers down my back. My black mammy would tell me in a coarse whisper about men she'd seen dangling from its limbs. Their bodies, she said, were quivering like gelatin, and their eyes were glaring like balls of fire."

"What a horrible experience for a child," Irene said.

"No, there was something fascinating about it," Prudence replied. "Don't you remember how as a child you adored 'Jack the Giant Killer,' 'Ali Baba,' and all sorts of stories about witches and goblins? Mammy could never tell me enough about those dangling men. I would always ask her to hold me tight and tell me more—my blood running cold all through me. Later, when the poor old soul was bedridden, she maintained to the end that the dangling men 'have put bad mouth on me!'"

"Why is that particular tree so ghostly?"

"Well, that goes back," Bob said, "to the time when the Red Coats passed through Cooperville."

"The *Red Coats!*" Priscilla shouted. "Is Cooperville as old as the Revolutionary War?"

"Yes, a little older, in fact." Bob continued: "It seems that back about 1760 a gentleman by the name of Thomas Cooper came over here from South Carolina, bringing his family and slaves as well as a few other families and their slaves. The Cooper home, in time, became the center of this planter village. I don't know whether my ancestor, Robert Lawson, had known Thomas Cooper before or not, but the records show that he soon followed him here, and a year or so later, married his daughter.

"It was this same Robert Lawson who built the old house over there. During the Revolution the Cooper house was burned by the Red Coats.

"In the battle of Brier Creek—fought in this county, by the way—the Patriot troops were defeated and scattered by the British. Then the bulk of the British army went toward Savannah by the road some miles to the east of here. But, straggling marauders took various routes, some of them through Cooperville. They sacked and burned the Cooper home and would have destroyed the Old Lawson house, but by the time they reached it a sort of spontaneous home guard, made up partly of slaves, had assembled and took them by surprise. One of the Red Coats was cornered and slain on the stair landing of the Old Lawson house. Two others were captured and hanged from a limb of the Ghost Oak. The rest of them got away.

"But the ones that were killed haven't left yet. They've been seen many, many times, generation after generation. Sometimes they wander off as though they might be looking for their buddies. But most times they appear just where they died."

At this point Mom Liza was seen passing through the shadows of the lawn mumbling to herself.

"Oh, Mom Liza," Bob called to her. "I have some guests here who say they don't believe in ghosts. *You* believe in them, don't you?"

Mom Liza ambled up to the porch. "Aw, Mister Bob, you're just tryin' to *use* me. You know what I believe."

"But, Mom Liza, I want you to help me prove to these people that place over there is haunted," Bob said placatingly.

"Well, all de provin' I can do is dat it just *is*."

"You've seen those men over there that were killed in the war?" Bob asked.

"Yes sir. I've seen dem dere and at plenty of other places too."

"How do you know they're the same ones, Mom Liza, when you see them other places?" Gordon asked.

"Humph! How you know Mister Bob when you see him? Besides, dey ain't no mistakin' dem *red coats* dey always wears."

"Aren't you afraid of them, Mom Liza?" Gordon pursued.

"Afraid? No sir. I know dem and dey know me. Dey know I ain't gonna bother dem, and I know dey ain't gonna bother me."

Mom Liza turned to go. Noticing a piece of glittering tin foil on the ground, she stopped and picked it up and walked on, mumbling, "Save all things, save all things."

In the course of the evening, a group of negros had gathered on the porch steps as Bob often had them do when he had guests. Usually they furnished entertainment—singing spirituals and folk songs or relating interesting plantation incidents and legends.

"Uncle Spode," Bob called through the screen.

"Yes sir, Mister Bob."

"Tell these people whether you've seen ghosts over there."

As Bob looked through the screen, he saw Taft beckoning to him to come out. Bob eased away from the group and slipped out another door to see what Taft wanted.

"Mister Bob, I hate to call you away from your party, but dere's somethin' I need to talk with you about." Taft ran over to Bob as soon as he saw him coming.

"Taft, you know that you're one of my best friends, but I do have guests to entertain," Bob answered.

"You don't need to worry about your guests for a little while, Mister Bob." Taft replied. "I've told Ruby and Br'er Burke to keep them entertained."

"This must be pretty serious business, then, Taft; so tell me your problem."

"Yes sir. I suppose you've heard dat Uncle Doctah died."

"Yes, Taft, I was sorry to hear about it, and I sure meant to come to his funeral. It's just that I have been so busy with these people I invited down from Atlanta."

"I know, Mister Bob. You're one of the best friends us colored folks ever had. You know dat de Lodge has been trying run dat divine healer out of the neighborhood. What I think you ought to know is I believe dat divine healer tried to kill Br'er Frank Lovett de very night Uncle Doctah died."

"Are you sure about that, Taft?"

"It's a long story; but, yes sir, I'm pretty sure. I was de first one at Uncle Doctah's house after he passed on. I was intendin' to pay him a social visit, knowin' dat he'd been ailin' for some time. When I got dere and walked up on de porch, I called, 'Uncle Doctah,' but I ain't heard nothin'. Den I called louder and I ain't hear a sound. About dat time somethin' told me Uncle Doctah's dead.

"So I peeped in de door and sure enough dere he lay on de bed, mouth wide open and eyes rolled back. Lordy, Mister Bob, I had de creepiest feelin' I ever has had in my life.

"While I was standin' dere, I found myself lookin' right square in de lookin' glass. Den I knew dat nobody ain't been dere to cover up de lookin' glass, and stop de clocks, and turn de pictures to de wall. My hair was standin' up almost straight.

You know, Mister Bob, I got a lot of children—about eleven, I guess. I say to myself, 'Taft, if you go into in dat house somebody in your house will sure die dis very year.'

"All dis time de old eight-day clock was goin' bang, bang, bang; and de little alarm clock was goin' tickety-tic, tickety-tic. Dere I was lookin' at myself in dat lookin' glass with no cover, listenin' to dem clocks, and lookin' at Uncle Doctah dead. I knew his ghost was snoopin' around and if he had called my name, I'd have died right dere in my tracks. I say to myself, 'Taft, you ain't got strength to stand dis long.'"

Taft was brave enough as long as he was dealing with tangible things, but ghosts were different. He had not been born with a caul; so he could never see the mystical things, but they were always in evidence in his subconscious mind. And he had never liked the idea of combating something he could not lay his hands on.

He went on: "About dat time I hear a rattlin' in de leaves in de yard, and I was afraid to look around for I say to myself, 'Dat's a ghost.' But, bless God, it was Br'er Frank Lovett. I ain't never been so glad to see anybody in all my life.

"'How's Uncle Doctah?' Br'er Frank ask.

"I say, 'Br'er Frank, he's made a die of it.'

"Den Br'er Frank ask me what I'm doin' out dere on de porch? I say, 'Br'er Frank, listen at dem clocks runnin', and look at dat lookin' glass dat ain't got no cover. And dem pictures dat ain't turn to de wall, and *a dead man in de house.* You know I got too much children to go in dat house. Some of us would sure die before de year's out.'

"Br'er Frank, he say, 'Br'er Taft, my children have all grown up and my wife is dead. I ain't got nobody to die in my house. De Lord ain't ready for me and de devil knows he can't get me. I'll get dem clocks and take dem out in de yard and we'll stop dem.'

"I say, 'Not *we*, Br'er Frank. You mean *you'll* stop dem, because I sure ain't gonna go messin' with dem.'

"Br'er Frank went in and got de clocks and bought dem out. He set de eight-day clock on a bench and held de pendulum and it stopped. But de Waterbury was contrary. Br'er Frank, he took off de crystal, and he tried to stop the hands, but it ran right on. Uncle Doctah used to give medicine by dat clock. It seemed like it knew something was wrong and it ain't want to stop.

"Now after a while Br'er Frank got dem stopped and he covered de lookin' glass and turned de pictures to de wall.

"Den we set about to lay de body out. We was feelin' powerful low, but dis mournful duty had to be performed. I got de tub and de water while Br'er Frank fixed up a coolin' board. Br'er Frank found de suit Uncle Doctah always wore to de Lodge and to church. I found his stiff-bosom shirt and high-standin' collar. About dat time Br'er Railroad Lawson come by; so we told him to go and spread de news dat Uncle Doctah was dead. I saw he was proud of his part and he ain't waste time gettin' away.

"Now, Mister Bob, dis is something I hate to tell because I'd injure Br'er Frank's reputation if it was known, since he is de senior deacon in de church. But I caught him drinkin' Uncle Doctah's moonshine. You know moonshine is a part of most medicine, and Uncle Doctah always kept some on hand. Well, Br'er Frank was sippin' it along and sippin' it along, and I notice he was gettin' bold and curious like, while I was actin' pious in de presence of de dead. Br'er Frank was puttin' de high-standin' collar around Uncle Doctah's neck. Br'er Frank act like Uncle Doctah's neck was swelled and he was havin' a time gettin' de collar on. About dat time i hear him say, 'Do dat feel too tight, Uncle Doctah?' I look around and he had de collar up over Uncle Doctah's chin and de bow tie almost settin' on his mouth."

Bob listened intently, but he became restless and hoped Taft would come to the point.

Taft continued, "I say, 'Br'er Frank, it's gettin' time for me to speak up. You're a Christian, but you're seekin' strength in moonshine in dis sad hour while I'm dependin' on de Lord to give us strength to lay Uncle Doctah out nice. If you don't mind how you squeeze Uncle Doctah's neck like dat, he's liable to lay his cold hands on *your neck* before dis night has passed.'

"By de time we get him laid out de people was comin' from everywhere. I knew we was in for some real spiritful worship when I seen my wife comin' with our whole family of children. Dey can sing, pray, and shout. Br'er Railroad built a fire in de yard to give light, and pretty soon Ruby began the singin'. All de rest of de people joined in singin' Uncle Doctah's favorite song, 'When de Saints Go Marchin' In.' Dey ain't finish half de song before everybody was singin'. De woods was ringin' with music, and when dey finish de song you couldn't hear a sound. Not a owl hoot in de swamp; not a whip-poor-will call. It seems like everything held its breath, waitin' for something.

"It took Parson Wilkes to start dat crowd to shoutin'. Dey say dat de parson was from de royal of Africa. He come into the crowd and walk right on in de house and stood lookin' like a king in de presence of de dead. His mustache was all combed out straight and his hair was brushed down like it was greased. His Prince Albert coat was all pressed out nice. De word went around dat Reverend Wilkes was gonna pray, and everybody got down on dey knees. De parson kneel down by a de body and pray all about what a great man Uncle Doctah had been, and how great a help he was to everybody. He say, 'We mourn our loss but we are happy because we know Uncle Doctah is reapin' a glorious reward.'

"About dat time Reverend Wilkes threw his head back, slap his hands on his knees, and start laughin' de holy laugh. He say, 'Lord, I know de angels are shoutin.'

"Mister Bob, you ain't seen nothin' like what happen den. Br'er Burke, he jump up and say 'Shout, you folks, shout! Wake up, you dry bones, and hear de word of de Lord and shout!' Everybody was shoutin', except Sister Lucindy Fawls. Some was cryin' for joy; some was laughin' de holy laugh. Br'er Frank Lovett was sittin' on a bench leanin' against a tree. You could tell he was feelin' de moonshine, but he was just laughin' de holy laugh.

"We must have shout about two hours before we began to settle down. Den Ruby start singin' 'Jesus, put your arms around me, and no evil thoughts can harm me; dear Lord, I'm in your care.' De congregation joined in and we all sang until daybreak."

"That must have been Tuesday night," Bob interjected. "I remember waking up in the night and thinking I was hearing the heavenly choir singing across the fields."

"Dat's right, Mister Bob. Then about daybreak I remembered we had to arrange for de funeral and get de pallbearers together; I looked around for Br'er Frank Lovett. But dey say he left about two o'clock. So I went over to Br'er Frank's house, about a mile. I could see his tracks in de sand headin' home. I could see dem plain, because all de other tracks were headin' for Uncle Doctah's. When I got past de Old Mill Creek I saw Br'er Frank had been runnin' and I knew something was runnin' after him, because I could see dose tracks, too.

"I got to Br'er Frank's house—de doors and windows were all open, but no Br'er Frank. I say to myself, 'I've gotta find him. He's de senior deacon and he's supposed to name de pallbearers.' So I went to de next house to see if he was dere. Sure enough he was sittin' in de door lookin' powerful down in de mouth.

"I said, 'Mornin, Br'er Frank: I thought you'd be home in your bed asleep.'

"The old man was so weak he couldn't hardly talk. He say, 'Br'er Taft, de Lord sure has punish me last night. I ain't more than got out of de light of de fire before I knew Uncle Doctah's ghost was follerin' me. I heard him comin' behind me and I stopped and turned around and sure enough I could see dat high-standin' collar and white-bosom shirt. And when I say, soft like "Uncle Doctah, is dat you?" he ain't say a word. When I walked faster, he walked faster. I say to myself dat I better get home as fast as I can, and, Br'er Taft, I'm tellin' you, I sure split de wind runnin'. When I got to de house, I fell across de bed, plumb give out. My heart seemed like it would stop beatin' and I felt like I was near 'bout dead.'

"Mister Bob, I'm tellin' you, Br'er Frank sure looked bad. His face was de color of wet ashes in de winter time and he was all drawn up with misery in his heart.

"He said, 'I ain't lay on dat bed long before I hear Uncle Doctah under de bed pickin' at the springs, like he was playin' on a harp. It seemed like he moved around and made a peculiar clickin' sound. Den I remembered what you say about him puttin' his hands on my neck before de night has passed, and no quicker had dat thought run across my mind when I felt his hand movin' around my throat. I yelled out, "Lord God, Uncle Doctah's got me." With dat I jumped up and down and dived through de window and I hit de ground runnin'. I come on over here to wait 'til day.'

"Den Br'er Frank and I started on back to Uncle Doctah's to get things in readiness for de funeral. Goin' along I told Br'er Frank dat Uncle Doctah's spirit ain't followed him last night; what he saw was dat divine healer after him. I say, 'Did you see Sister Lucindy Fawls last night? Did you see dat she was de only one dat ain't shout? And did you see her keep goin' out in de dark and stayin' a while, den she come in, and directly she go out again?' Br'er Frank say dat he ain't notice her. I told him 'de Lord ain't give me dese eyes for nothin'.' I say, 'Dat woman was goin' out in dat dark to meet dat divine healer what got all de money to build dat college, and ain't built nothin' and ain't gonna build nothin'. He's had feelin's against you ever since we had dat meetin' of de Lodge and you told him to get started buildin' or give all de money back or someone might get careless on his head with a stick. I saw dat same divine healer stain' at de window lookin' in when we was layin' Uncle Doctah out. He was de one dat pick at dem bed springs, and he was de one dat put his hands on your neck; and what you heard clickin' was probably his knife openin'. I saw de tracks of his patent leather shoes with de heels under your window dis very mornin'. *He aimed to kill you, Br'er Frank.* You been askin' too many questions about what become of de money for de college.'"

"Don't go making any accusations, Taft," Bob told him, "I know that Reverend Starkes has been a problem. I had no idea that he had caused that much trouble. But I think we had better handle him the legal way."

"Dat's more of de problem, Mister Bob, we've sent a committee from the Lodge to investigate, and it's all true about dat healer settin' up a hospital at Sister Lucindy Fawls's house. And we've told him to get out of here by Saturday night. Now dat divine healer says he is goin' to have us all arrested for interfering with divine worship."

"Don't worry, Taft, I was in Sylvania this morning," Bob assured him. "Sheriff Satterfield had asked me to come by his office. He told me about Reverend Starkes asking him to have your people arrested, and I told him that if this Reverend Starkes caused any more trouble, I wanted him arrested for practicing medicine without a license."

"Mister Bob," Taft said, "dat sure makes me feel better. I'll tell the brothers dat you've done taken action to help us. But, we still want to run dat divine healer out of here."

"I think he has gotten the message from the sheriff that he had better not cause any more trouble. If you and your brothers want him out of here, just tell him the law is on your side, and he had better leave by Saturday night. Now I must get back to my guests."

Taft was right. His friends had kept Bob's guests so fascinated with their tales of ghosts and haunted places that they had not noticed that Bob was not with them.

"Yes sir, I sure have seen dem ghosts. I've seen dem plenty of times," Uncle Spode almost seemed to be bragging.

Priscilla put her empty glass on the table, moved over, and stood against the screen. "Tell us about them, Uncle Spode. What do they do?"

"Dey sometimes wanders around, Miss. I've seen dem once in a while in different places around here. But dey ain't wander much. Most generally dey stay mighty close to one spot. And when dey do go away, dey always have to come back before daylight to de place where dey died."

"Why is that, Uncle Spode?" Priscilla asked.

"It's just always dat way with spirits, Miss; dey can't help it."

"Have *you* ever seen them anywhere except around the Lawson grounds?" Gordon inquired.

"Yes sir. De furthest I've ever seen dem away from here was down to de Old Mill Creek. I'd been fishin' and first thing I knew it was gettin' dark; and before I knew it, it was good and dark. And dat's a scary place even in de daytime, 'specially when dey ain't nobody with you.

"And so I begin to feel one of dem creepy feelings comin' over me, and I knew de spirits was stirrin'! Before I could get out of dat swamp, dere was dem Red Coats sort of walkin' backwards like ahead of me. I allowed I'd better see could I call for a little help, but my talk just hung in my jaws."

"What did you do then, Uncle Spode?" Allen Harvey had roused from his languor, his reddish face looking almost bronze in the dim light.

"Do? I got out of dat swamp right den, sir. I'm tellin' you I did. And de faster I ran, de faster dem spirits ran—backwards. I'm tellin' you, *backwards!* And just before we got to where it was a little bit light dey was gone, plumb gone, dat's all. Dey can't stand de light. No sir, dey just can't—dat's all."

"Did you see them plainly? Or were they just misty-like?" Allen asked.

"I seen dem just about as plain as I see you all now. Yes sir, I seen dem good and plain."

"Now, Uncle Spode, tell our guests about the time you thought you saw the two in the Ghost Oak, the two that were hanged," Prudence said.

"Which time, Miss Prudence? You know I've seen dem more than once."

"Well, tell us how they looked."

"Dey were just hangin' dere by dey necks, and de ropes were chokin' dem. Dey eyes looked like dey would pop out of dey heads and dey tongues were hangin' out about five or six inches from dey mouths. And dey looked mad enough to kill everybody around. Most generally it's just before daylight when you see dem like dat."

"Did they say anything?" Gordon asked.

"Mister Tyler, you know dey didn't. Dey were so choked dey just *couldn't* say nothin'. Leastways I don't reckon dey could; besides, I ain't give dem time. I was gone from dere fast as I could go."

"Uncle Spode, why is it Mrs. Morris has lived here all her life and has never seen a ghost at all?" Irene asked triumphantly as she crushed out the butt of her cigarette.

"Dat's because Miss Prudence, she wasn't born with no caul. Only dem what's born with a caul is got a seein' eye. And any dem dat's got a seein' eye can see spirits."

"A caul? What's that?" Priscilla asked.

"A *caul*," Uncle Spode said, "dat's like a wedding veil over the face of a newborn baby."

"Were you born with a caul, Uncle Spode?" Priscilla asked.

"Who, me? Yes, ma'am, I sure was. If I wasn't I couldn't see dem ghosts."

"Uncle Spode, have you ever seen the one that was killed on the stairway?" Even Wormser had broken his silence. He lighted his pipe and moved nearer the steps where the negroes were grouped.

"Not dere; no sir. I ain't never been about dem stairs when dey wasn't no light dere."

"What about Taft, does he claim to have a seeing eye?" Irene asked.

"Br'er Taft ain't here, ma'am; but he wasn't born with no caul."

"Who else is here that was?"

"Br'er Frank Lovett and Uncle Jud Williams."

"I guess I've seen pretty nigh all de spirits dat's around here," Br'er Frank Lovett volunteered. "But I ain't seen many at a time. An' de tallest runnin' I ever done was to give dem de road."

"*Now* you're talkin', Br'er Frank. I sure have seen you burnin' de wind." Uncle Jud walled his eyes at Br'er Frank Lovett.

"Humph! You ain't got no room to talk yourself, Uncle Jud," Br'er Frank came back at him.

"But I ain't never run like you did de night Uncle Doctah's ghost was after you."

"Sh-h-h!" Irene interrupted. "What's that?"

From across the fields and woods came the monotonous drone of a deep bass voice. Priscilla drew in her breath and moved over close to Allen. Irene shifted her position impatiently and asked: "Is that one of your ghosts?"

"Oh, that's an old fellow, Sam Holloman, who lives over in the pine barrens," Prudence explained. "A very religious man who seems to find a great comfort in praying as loud as he can."

"Bob was telling me about him this morning," Priscilla said. "I feel so sorry for him, living alone as he does."

"You're wasting your sympathy, Priscilla," Prudence consoled. "He's probably happier than the majority of people, for he's living exactly the sort of life he prefers. So many people are unhappy because they have to live according to patterns that are imposed upon them."

"You certainly have plenty of diversions down here—with your ghosts and haunted houses and all manner of freaks," Irene concluded and leaned her head on the back of the chair.

"Queen, you said a mouthful," Lester blurted from the background.

"Irene," Bob said, "that's what *makes* this place. It has a character all its own. And it takes all these varied elements to make it what it is. These things that appear odd to you are part of our life here, like our friends and our religion. I have always been fascinated by unusual people and things." Bob had just returned to the group. They had been so interested in talking about ghosts that they had not noticed he had been missing.

"Well, Bob, above all, it's surprising to me that you'd be credulous about ghosts."

"All right, Irene, do you think you could walk alone through that old house over there tonight without any sense of fear?"

"I *know* I could. I'm more afraid of that crazy yelling man than I am of any ghost."

"Then prove it."

"I don't feel that my imperviousness to superstition demands such a test."

"Or, as the negroes say, there are always plenty of excuses when you don't want to do something," Bob challenged.

"It's not that I'm afraid to do it, goodness knows!" She rose to her full height, Irene the undaunted. "And, to prove my point, I *will* do it." She started with long strides toward the screen door.

"What a blast!" Lester exclaimed as he watched the party adjourn to the yard of the old Lawson place.

"Hold on a minute!" Bob stepped in front of Irene. "I want Gordon to count your pulse before you go and again when you return."

Irene submitted her wrist with a shrug.

Gordon counted . . . "Seventy-four," he said.

"Now, go in through the front door and up the front stair to the landing that's guarded by the Red Coats," Bob directed. "On the right side of the landing is a door leading to a back stair. Go down that stair, out by the Ghost Oak, and back to us. Take it easy, Irene; I don't want you to say that any variation in your pulse was caused by exertion."

Irene went toward the front door with an air of bravado.

Allen excused himself to write an important letter and went back to Linger-long to the library.

Presently the rest of the guests saw her disappear into the gaping hulk. A few minutes later she reappeared in the dark shadows of the back yard, strode over and slapped the Ghost Oak, then rejoined the group.

"Another pulse count," Bob ordered, producing a flashlight.

When the count was made, Gordon looked up in surprise. Despite her boldness, Irene's pulse had gone up twenty-four beats.

"Oh-oh, Irene," Gordon said, "I can do better than that—I who don't believe in ghosts but all my life have been afraid of them." And he put out his wrist for Prudence to take his pulse.

When Gordon returned, it was found that the effect upon him was about the same as upon Irene.

No one there except Bob would acknowledge it, but Schopenhauer was right. Nothing but a spirit of bravado and iron grip on the nerves cold have carried any one of them through that ordeal. Each one knew it; each one concealed it—more or less.

"You try it, Priscilla," Gordon said daringly.

"Not alone," she pleaded.

"Don't be a sissy!" Gordon urged.

Priscilla eased out her wrist for the count. . . . Then, she walked hesitantly up to the wide double door of the old house, stood for a moment on the threshold, and disappeared within.

A momentary breeze swept across the old lawn and the long wisps of Spanish moss stirred like dying wings. The distant drone of Holloman's voice became clearer and more plaintive. From high up in the Ghost Oak came the unearthly cry of a screech owl.

Suddenly Priscilla ran back through the front door, screaming: "Ooooh! I saw it, I saw it! The Red Coat! He's there!"

Wormser dashed into the old house.

"Prude," Bob said, "you'd better take Pris in and give her a good stiff bracer."

"Oh, I'll be all right. I want to stay and see what happens," said Priscilla, putting her arm around Prudence.

"What did he look like, Priscilla?" Gordon asked.

"Please, Gordon, I'd rather not talk about it now."

Prudence could feel the pounding of Priscilla's heart.

Bob turned toward the old ruins. "I'm going to take a look myself," he said and followed Wormser.

Presently Wormser reappeared from the backyard. "Nothing there, not a sign . . . Are you all right, Mrs. Harvey?"

"I think so." Priscilla's voice was not entirely natural.

"I believe you were feigning."

"No, Mr. Wormser, but I'd rather not talk about it now."

"Well, I grant you, it is a ghastly place in there."

"I wonder why Bob doesn't come on out? Did you see him, Mr. Wormser?" Prudence asked.

"No, I didn't."

After the group had waited for several minutes, Prudence proposed that someone go look for him.

"I'll go," Gordon volunteered. "But I want the flashlight this time."

"Here it is." Prudence handed it to him. "But if you're going to take the light, let's all go."

They climbed the steps to the landing, then peered down the back stairs as Gordon held the light. About halfway down a loose banister leaned slantingly across the steps.

Gordon shifted the light. And there at the bottom of the stair Bob lay sprawled in a heap. Prudence and Priscilla both screamed. Gordon and Wormser carried his limp body out into the open air.

"Water, water! Ruby, water!" Prudence called as she ran toward Linger-long.

"Do you think we should give him artificial respiration?" Gordon asked.

"No." Wormser was emphatic. "There may be some injury that we might accentuate. Besides, he's still breathing."

"Bob, Bob!" Priscilla kept calling.

Ruby ran up with a flower sprinkler of water. Irene took it and emptied it into Bob's face.

"What's happened?" Bob asked, his consciousness returning.

"Never mind that now," said Prudence, wiping the water from him. "Are you hurt?"

"Not badly, I think."

"You must have had an awful wallop." Priscilla's voice was a-quiver.

Gordon said, "It's strange that no one else tripped on that banister."

"It wasn't there when I went down," Wormser declared.

V
Midnight Talk

Late Friday night

"Yes, Dr. Evans, I'll put an ice pack on his head right away. And I'll be sure to check the pupils of his eyes." Prudence had called Dr. Evans as soon as the group returned to Linger-long. "Yes, I'll call again if I notice any of the symptoms you mentioned. Bob seems fine now, but I will see that he stays awake for a couple of hours. I'm sorry to have called you so late at night, but I knew you'd understand, Dr. Evans."

"Prude, did you call Dr. Evans?" Bob's voice seemed agitated. "You know I'm all right," Bob said as he sank into his easy chair in the library.

"And you know that I just wanted to take care of you," Prudence answered.

"But I'm not hurt. You didn't need to bother him," Bob countered.

"Well, he did give me some good advice," Prude said. "He said to check the pupils of your eyes to make sure they are evenly dilated and to get a flashlight and see if they can contract in the light. You can tell by the pupils of your eyes whether there is a concussion. I know you will need an ice pack, so I'll bring the flashlight when I bring the ice pack."

"You make me feel like an invalid," Bob shouted after her as she left the room.

"You are okay aren't you," Priscilla asked as the guests began to gather in the library with Bob. The library was a large room across from the living room. The floor-to-ceiling bookcases on two walls were filled with books that the Lawson family had collected over several generations. Bob's office-sized desk, which was usually piled with papers, was cleared to look neat for his guests. The room served as a conference room as well as an office, so it was equipped with leather upholstered overstuffed chairs and a sofa. Bob sank into his easy chair, reclined it to a comfortable position, and rested his head on the back of the chair.

"Of course I'm okay," Bob answered with determination. "It may not have been the best way for the perfect host to behave, but there is really no damage done. Dr. Evans says for me to stay awake for a couple of hours, but I have to do that anyway because Lester is out on the town again and I want to see him when he gets in."

"I'll wait up with you," Gordon volunteered. "We need to get caught up on old times."

"Well, I guess I can get my beauty sleep," said Irene as she went toward her room. Allen and Priscilla told Bob that they hoped he would be better by morning, and headed toward their room.

"Well, I guess you don't need me," Wormser said as he disappeared down the hall.

Prudence returned with the ice pack and the flashlight. "Well, if it isn't Florence Nightingale," Gordon ventured. "May I help you with the diagnosis?"

Bob was quick to respond. "That ice pack might feel pretty good, but forget the flashlight. I told you I'm all right."

Gordon took the flashlight and turned it on. "This isn't going to hurt, and it will put our minds at ease. Relax, Bob." Gordon held the flashlight while Prudence inspected the contractions of Bob's pupils.

"Your eyes seem to be reacting normally, thank goodness," Prudence reassured Bob.

"Then you don't need to lose any more sleep over me," Bob told her.

Bob sank back in his easy chair and positioned the ice pack on his head. "Sit down, Gordon," Bob suggested as he motioned toward the sofa.

"I might as well, if we are going to be staying up," Gordon replied as he slouched into the corner of the sofa. "The last time I remember staying up until two in the morning with you was on the roof of the drama center at college," Gordon began.

"Do you mean the night we were watching Mary Jane Lovett and her troupe practice ballet?" Bob chuckled.

"Mary Jane was quite a girl. I remember I would do most anything just to see her. Somehow she never felt the same about me."

"I can't imagine why. You were a handsome young man in those days—and brilliant, too."

"Well, that was just the way it was. She was stuck on that goofball football player. I can't even remember what his name was."

"Sam something, I think, but that doesn't matter," Bob was hoping to loosen Gordon up. "It was your idea to climb up on the catwalk above the stage in the auditorium and look down to watch Mary Jane do her pirouettes and arabesques. I don't know why I went with you."

"Friendship," Gordon said. "Or maybe I dared you. But, anyway, it was quite a climb to get up there. I'm still not sure how we made it. Then just as soon as we settled on a beam where we could look down and see Mary Jane, that stupid fire alarm went off."

"I remember saying to you, 'Funny time to have a fire drill.' And all you could say was 'How the hell can we get down from here without being seen?' And, genius that you were, you added 'It's only a fire drill, so why don't we hide up here until its over.' "

"It seemed like a good idea," Gordon chimed in, "until we began to smell smoke."

"It really was smoke. Tons of it. We had to get the heck out of there fast. So we climbed out onto the roof and kind of hunkered down, hoping we wouldn't be seen. And there on the ground was Mary Jane pointing up at us and laughing." Gordon put his hands over his face and a muffled laugh escaped as he listened to Bob. "But, the worst part was that we had to be rescued by the firemen. I'll never forget going down that ladder, a steep one too. I wanted to run the minute I hit the ground."

"You wanted to run? I would have, but the firemen held us for questioning. I don't remember what they asked us. I only remember that by that time Mary Jane had seen me make a fool of myself."

"That wasn't the only time," Bob reminded Gordon. "Remember the time we Sigma Chi's decided to dump a can of green paint all over the stone lion in front of the Sigma Nu house,"

"Don't even mention that," Gordon admonished, and then proceeded to tell the story. "Painting the Sigma Nu lion was a spring ritual. Other people got away with it. But just let Gordon and Bob try something, and they'd get caught. We had hardly finished emptying the can when a spotlight from the upstairs of the house blinded us. We took off running like a pair of scared dogs and jumped over the fence in the back of the house. The plan was okay, but we hadn't counted on my pants catching on a nail in the fence."

Bob was beginning to chuckle now. He usually responded to humor with a wry grin, but he was remembering what happened next. "So we had to walk back to back like a pair of Siamese twins to cover up the tear in your pants made by the nail."

"And to get to the Sigma Chi house we had to pass near the auditorium. And, sure enough, it was Mary Jane's night to practice. She was on the way back to her dorm with Alice Bazemore and we all but bumped into them, still walking like Siamese twins."

"It would have been a perfect time to have a foursome," Bob added. "I always thought Alice kind of liked me."

"But there I was with that damn hole in my pants, making a fool of myself, again."

Bob looked at Gordon and asked, "So, what finally happened with you and Mary Jane?"

"Why do you ask that? You know that I carried a torch for all her through college, but she never showed any interest in me. Then, we graduated from college, and I found myself in the real world, still playing the field."

"Gordon," Bob became reflective again, "we had some good times in those days. Even after we graduated from college, you were as ready as I was to have fun doing the unusual. Remember we were just out of college and selling life insurance for that company with a branch office in Augusta? That car we used barely escaped from the junkyard. But we drove it all over southeastern Georgia. And we did pretty well for young men just out of college. At least we made enough money to live on."

"Money?" questioned Gordon. "Don't you remember the number of policies we traded for chickens and goats as a first payment?"

"But we made money on the chickens and goats at the farmers' market," Bob countered.

"Not that one goat I remember," Gordon reminded him. "Don't you recall the day two half-starved young men built a fire, put up a spit, and resolved to make a meal of a tough old nanny?"

"Yes, but you didn't have the nerve to kill the goat. You took one look at the knife and the neck of the goat and handed me the knife. Then it was a case of 'you do it,' 'no, you do it,' 'not me, you do it.'"

"Neither of us could make ourselves commit murder on a goat. So, we went fishing instead."

"And it was a good thing," Bob reminded him. "When we got back from fishing, old nanny had dropped a kid."

"I know. So we were nursemaids for a couple of goats until the kid got old enough to sell. It wasn't easy selling life insurance with a couple of goats in the car. But, we did pretty well that month. Then we were able to sell the goats. Thanks to the depressed insurance market that summer, we were high salesmen for that month. I think maybe that's what gave us our real start in life insurance as a career."

"I wish Lester would get home," Bob said as he looked at his watch. "Not that I'm not enjoying reliving old times with you, but I have something important I have to talk with him about."

"Lester is going to inherit this spread, isn't he?"

"He thinks so, but he's going to have to learn how to manage the farm if he expects to get it. And he's also going to have to learn to quit spending so much money. I have been talking with Prudence about putting the estate in a trust until he shows some sense of responsibility. And staying out to all hours isn't the way to manage a farm."

"Well, I guess that isn't any of my business," Gordon replied. Then, he changed the subject. "We did go up pretty fast in the life insurance business. I remember when you left the company to start your own company. You always were an independent cuss."

"I just never like working for somebody else. But even after I left the company, we had good times together—like when I was best man at your wedding."

"Yes, I thought I was pretty lucky when Irene and I were married. Irene was no Mary Jane, but she always looked as if she had just stepped off the cover of *Vogue* magazine. And when I was close to her, there was an aroma of French perfume. I guess it was love. Anyway I liked being around her, and my business associates were always impressed by her style. She's still a good looker." Gordon paused a minute and then asked, "Bob, why didn't you ever get married?"

"I guess I never met the right girl until it was too late," Bob said in a curt fashion, hoping to end that phase of the conversation. He paused a minute, adjusted the ice pack on his head, and then opened a new subject. "Remember the summer we bought those awful Hawaiian shirts."

"You talked me into that. I never expected to wear mine. Irene would have died if she had seen me in it. But then there was that hot summer day when we took the train from Atlanta to Augusta together. You dared me to wear mine and said you would wear yours." There was a chastising tone in Gordon's voice.

"Well, they were cool," Bob said, "and we had time to change before our appointments."

"Then the train stopped and an institutional guard got on with a group of inmates from an insane asylum he was transporting to the asylum in Augusta. Before the train could start he had to count to make sure all his people were on the train."

"I remember," Bob said. "So he started counting. At nine he came to us in those awful shirts. He looked at me and I said, 'I'm President of the Georgia Life Insurance Company and this is my friend who is also in the life insurance business.' The guard pointed to me and said ten and then he pointed to you and said eleven and passed on down the aisle counting. I saw him scratch his head when he finished counting. He seemed to have more charges than he started with." Gordon remembered and laughed loudly, slapping his knees as he laughed.

"Gordon, it's good to see you laugh again. There is so much to enjoy in life that I can't understand why you've become so somber lately. Until tonight, when we were reliving the past, you have been so distant. It's as though you were preoccupied with things that sap your zest for living. It seems that you've changed."

Gordon did not have a chance to reply, because they heard the front door open and out of the corner of his eye Bob could see Lester trying to sneak into his room.

"Lester," he called. "Come here a minute."

Lester was obviously taken aback. "Oh," he said as he entered the room, "Uncle Bob, I didn't know you'd still be up." Then he looked from Bob to Gordon and back to Bob. "What's with the ice pack? Isn't this a weird time of the night to be having a hangover?"

"It's hardly a hangover," Bob replied. I tripped on a banister going down the stairs at the old Lawson place."

"We were trying to prove that we were not afraid of imaginary ghosts," Gordon added, "by going in the front door and up the stairs and down the back stairs and out the back door."

"So, that's what you did after I left," Lester volunteered.

"Somehow a banister on the back stairs fell across the stairs, and I tripped over it. I took a tumble, but I'm okay now," Bob explained.

"Probably one of your ghosts pulled it loose, Uncle Bob. As you say, ghosts are that way. You never can tell what they will do." Lester was a bit sarcastic, but then he changed his mood. "Are you sure you're all right?"

"Of course I am. Gordon and I have been talking over old times. We didn't notice how late it had gotten."

"Well I don't want to interrupt you, so I'll just go get some shut-eye," Lester told them.

"Hold on a minute, young man. I want to talk to you," Bob said in an emphatic tone.

"At two in the morning?" Lester protested.

"At two in the morning," Bob confirmed.

"I'll see you in the morning," Gordon said. "I enjoyed keeping you company, but I'd better go check on Irene." Gordon remembered that Bob had wanted to talk with Lester.

"Good night, Gordon," Bob said.

"Good night, Mr. Tyler," Lester added as Gordon retreated from the room.

"Sit down, Lester," Bob began.

"But, Uncle Bob, it's after our bedtime," Lester protested.

"I know it's after bedtime, a long time after bedtime, and that's what I want to talk with you about."

"You've got to be kidding, Uncle Bob. What's there to talk about?"

"For one thing these hours you've been keeping—up 'til all hours of the night, sleeping all morning, listening to the radio all afternoon, and doing nothing to learn about the management of this farm."

"What do you want me to do? Start out at daybreak with a hoe and move some dirt around?"

"I'm in no mood for any of your back talk," Bob chastised.

"But, Uncle Bob," Lester interrupted.

"Just listen to me, young man. You know that you are the only heir that Prudence and I have. But don't get any ideas about inheriting this farm if you don't know how to manage it. I've worked too hard to make the cattle and the timber into paying businesses, and I don't intend to let some irresponsible person take over and lose it all."

"Don't call me irresponsible," Lester raised his voice. "What the hell is there to do here but see that those niggers you have working here do their jobs."

"Don't let me hear you say that word again. My employees are my friends, and I want them treated as friends."

"So I have to kiss ass with some colored folks. I don't see what that has to do with me taking time off to be with my friends."

"You need to know what each person's job is and how they do their jobs. More than that, you need to be aware of the latest farming methods, why I fertilize my pastures, what is a balanced diet for black angus cattle, when to immunize the cattle, how to care for a sick cow, how to deliver a calf, and more. As years go by there may be new and better ways of raising cattle, so you need to study livestock development."

"I suppose I have to feed and care for the trees, too?"

"They take more care than you might think. You need to know where to plow fire lanes, how to identify and treat bark beetle, and when to thin the forest. So far all I've seen you do is spend the money we make on this plantation."

"Uncle Bob, that's not fair. You fuss at me for staying out at night but it's you that's having this big house party and I bet it's costing you plenty."

"You might say that I'm mixing a little business with pleasure."

"Especially pleasure, with that Mrs. Harvey," Lester retorted.

"Be careful what you say, young man. We're talking about your responsibility around here."

Lester raised his voice, "I'm just finishing high school, and you expect me to know all that stuff you were talking about."

"Just calm down. We'll take one thing at a time, but I expect you to be trying to learn this business, not running off all the time with your friends. You know that your grades in school are so bad that we are not sure you can be admitted to an agricultural college."

"So it's my fault that I don't like math, and that reading all that hogwash about history and stuff is boring."

"You always have an excuse for doing what you want to do and not doing what you should do. I'm getting sick and tired of your playboy ways. I want you to shape up, beginning right now."

"Uncle Bob," Lester protested, "you act like you were never young yourself. And you say you and Gordon were talking over old times. I bet you had some fun in those days."

"We did, but we worked, too. We worked pretty damn hard selling life insurance while we were in school and after we finished college. Don't get me wrong. I don't mind your having fun, but if you don't settle down and spend some time learning how to manage this farm, your mother and I will have to will it to a management trust and the trust will control your income."

"The hell you say," Lester retorted. "I know what my rights are. Mom would never do that to me, and who are you to tell her what to do?"

"I'm just telling you to shape up or face the consequences."

"Good Lord, you're trying to make me an old man before my time."

"Not an old man, a responsible person," Bob replied. "Now you can go think about what I've said. I'll know whether you got the message when I see you working on the farm."

"Gee, whiz. Can I go now, Uncle Bob?"

"I guess it's time we both got some sleep," Bob said, and then added, "I'll see you in the morning."

As Bob got up to go to his room, he could hear Gordon and Irene arguing. "I thought Irene would be asleep," he remarked under his breath as he passed their closed door.

Irene had not been to sleep at all. She was pacing the floor when Gordon came into the room. "Irene, honey, I was sure you were asleep or I wouldn't have stayed away so long."

"Asleep? How could I sleep when I knew you were trying to get Bob to put his company into your holding company. That's the most important thing in our lives right now. Did he agree? Did he agree?"

"As a matter of fact, I didn't think tonight was an appropriate time to broach that subject."

"Are you kidding? You had him all alone. How could you miss a chance like that?" Irene's eyes were flashing green and her voice was angry.

"Bob had just taken a nasty fall. You don't hit a man when he's down. At least I don't," Gordon told her.

"You just don't have the gumption," Irene countered. "Sometimes I wonder why I married a dope like you. Did you see those pearls Prudence was wearing? It was a long rope of pearls, and real ones, too. And here I am with Majorca imitation pearls. I'm sick and tired of second best. I'm sick and tired of wearing last year's clothes. I want to look like the wife of an insurance magnate. I want—"

"Hold on a minute, honey—"

"Don't you 'honey' me. You know we came down here to get Bob to add his firm to your holding company, and you've blown your best chance." Irene marched over to the window and blew a puff of smoke from her cigarette out into the night air. Then she turned around and said, "Look at this room. It would look good in the best of mansions, and our room back home has just any old kind of furniture in it."

Gordon sat down on the edge of the bed. It was an antique four poster finished with a shine that made the wood look like satin. He looked around the room. The ruffled canopy and the bedspread reflected the sky blue from the flowers in the wallpaper. He had never particularly noticed things like that before. It was tastefully, and expensively decorated.

"I know how much you like nice things," Gordon told her. "Some day I will dress you like a queen. It takes time to build an insurance empire, but when I do, you'll be the queen."

"Or dead," Irene retorted. "You've been making promises like that until I'm tired of listening to your promises. Sometimes I wonder why I stay around and wait. There are other fish in the sea."

"Don't say things like that, Irene. I'm really trying. That deal I made last week was pretty good. Our company is coming along real well, and tomorrow Bob and I plan to go to Savannah. I had it in my mind to talk with him then."

"You'd better do some fast talking, because I don't intend to spend the rest of my life waiting for something to happen."

"I have all the facts and figures to show Bob that it is to his advantage to join with me. They're right here in this brief case," Gordon gestured toward a brief case leaned up against the chest at the foot of the bed. "So, give me a chance to get some sleep, and I will make you proud of me tomorrow."

"I hope that is not just another promise," Irene said as she sat down on her side of the bed and removed the slippers.

As soon as Gordon had gotten ready for bed, he noticed that Irene was turned to sleep with her back toward him. He lay down on his side of the bed quietly and was soon resting in a troubled sleep.

VI
Another Side of the Triangle

Friday night

Priscilla lay awake that night long after she and Allen had gone to bed. She could not close her eyes after the experiences of the day—the day that had crystallized for her a feeling that she had held, undefined, for years. She had felt it when Allen had kissed her hurriedly and absently in the mornings and, without even looking back, left her standing at the door. She had felt it on those long evenings that he spent in his study writing letters or reading business manuals. She had felt it most keenly during the last two years, when he brought her expensive presents and didn't wait for her to open them before he began reading the exchange lists in the evening paper. She had felt it last when he allowed a business detail to delay his trip to Linger-long.

It was a feeling of unfulfillment. Yet she had not been able quite to grasp it or to find any concrete experience that she could hold before her and say: This is what would make any life meaningful. On this night in Linger-long she could close her eyes and see pictured before her the moss-hung oaks moving slowly by as she rode along in the road cart. She could hear the symphonies of bird song from enchanted woods. She could smell again the odor of the twilight and feel Bob's lips pressed against hers. She knew now that it was Bob's keen appreciation of such things that had revealed to her what it was that would make her life complete. She remembered the night that seemed so long ago, when Allen had first said he loved her. She had known the feeling then too, and for some months thereafter. She had felt the fulfillment of her whole desire for being. Then, it had slipped away. And she had felt that Allen's love for her had not grown in richness like some antique jewel, mellowed and more treasured with age. Rather, as a pearl loses its lustre when it is not worn, his love had lost its charm.

The day at Linger-long had told her what was unfulfilled. She could see it now, and hold it. All the foggy subconsciousness of dissatisfaction had been clarified. She knew now her inner feelings. She could see them symbolized in the little duck or in the bluebird. Or, again, in the falling star she and Allen had seen on the night that he first kissed her. But that seemed so long ago.

"Pris, you are not asleep!" Allen said in an accusatory voice.

"Well, what of it? Neither are you?" Priscilla had been aware that Allen also was wakeful.

"That's just it, 'What of it?' You usually fall asleep like a kitten and I never know when my last foot hits the bed. Why should we lie awake for hours?"

"I had never thought to wonder why I am not asleep," Priscilla yawned. "It's so peaceful down here. I am quiet and comfortable, and I don't feel the need of anything else right now. In fact, I'm not so sure but that I may have been dreaming."

Allen turned over in his bed, his mind a tumult of conflicting impulses. He was eager to question her about Bob and herself. But he was constrained by a sense that the occasion demanded the utmost discretion. *No*, he thought, *I'll not do that now. It might break something in both of us.*

But the silence was breaking him. Feeling as he did, he could not bear to lie five feet away from her and remain quiet. He turned, facing her bed. "Baby, you are still awake!"

"How did you know?"

"A little bird told me."

At the mention of bird, Priscilla felt that the marrow in her bones was melting. Her cheeks were burning. She thanked her stars the moonlight was unrevealing. "Oh," she half whispered.

"You know as well as I do why we're both awake. You're expecting me to ask you why you and Bob were out so late this afternoon."

"Oh, we just went by the old swimming hole that he had told us so much about. I wanted to see it."

"Of course, I know that I have no way of keeping you and Bob apart, if you want to see each other. I'll have to depend on your honesty with yourself and with me for what goes on between you."

Allen was in a cold sweat. He hadn't meant to say that. He wondered why he had said it.

"That's a very sane attitude. I have not tried to conceal anything from you. Bob and I have had a lot of fun together. He's a swell sport and enjoyable company. You've known that longer than I have," Priscilla answered, hoping Allen would let the matter end there.

"But it seems to me, Pris, that it has become more than that between you and Bob."

Priscilla could not answer him. Her heart was beating rapidly and there was a pounding of the pulse about her throat.

Allen got up and slumped down on the side of her bed.

"Baby," he said, "you know I love you more than anything in the world. I'd do anything for you, anything that would make you happy."

"I know—that is, if you could understand what it takes to me happy."

Priscilla felt sorry for Allen—and for herself. Their interests were so different. She had never been able to bring herself even to a halfway interest in his business as a broker. It seemed such a prosaic sort of thing. Now, she realized that they had matured separately instead of together. *Perhaps*, she thought, *we are both to blame for that.*

"Pris, you've expected a perpetual honeymoon out of marriage." Allen sat upright. "But that honeymoon excitement can't keep up. It's like champagne—so exciting, so intoxicating—but it isn't normal for people to go on like that."

"That's just the trouble. Since those honeymoon days you have had your business to keep you stimulated, something to live for that's outside our relationship. But I've had to stay home and play out my restlessness by joining bridge clubs and the like. And that has not kept me happy. Do try to understand when I tell you that I've learned today something of the inner meaning of life that I had once known with you but had forgotten."

"Then, you do love Bob?"

Priscilla could feel his plump body go taut.

"Y-yes, but not in the same way I love you." She felt her answer was reassuring.

"What do you mean by 'not in the same way'?"

"I'm not sure that I can make you understand," Priscilla said with deliberation. "I'm devoted to you, you can never doubt that. There naturally grows a strong attachment between people who live as you and I have. You have been very generous to me. You have given me all the material things I've wanted. And I sincerely appreciate all that."

"You should," Allen interrupted.

"But somehow—well, after our early experiences together, you seemed to grow more interested in your business than you were in me; you seemed to regard me as a part of your property—something that would show off well among your business and social acquaintances. Then, you seemed to forget how to say all the clever things I enjoy, and the beautiful things I love.

I feel," Priscilla hesitated, "as if you'd given me second place in your life."

"Second place?" Allen was livid. "After all the things I have done for you over the years?"

"I appreciate what you have done for me, and I know you've been pleased with me; that is, I think you have. You have proudly rewarded me with houses and cars and roses—which have their place. But there are some desires in my life that such things can't fulfill. I am not sure that I am making myself clear. It's a matter of feeling, of understanding."

"But, Baby, you know I have shown my devotion for you in a great many ways."

"Yes, you have. But in your very giving, something has been lost. You are no longer the same Allen that I married."

"Pris, those are hard words. . . . I had hoped that this affair with Bob was just a passing fancy, but I'm afraid it's more than that. You are not only in love with Bob, but you are trying to justify it by making me the goat," Allen said with impatience.

"No, Allen, I don't need any goat. I feel no sense of guilt. I believe as a great many believe, that a woman can love more than one man and that a man can love more than one woman, but love them in different ways. There are doubtless some people who find all the attractions they desire in one person, but there are others who do not. Do you see what I mean?"

"No."

"If I must be specific, I love you for what you are: for your utter sincerity, the good times we have together, the places we go, the people we meet, and all the lovely things you have done for me. . . ."

"And isn't that enough?" Allen was becoming more agitated.

"Yes, it's enough in your way of doing things, but you still don't get the point. Bob . . . I love him because he shows me beauty that I never knew existed, an intangible something that reaches beyond ordinary things. He gives life a new meaning for me. The way he tells me about flowers, or roads, or friends. The paths I walk with you are securely cemented and safe; the paths I walk with Bob are vibrating, pulsating with the love of life."

"So-o . . . It's one of those businesses in which I hold the body and Bob holds the soul!" Allen said resentfully.

"Allen, you're downright unfair! You're not yourself tonight."

"Pris, it's you who are not yourself. You are giving Bob the place in your heart that rightfully belongs to me."

"Won't you believe me when I say that my feeling for Bob takes nothing away from my feeling for you?"

"Pris, you're lying," Allen's voice showed anger.

"No, Allen. Remember the first night you kissed me, and how we sat out in the night for so long and counted falling stars?"

"You've kissed Bob!" Allen's anger was increasing.

"That isn't the point. You hadn't thought of that night in years. I hadn't either. But I remembered it today. And I remembered I love you."

"You've kissed Bob! Say it! Say it! You've kissed him, haven't you?" Allen had lifted Priscilla from her pillow and was holding her at arms' length in front of him.

"What does it matter whether I kissed him? He's driven away all that restless feeling in me. He's shown me what my life means. He's shown me how to love and how to feel. Don't you ever want to feel? Don't you ever get tired of living on and on without feeling glad, or sad, or so happy that you could burst with excitement?"

"He can't take you away from me!" Allen's arms were vibrating. His blood ran hot as he waited for her answer.

Priscilla did not answer immediately. She began slowly with a calmness that emphasized the tenseness of the situation.

"Allen, please try to understand that my love for you has grown today, because I have learned again what it was meant to be."

"You little liar! You're in love with Bob. But he can't have you. You're mine! *I'll see Bob Lawson in hell before I'll let him take you away from me!*"

Before Priscilla was aware of what was happening, she heard Allen stumble through the door as he walked out into the night. She knew he had not understood. But, she knew she could not have explained her feelings more clearly. And now, she thought, he might try to keep her away from Bob or make a scene with him about her. Perhaps he would stay on there and make all three of them uncomfortable. Or perhaps he would calm down by morning and go along in his usual undemonstrative way.

Suddenly, Priscilla could bear the darkness no longer. Turning on the light beside her bed, she saw the little duck she had rescued from the swimming hole. It was lying on its back. As she picked it up, she realized it was dead. That was what Allen had stumbled over, she thought. She wrapped it in tissue and placed it in an empty candy box. For a long time she stood still, staring at objects in the room without seeing anything until her focus fell upon the vase of daisies on the dressing table. It seemed years since the late afternoon when she put them there. As a reflex from childhood, she began slowly pulling off the petals and letting them fall to the floor. . . .

"He loves me, he loves me not; he loves me, he loves me not; he loves me. . . ."

VII
Other People's Money

Saturday

The next morning Bob joined the group at the breakfast table, little the worse for his fall the night before—a knot on his head and a few bruises of little consequence were all that remained. The experience had in no way dampened his feeling for the old place.

"All sentiment aside," he said, "the old Lawson house has a definite function to perform in my little orbit. A southern gentleman must have his liquor, as you all know. And that house has a cellar which is ideal for storage purposes—walls of such masonry as you rarely find today, and old-fashioned locks with keys that could hardly be duplicated. The awe in which the place is held makes it pretty safe anyhow. I don't dare keep much liquor at a time over *here* where so many servants have the run of the house. Liquor is the *one* thing that our servants will take, however honest they may be in other things."

"Bob, your statement is too sweeping," Prudence corrected. "You know very well there are some who never taste it."

"Maybe," Bob went on. "The place also offers me perfect seclusion for meeting with my bootlegger. I hate such clandestine dealings, but the laws have forced these things upon us. 'There must be a law, *there must be a law!*' Hence there must be bootleggers."

"Don't they sell liquor in Savannah?" Irene asked.

"Certainly! Barrels of it, rivers of it—enough to float the Atlantic fleet. But a gentleman who values his reputation in these parts will not go hauling liquor through dry counties.

"When Walt Hendrix, my bootlegger, gets in with a new cargo of imported stuff (more or less imported) he informs me in code, and, if I'm in the market for it, we meet at the old place at an appointed time—always, of course, at night. The liquor usually appears per schedule. I take it on faith, but on faith that is never too high, for sometimes it's fake or heavily cut. He's a scoundrel of a fellow. The last time I saw him I threatened to sic the federal authorities in Savannah onto him if he palmed off any more fake stuff on me."

"Why don't you buy from somebody else?" Gordon asked.

"For the simple reason that he's the only bootlegger within reach who even pretends to carry first class stuff. As a matter of fact," Bob remarked casually, "I am to keep a rendezvous with him tonight. Not that I'm out yet, but I want to be prepared for all emergencies. There are snakes in these woods, you know, and we have to be prepared with what's good for snake-bite."

When the laughter subsided, Prudence inquired of Bob: "You are still planning to go down to Savannah today?"

"Yes. Gordon and Mr. Wormser are going with me. Allen, won't you change your mind and join us?"

"Thanks, Bob, you forgot that I have a business engagement in Sylvania this afternoon and evening."

"You'll go in the Lincoln, won't you, Bob?" Prudence asked.

"No, I'm leaving that for you all. It's going to be a fine day, and I thought those of you who stay here would enjoy having Taft drive you over some of our beautiful countryside—down the Louisville Road, for example, at least as far as Oliver. You know there's not a prettier stretch this side of heaven. Be sure not to miss the huge oak in front of the old Cameron place. That tree actually has a spread of a hundred and forty feet, I've measured it." Bob motioned broadly with his hands and added facetiously, "And I want particularly to call Irene's attention to the old family graveyards and to the remains of deserted mansions along the road."

Irene inhaled long drafts from her cigarette and blew out the smoke with cool disdain.

"Why don't you use the Lincoln?" Prudence insisted. "We can all go in the roadster, if we use the rumble seat."

"No, Prude, we have decided to go on the train. The detours on the highway to Savannah are terrible. The last time I was over them they were almost impassable in places. Lester, how did you find them Thursday?"

Lester dropped his eyes sullenly and did not answer at once. This was a sore point with him.

Bob said parenthetically, "Lester stole a march on us Thursday and went on a wild party to Savannah Beach."

"*Sufferin'* cats, Uncle Bob! How do you get that way! Every time I go off with my friends you have to call it a wild party."

"We'll settle that later, young sprout. Will you answer my question?"

"About the detours? They're plenty bad. We got stuck several times. One time comin' back we had to get some niggers to push us out."

Prudence put her hand to her mouth and gasped. "Lester, haven't I told you never to use that word. They are negroes," she admonished.

"Oh, Mom, when are you going to quit trying to control me?" Lester threw back at her.

"If the detours are that bad," Gordon went back to the original subject, "we're wise in going by train."

"What time will you get back tonight?" Allen inquired, apparently thinking he might meet the train.

"The train is due at Dover at ten-twenty-eight," Bob replied. "It's the night train for Atlanta and is usually on time. It better not be too late, for my appointment with Hendrix is at eleven tonight."

Gordon looked at his watch. "Bob, do you realize that it's nine-fifteen? We have only twenty minutes to make our train."

The three men rose from the table, grabbed their hats and brief cases, and hurried to the car which Taft had waiting for them in the driveway.

As they arrived in Dover, the train for Savannah was just pulling in. The three men found a four seat compartment. "Just made it," Gordon said nervously.

"I knew our timing was good," Bob said as he handed each of them a copy of the morning newspaper which he had picked up in the station when he stopped for his mail.

After spending about fifteen minutes browsing through the headlines, Mr. Wormser, who was seated next to Bob, asked, "Bob, why is it that you seem to have a strange influence over the people around here?"

The corners of Bob's mouth turned up in a smile. "What makes you say that?" he asked.

"Well," Wormser replied, "just listening to people talk. Like in Sylvania yesterday, and then this morning. I was taking my early morning walk. I went down through the orchard, and I heard a man and a boy arguing. I wasn't close enough to catch every word, but the man was fussing at the boy for stealing tobacco. Then I heard the boy yell, 'You act like you own the world, but Bob Lawson's back here now, and you'll see who's boss'—or something to that effect."

Bob was mildly amused. "That was mostly just talk. But the Coopers and the Lawsons did found the settlement here, and I suppose that adds respect to the name. And I have a lot of friends, but I would doubt that I have any special influence."

Gordon looked up from his paper, "Ever think of running for political office?"

"Hardly," Bob answered. "I have my hands full with Prudence and Lester and the farm."

"From what I saw of the farm yesterday, it does seem like a full-time job," Gordon said, thinking of the added responsibility of Georgia Life, but he said no more at that time. He considered broaching the subject of the merger, but he decided to wait until he could get more information in Savannah. The men rode on in silence lulled by the rhythm of the train wheels against the track.

In Savannah, the men agreed to separate, each to look after his own affairs, with the understanding that they would meet on the train that evening. During the day they caught only glimpses of one another trailing in and out of banks and other business places.

When the train for Atlanta pulled out from the Savannah station at exactly eight-forty that night, Bob and Gordon were seated together in a Pullman car. Wormser was on the opposite seat. They exchanged a few favorite jokes and chatted a while about nothing in particular. Then they fell silent, each browsing over the columns of the *Savannah Evening Press*.

But, Gordon was restless. He kept chewing an unlighted cigar and shifting his paper back and forth among the front page headlines, the editorial columns, and the stock market reports. But he appeared unable to concentrate on any of them. Bob watched him from behind the corner of the newspaper. *Gordon is losing that athletic figure he used to be so proud of when we were at Tech,* he thought; *I hate to see him getting fat and bald.* Finally, Gordon reopened the question most on his mind—that of bringing Georgia Life into his empire.

"You can't do it, Gordon! You can't do it! And you know perfectly well I can stop you." Bob was polite but positive.

"I'm not so sure, Bob, I've been doing some talking the same as you."

"No doubt; but I have the better case and I think I've been more convincing."

"Bob, it's a strange thing to me that, as good a business man as you are, you sometimes act like a babe in the woods."

"I may seem that way to you, but I'm no babe at *this* game. I know what your holding company proposition would mean. It would milk Georgia Life all but dry, to the detriment of thousands of stockholders and policy holders who have placed their confidence in me.

"When Georgia Life was first launched, I sold many thousands of dollars worth of stock, all told, to trusted friends and relatives. I later persuaded my own sister to invest in its stock and she put the greater part of the small fortune her husband had left her in the company. Directly or indirectly, I am likewise responsible to thousands of its policy holders."

"But Bob—" Gordon tried to interrupt.

"You may sneer at the sob stuff about 'widows and orphans' if you like, but I have enough of the Old South spirit of *noblesse oblige* to feel a personal responsibility to these people who have trusted me. And I can't be lured by a half-million-dollar slice in your melon cutting any more than I can be convinced by your ingenious arguments of value received."

"You're over-conservative, Bob. In fact, on this subject I might say you're antiquated. This is a new age. Business relationship have changed—"

"Remember, Gordon, that I'm not a believer in much that characterizes our new business age."

"Bob, you're a visionary. You are trying to tie a dead past to a utopia that never was and never will be. Your idealism stands in your own light. You have a chance to make big money, and you won't take it." Gordon opened his brief case. "Look at these charts and figures. Can't you see that—look here—both our companies would profit."

Bob studied the charts carefully. Then he spoke with certainty. "But, Gordon, your proposition to me means taking other people's money. I can't do it. I won't do it. And I won't sanction it. I'll slop my hogs and fatten my steers, preserve my self respect, and die with a gentleman's conscience."

"Well, I maintain that the small company is doomed unless it falls in line. Coordinating agencies are imperative. The holding company, you must understand, has a definite service to render. It is indispensable."

"Not for Georgia Life. It has its own sphere of influence, its own clientele, it is doing well in its own right, and I intend to see to it that it shall not be milked dry by any holding company. I hope you'll understand, Gordon, that there's nothing personal in this. I don't impugn you own motives. I simply feel that you are hipped with this holding company idea. You may be blinded somewhat by the prospect of millions in personal gain—"

Gordon broke in: "It's all right for you to say that. You don't have a wife to support. A woman these days can't wear the same clothes year in and year out. She can't sit at home and wait until you can bring the family car to her. And when all her friends go off to Florida or Cuba for the winter, she can't stay calmly in the old home town and twiddle her thumbs. Irene's not a simple country girl. She's not used to the small town idea of just living from day to day."

Bob was convinced now of what he had suspected earlier. It was Irene who had changed his college pal into a grasping, overaggressive financier.

"But in any case," Bob maintained, "there are interests which I feel honor-bound to protect, and am determined to protect. So, definitely and finally, Gordon, I shall fight your scheme to the bitter end, and if, as a last resort, I have to, I will divulge some facts that you would give an awful lot to keep off the records."

"Bob!" Gordon was obviously irritated, but was weighing his words. "If it were anyone but you, Bob, I'd call that blackmail."

"That's an ugly word, Gordon, especially between friends such as we have been—since our days at Tech together. Don't you see, can't you see that I feel a personal responsibility toward those whom I am sure a holding company would injure?"

"My Lord, Bob! For every dollar it would take from Georgia Life it would give value received and more. You know very well that its coordinating service would—"

"I know nothing of the kind! But we've gone over all that time and time again. Let's not rehash it now. You know how I stand. I have told you my decision and that's final."

During the conversation, Wormser sat in apparent listlessness, now turning through the newspaper, now peering through the window, or shifting his eyes absently among the other passengers.

They rode on in silence.

VIII
Rendezvous with a Bootlegger

Saturday night

The train puffed noisily past the crowd of tenant farmers, hired hands, and small landowners such as generally assembles at way stations, especially on Saturday nights. Then, it came to a stop, its day coaches flanking the crowd. As Bob, Gordon, and Wormser descended and walked along the gravel platform they met Dr. Evans.

"How do you do, Dr. Evans," Bob greeted cordially. "I want you to meet my guests, Mr. Tyler and Mr. Wormser.... Dr. Evans is the guardian angel of Cooperville." The men exchanged greetings.

Dr. Evans, of a locally prominent family, was a combination of planter, physician, and coroner. One of the most poised and cultured men thereabouts, his opinions, in all matters in which he would venture an opinion, were given great weight. He was tall and straight and, despite his threadbare attire, looked the part of the old-southern gentleman more completely than anyone else in the community.

"You all are to ride home with me, Bob," the doctor said. "I had dinner with Prudence and your other guests today, and I told her that I had to come here anyway, that she needn't bother to send a car."

"You are very thoughtful, Doctor, as you always are. But, if you'll take my guests, I believe I'll walk home through the woods. I often prefer to walk, you know. Besides, as my guests understand," Bob said with a telling wink, "I have an appointment en route."

"But there's a dark cloud rising, Bob, you'd better come with us. If my understanding is correct you can reach your appointment just as easily—"

"Storms hold no terrors for me, Doctor. In fact, I rather like them," Bob said, knowing that his real reason was that he wanted to be alone.

Across the way, on the porch of Mason's General Store, a group of rowdy loafers, black and white, were indulging in their usual Saturday night's dissipation—drinking, dirty-joking, swearing, carousing in general.

Every country store in that region had a commodious front porch with seats for loafers. Such people were welcomed because they furnished a trickle of trade in the way of tobacco, soft drinks, and knickknacks. There is always a group of such loafers, and usually in the late afternoon and evening there are larger numbers, frequently boisterous.

On this occasion, Will Sorrel had been making himself the center of attention, as he often did when he was "in his shine." Will was a mean one. His chief joy was in his hatreds. He was a poor white from a family that for generations had struggled to eke out a sorry existence on a patch of worn-out, sandy land. From childhood, he had developed a pronounced inferiority complex. He hated those whom he envied and enjoyed lording it over those whom he felt to be his inferiors.

Among his hatreds, by far the bitterest was that against Bob Lawson. Will's father before him had held a similar hatred against Bob's father—a hatred which sprang from incidents which the elder Mr. Lawson had regarded as trivial. He had tried repeatedly to placate Mr. Sorrel and, failing that, had sought to ignore him. But Mr. Lawson was high tempered and his patience with Mr. Sorrel often came near the breaking point.

One day, when Bob and Will were still boys in their teens, the two fathers had encountered each other in the courthouse yard in Sylvania. Mr. Sorrel, who was drinking heavily, became vituperative. Mr. Lawson was stirred to wrath and said things that he afterward regretted. Both men had long gone armed. Mr. Sorrel drew his pistol. Mr. Lawson was quicker on the trigger. The jury pronounced it self-defense, and all reputable people thereabouts agreed with the verdict. But, the fact that he had killed a man, even a Sorrel, bore heavily on Mr. Lawson's mind and, some said, hastened his death a few years later.

Even though this affair involved a Cooperville man, it had never been accepted by Cooperville people as part of their village traditions, for it had happened in Sylvania and during the abnormal atmosphere of court week. It is well known that almost anything may happen in a rural county seat during court week, when so many people of all different kinds are on hand, many of them in various stages of intoxication and scarcely responsible for their emotional reactions.

As Bob stood there by the train, excusing himself from his guests and Dr. Evans, he was aware of Sorrel's ranting. He heard bursts of profanity, which he more than suspected were directed toward him. Without even looking in that direction, however, he crossed the tracks behind the departing train and was lost in the shadows of the Old Dover Road.

This had once been *the* Dover Road. But, because of the fact that the portion of it leading out from the station was so low-lying and marshy, the new, sand-clay highway to Sylvania had been rerouted. The old road had become virtually impassible to cars and was little used at all. But, Bob preferred to take this road when walking because of the solitude it afforded.

After he passed out of range of the station's lights, he had to use his flashlight and pick his way carefully until he emerged from the dense wood into the open country beyond. The sky was almost black except when occasionally rent by flashes of lightning—dazzling for an instant—then followed by contrasting blackness. But this was nothing new to Bob, he loved it.

Lingering in his mind was the picture of Will Sorrel, swaggering and mouthing what Bob felt sure were execrations upon him. For the first time in years, Bob permitted himself to reflect upon the whole Sorrel affair.

He recalled his earliest years in the Cooperville school and his first contacts with Will and the other Sorrel children. He was momentarily amused as he thought of an incident that occurred when he and Will were in the primary grades: lice were found in the hairbrush used in common by the school children. It was one of the snooty Wilkes girls who had made the discovery, but she was from a family that *rated,* and certainly no one would ever have suspected her of being lousy. But the Sorrels were the kind upon whom suspicion would naturally fall, upon whom, as a matter of course, it inevitably did fall. Not merely a suspicion, but open accusations. There was no evidence that the Sorrels were guilty, except for the fact that they were poor whites, and lice were naturally associated with the poor whites, just as dirt-eating was.

Bob had developed no sense of class distinctions, and he well remembered how at the time he had resented the derision heaped upon these poor children when there was no real proof of their guilt. He had wondered at the time why the Wilkes girl, who had used the brush last, was not suspected at all.

But this early tendency to pity the Sorrels did not last long. In time, there developed a sharp personality clash between him and Will. In the years of their adolescence, Bob came to be bitterly riled by this red-headed, freckle-faced, contemptible blusterer. Will was so damn boastful, for one who had nothing to boast of, and resentful of all gentility. He was ready to fight to maintain his exceedingly doubtful status. Bob, too, was quick-tempered in those years. And so, this clash of personality lay the basis for inevitable fights. Bitter fights! Bob was the hardier boy, and on several occasions he beat Will rather badly. But, Will was never conquered.

As Bob matured, he came to feel that such fights were beneath his dignity and social standing. He simply ignored Will. Then, of course, after Bob's career in college and the business world, the chasm between them had grown wider and deeper. It had been while Bob was in college that the fatal fight between their fathers had occurred. After that, Will, of course, was all the more bitter, but now that Bob had become a power to be seriously reckoned with, Will no longer bantered him to his face. But he often cursed Bob vilely behind his back, sometimes even daring to do so within hearing distance.

Hell! Why can't the man see the futility of trying to perpetuate a one-sided squabble? Bob thought. It was not that he had any real fear of Will; the fellow was simply a pest.

In the spasmodic light Bob could see wide fields of growing cotton on either side of him as he trudged through a sandy stretch of the Old Dover Road. Outlined against the horizon some distance ahead of him were the tall oaks of the Lawson grounds. He was again impressed with the gigantic size of the Ghost Oak standing like a sentinel over the place. *It's strange,* he thought, *that it should have grown so much bigger than the other trees around here.*

This reverie was broken by the weird howls of Starvation between the intervals of thunder. Starvation—Bob's heart warmed at the thought of the dog's devotion to him.

The sky was growing blacker, the atmosphere more oppressive; the lightning was more frequent and move vivid; the rumbles of thunder were turning into violent crashes. Great drops of rain that heralded the shower splashed coolly on Bob's face. He remembered how he and Taft as boys had dared each other to run out into the rain until they were drenched. *Good old Taft,* he thought. A herd of cattle was running pell-mell before him, seeking shelter under the great oaks. The roaring of the wind in the clouds sounded almost cyclonic.

Bob had now reached the old Lawson place. As he groped his way onto the old grounds to keep his rendezvous with the bootlegger, his eyes were blinded by lurid flashes of lightning and his ears were rent by deafening crescendos of thunder.

IX

In the Old Lawson Yard

Sunday morning

Cooperville was always placid. On this particular Sunday morning it was especially quiet and serene. Everyone had slept later than usual, for the shower the night before had left the atmosphere cool and restful.

As Taft walked slowly up the Old Dover Road toward Linger-long, he was conscious of the raindrops that still clung to the leaves and grass and glittered in the sunshine. Somehow they reminded him of the diamonds that Bob and Prudence wore, treasured heirlooms of the Lawson family.

When he reached the stretch of the Old Dover Road that ran between Linger-long and the old Lawson place, he was interrupted by Starvation, barking and whining persistently. Pushed aside with a kindly but positive "be gone," the dog became all the more persistent, jumping up on the man then running back into the old yard. When Starvation had repeated this action several times, Taft was impelled to follow the dog's retreat.

"Blessed Jesus!" Taft gasped, as his eyes fell upon the body of Bob Lawson lying sprawled before him.

"Mister Bob! Mister Bob! *Oh, my God, Mister Bob!*" Taft knew at once that Bob Lawson was dead. There was no use to question. There was no use to hope. A gaping slash across the throat, dark, reddish-brown patches of blood on the grass where he lay, and the sickening drone of flies against the stillness of the morning told Taft to expect no response from "Mister Bob."

Taft fell upon his knees beside the dead body. "Dear Jesus," he sobbed. "De best friend us colored people ever had."

He took off his Sunday coat and spread it over Bob Lawson's face.

"How can I ever tell Miss Prudence! How *can* I tell her! How can she stand it!" Taft moaned as he rose and ran toward Linger-long. "I gotta be a man! Mister Bob trusted me, and right now he's lookin' down on me from de sky . . . I *is* a man!"

He put his hand against his pounding heart when he saw Prudence Morris, already up, on the back porch arranging flowers for the breakfast table. She was startled by Taft's rapidly approaching footsteps and as she turned she felt the terror in his eyes.

"What on earth's the matter, Taft?" Prudence asked anxiously. "Something terrible must have happened to you."

"It's about Mister Bob, Miss Prudence." Taft's face was drawn in painful confusion.

"Taft?"

"He's dead, Miss Prudence, he's dead . . . And what's more, he's been killed," Taft said brokenly, his eyes fixed on Prudence's blanched face. "Yes, ma'am, Miss Prudence, dey ain't no doubt. . . . Mister Bob's lying dead under de Ghost Oak with his throat cut." When he could no longer hear the sound of his own voice, Taft wondered what he had said.

Prudence stood in a daze, bracing herself against a pillar. A sense of helplessness—helplessness in the presence of death—held her motionless and silent. A crash from the bowl of flowers as it fell from her hands brought her back to the tragic situation. *I must be brave,* she thought, *Bob would want me to be.* She looked at Taft. He was standing in the same tracks, his distraught expression unchanged.

"Taft, go to Dr. Evans and tell him to come over here at once." Prudence's voice was that of one straining to affect calmness.

Lester Morris, half asleep, in house shoes and pajamas, staggered onto the porch, his sunburned hair awry, his pimpled face in a frown.

"What the hell's goin' on here?" He asked as if stupefied. "Has the so-called divine healer been workin' on Taft's wife?"

Prudence glanced up and saw that Taft was out of hearing. "Son!" Under any circumstance she was always sweetly affectionate when she spoke to Lester. "It's your Uncle Bob..." Prudence found it difficult to believe what she was saying. "He was killed last night. In the old Lawson yard—"

"Are you sure?" Lester questioned. "Who's seen him besides Taft? You know how these colored folks are about that old place—always imaginin' they see things there. Besides, who'd want to kill Uncle Bob?"

"*Oh, Sonny-Boy!* Your Uncle Bob is *dead....*" Prudence thought: *If I had only held out and had that old house torn down, maybe this wouldn't have—* "I must call Colonel Livingston and tell him what has happened," she said, "and ask him to come out here as soon as he possibly can—or will you do that for me, Son?"

"Okay, Mom."

Prudence's mind went blank again as she heard Lester ringing for Colonel Livingston, first one ring for Sylvania. She could not for the soul of her remember what she had told him to say. But what did it matter what she had said? Bob was dead.... What did anything matter? She wished Dr. Evans would hurry.... Who was that whistling in the bathroom? Who had the heart to whistle? The guests—how would she ever tell them? The Tylers, the Harveys, Mr. Wormser—what a terrible greeting for Sunday morning!

"Prudence," Dr. Evans called gently as he came up to the back door. He had taken time to go by the old Lawson grounds, verify Taft's report, and leave him to guard the place; so he came from an unexpected direction.

"Oh, Dr. Evans, I'm so glad you're here!"

The doctor had come onto the porch and was standing beside Prudence. "It's a dreadful blow, my dear; but you're strong and brave, remember you're a Lawson."

It was remarkable how Dr. Evan's presence brought a change in atmosphere. The tension and pent-up excitement gave way to calm assurance and stoical resignation.

"Have the officers in Sylvania been notified?" he asked.

"Yes, Lester called Colonel Livingston, and he'll know what else to do."

"Did anyone outside our group know that Bob was going to that place last night?"

"Not so far as I know—except Walt Hendrix, of course."

Wormser, coming up from across the yard, suddenly stopped when he saw Dr. Evans. "Good morning, Doctor, you're making calls early this morning." Then he saw Prudence and seemed a little confused, as though he might be intruding upon a private conversation.

"Unfortunately, Mr. Wormser," Dr. Evans was grave—"I am not here for a medical call. I was summoned here by your hostess because of the strange death of your host."

"*Dead?* Bob Lawson dead? How on Earth could that be?" Wormser exclaimed.

"Murdered—in the old Lawson yard."

There was a general stir upstairs. The other guests had overheard enough to be aware of what had happened. They were hurriedly grabbing the first clothes in sight, or coming down as they were. Irene was already dressed; Priscilla, her hair falling in loose, tousled curls about her face, was holding her negligee together; Gordon was struggling with a wrong-side-out sleeve of his bathrobe; and Allen, half-shaven, was in his pajamas.

Priscilla, looking like a hunted animal, was the first to speak. "Tell me it isn't true! It *can't* be true! Nobody could possibly have killed Bob."

"I never would have thought Bob had an enemy so heartless," Gordon said, as though to himself.

Irene and Allen were gravely silent.

Presently Dr. Evans excused himself and walked toward the scene of the crime.

Colonel John Livingston, prosecuting attorney,* and Sheriff Joe Satterfield were on the scene in record time. After a brief conference with Prudence, they edged their way through groups of neighbors and plantation negroes and joined Dr. Evans, who was waiting for them in the old Lawson yard. With little ado the doctor showed them the body.

"Dastardly! And who on earth could have done such a thing?" said Colonel Livingston, deeply moved. The Colonel (every lawyer in that region is a "colonel"; the title seems to go with the legal profession as uniformly as "doctor" with the medical and dental professions.) was a smallish man with dark hair and skin darkened by the summer sun. He was mild-mannered and soft-spoken; but behind that calm appearance lay exceptional judgement and firmness of decision. And he could be fiery enough when the occasion demanded.

He noticed a streak of untanned skin on one of the lifeless fingers and thought of the diamond ring that Bob had habitually worn.

"Looks like a case of robbery as well as a murder," he said.

"Yes, John, I had noticed that his ring was gone, also his watch," Dr. Evans replied.

---

*In Georgia known as solicitor general.

The Colonel eased back Bob's coat sleeve and saw the mark where the watch band had been. "Joe, search the body," he said.

Sheriff Satterfield pulled aside the bloodstained coat and went through Bob's pockets. Starvation stood watching every movement with sadly bewildered eyes.

"No wallet?" the Colonel asked.

"No nothin'," the Sheriff barked. "And I'll bet my bottom dollar he had plenty of dough in them pockets."

"Yes," Dr. Evans said, "he usually brought back several hundred dollars from Savannah; he did most of his banking there."

"Was it well known that he carried so much money?" the Colonel inquired.

"I think it was rather generally known around here."

"Look here!" the Sheriff was examining Bob's wrist where he had worn his watch. There was a definite gash, showing that the leather wrist band had been cut from the wrist. "Whoever took that watch sure was in a helluva hurry," he deduced.

"Any murderer would try to make a speedy get-away from the scene of the crime," the Colonel stated.

"It has occurred to me, John," Dr. Evans said, "that robbery may have had little or nothing to do with Bob's murder. It is possible that the robbing of the body was committed later by someone other than the murderer. But, that is unlikely," he reasoned, "in view of the superstitious awe in which this old place is so widely held."

"Haven't you found any clues at all, Doctor?" Colonel Livingston asked.

"Not yet, John. There seems to be no chance of fingerprints and the weapon used is nowhere around."

"What sort of weapon do you think was used?"

"Oh, anything sharp—a pocket knife, a butcher knife, a razor—"

"What about tracks? Have you found any evidence of that sort?" the Colonel continued as they walked out toward the Old Dover Road.

"No, I have been looking for traces in the road, but unfortunately, before I came out here to see that the place was guarded, there had already been so much tramping around that the sand was too churned up to distinguish anything but a mingling of fresh tracks...."

Screven County stock roamed at will over the roads and woods. Only the fields, a few pastures, and the yards were fenced. The portion of the Old Dover Road that ran through the Lawson plantation was used considerably for local plantation traffic.

"As you see, I have the place cleared now," the doctor concluded.

The officers looked toward the road and saw Taft and Br'er Burke standing guard.

"Well, let's look a little further," Colonel Livingston suggested.

They eased along the flank of the old road in the Dover direction, watching closely for some evidence of distinguishable tracks—of person, mule, or horse. About sixty to seventy yards beyond the Ghost Oak they found several hoof prints of a mule, which evidently had walked mainly on the deep-tufted wire grass, but had made a few stray steps on the firmer top soil that appeared between gaps in the grass, just off the roadway. Although these were largely protected by the overspreading oaks, they were sufficiently dented by rain drops to show they had been made before the thunder shower.

"Mule tracks! Pointed toward the old Lawson place, and made *before the shower*. We must get impressions of these." Colonel Livingston called to one of the neighbors and asked him to stand guard over the tracks.

The officers turned and walked toward the Louisville Road, still keeping on the grass, their eyes alert for such gaps as might reveal similar evidence. They had almost reached that road when they discovered similar prints headed toward the road. These, interestingly enough, were quite evidently made *after* the shower.

"Telltale evidence—if we can only find the mule that made them," Dr. Evans said. "The rider evidently came up before the rain and left after it was over. . . . I have plaster of Paris in my office. I'll step over and get some and we'll make casts right away."

"Joe, get your bloodhounds out here," Colonel Livingston ordered when Dr. Evans had gone.

Sheriff Satterfield was a burly, good-natured sort of fellow. His pot belly shook with amusement at the mention of his bloodhounds, and despite the tragic occasion he grunted in suppressed laughter.

"What? Them pups? Why we ain't even learned them how to trail niggers yet."

"Well, send over to Statesboro, Swainsboro, or—"

"Tain't a bit o' use, Colonel. They ain't no bloodhounds I ever knowed can trail a mule's track, and that's all you got to go by, ain't it?"

Dr. Evans returned presently with his plaster preparation and proceeded to pour it into the tracks, cautioning the guards to see that everything was kept undisturbed.

"Who you think you're making them casts for, Doctor?" the Sheriff blurted.

"If we knew that, Joe, we might know who did the killing."

"There sure is a heap of mules around here to try to match them up to, but I guess it's our job to find the Cinderella that wore them slippers."

When further canvassing of the grounds showed no more clues, the sheriff was left with the body, while the doctor and the Colonel went in to question everyone at Linger-long, hoping that someone there might be able to throw light on the matter. They were prepared to seek out private details of information that might not be revealed at a public inquest.

Ruby met the gentleman at the front door and led them directly to Prudence, who was, at the moment, alone in the library. She could think of nothing to tell them beyond what they already knew, except to confirm Dr. Evans's impression that Bob was to meet Walt Hendrix at the old Lawson place about eleven o'clock the night before.

They asked her where they might talk with each of the others in the house.

"Right here in the library would probably be the best place," she said. "I'll ask Lester to page them for you."

The Lawson library, across the hall from the living room, was where Bob had held his business conferences. The room was not as large as the living room, but the furniture was commodious and comfortable; and it afforded the necessary privacy for questioning the house guests. The officers were seated on the leather-covered sofa.

When Lester came in, a minute later, he was able to give them several leads. He said, "Uncle Bob had been playin' around with Mrs. Harvey and I don't think Mr. Harvey liked it any too well." He also told them that Bob and Mr. Tyler had been having some sort of dispute about the affairs of Georgia Life, and that each one seemed hell-bent to have his way. Questioned as to Mr. Wormser he said, "All I know about him is that he's a friend of the Tylers. At least Mr. Wormser brought them down in his car. I don't know for sure, but I don't think Uncle Bob had invited Mr. Wormser."

Lester agreed to call in the guests as requested, and retired from the room.

"Before we call in Mr. Wormser and Mr. Tyler," Dr. Evans said, "I think I can tell you what their alibis will be. I brought them home with me from Dover last night. I invited them both to come in and have whiskey and sodas. Mr. Wormser declined and went across toward Linger-long. But Mr. Tyler came in and stayed until it stopped raining."

Wormser accounted for his movements just as Dr. Evans had said he would, adding that when he left the doctor's place he went directly to his room and went to bed.

"Did you see anyone from the time you left Dr. Evans's until you reached your room?" Colonel Livingston asked.

"No one, so far as I can recall."

When Gordon Tyler came in, he too gave his alibi just as Dr. Evans had predicted, up to the time of his leaving the doctor's house. After that, he claimed to have gone directly to his room, seeing no one on his way. These questions settled, Colonel Livingston asked: "Mr. Tyler, is it not a fact that you and Mr. Lawson had had a disagreement with reference to Georgia Life which had recently developed into considerable animus between you?"

"Animus? Between me and Bob Lawson? Why, we have been the most devoted friends ever since we were in college together. There could never have been any real unfriendliness between us."

"You acknowledge that there had been some disagreement?"

"It was merely a difference of viewpoints regarding a certain business matter."

"Will you tell us what the disagreement was about? That is, what the nature of it was."

"I believe that I have the right not to answer that question now, have I not?"

"Yes, but you may be compelled to answer it later."

"Then I prefer to say no more about it at present."

When Gordon had left the room, Colonel Livingston said, "I can find out all we need to know about that from Mr. Underhill at the bank. He is on the board of directors of Georgia Life Insurance Company."

Next, came Allen Harvey. He said that he had driven in from Sylvania and had gone to his room after the shower. As he entered the house, he had noticed Mr. Wormser in the library, absorbed in a game of solitaire and had not disturbed him. Questioned about the alleged love triangle, Allen acknowledged that Priscilla had been rather fascinated with Bob. "But surely, gentlemen," he said, his steely eyes spitting fire, "you couldn't suspect me of killing Bob!"

"Please understand, Mr. Harvey, that we're accusing no one; we hardly have grounds for definite suspicion of anyone as yet."

"I'm sorry, Colonel Livingston." Allen dropped his head. "I should have remembered this sort of questioning is a necessary part of the routine required of you in such cases," he said apologetically.

"I understand, Mr. Harvey. That's all for today."

The officers didn't hold Priscilla and Irene long for questioning. Priscilla's big, blue eyes were remindful of a startled fawn. She could give them no information other than that she had been out on the lawn with Irene and Prudence until about ten-thirty, and after that, she had read in bed until Allen came in.

Irene lit a cigarette as she came in and sat down. She kept blowing ill-formed smoke rings, but listened carefully to all that was said. She explained that she had gone to bed about ten-thirty, and except for an interval during the thunderstorm, had slept soundly all night. When pressed with further questions, she answered, "You're not getting me mixed up in this. I've got my reputation in Atlanta to think about."

Each of the persons questioned had been told to appear at the inquest next day; also, not to leave the jurisdiction of the court until given legal permission to do so.

Left alone in the library, the Colonel and the doctor discussed the testimony together.

"We have at least two people who have had motives but there must be a lot more evidence before we can make a case," Colonel Livingston said.

"I think, John, our next move is to have the premises searched for any possible trace of the stolen valuables," Dr. Evans suggested.

"I shall see to that at once," the Colonel replied.

"Then we should get in touch with the authorities in Atlanta and see what we can find out from that end of the line. It might be well for us to employ a private detective there," Dr. Evans said.

"Yes, I think we should," the Colonel agreed and added: "We must offer a sizeable reward. You know, money talks. From the evidence we've gotten so far, there's not a substantial alibi amongst the whole bunch. We merely have their own statements to go by. Any one of them could have slipped out of this house last night after going to his or her room. And all of them knew that Bob was to be over there at that time. Harvey said that he saw Wormser in the library when he came in. But Wormser, you recall, had said that he went straight to his room and went to bed. Either Wormser tried to deceive us, or else Harvey was in error. Assuming that Wormser was there, as Harvey said, where had he been in the interval after leaving your house? How can Harvey prove what time he drove into the garage? How much later was it when he went to this room? And what did he do in the meantime? Then, too, we have only Tyler's word that he went directly to bed from your house, for Mrs. Tyler said that she was asleep when he came in." Both men felt that their investigation of the morning had left them little that was definite to work on.

Colonel Livingston and Sheriff Satterfield, under existing conditions, declined all invitations to have Sunday dinner in Cooperville. They drove back to Sylvania with the understanding that they would return in the early afternoon, call for Dr. Evans, and drive over toward Statesboro to interview bootlegger Hendrix.

While all these questions and consultations were going on in the library, the undertaker from Sylvania had quietly taken the body away. Of those who watched the departing service car, none was more deeply grieved than Taft. He had been pondering as he stood apart from the milling crowd. "I kind of believe I know de killer," he muttered, "but I'd better study a little bit more, before I say what's on my mind."

X
At the Hendrix Distillery

Early Sunday afternoon

Colonel Livingston, with Sheriff Satterfield aboard, stopped his car on the circular driveway in front of the coroner's home promptly at two o'clock Sunday afternoon.

The Evanses' home followed one of the oldest Savannah styles. The main story, fronted by a pillared veranda, was actually, though not apparently, the second floor. Leading from the ground up to the veranda was a long flight of steps, on either side of which were tall masses of shrubbery. The shrubbery and the steps concealed a flagstone terrace and a full length basement floor at ground level. Scarcely perceptible in the background were outhouses and several negro cabins, remindful of the quarters of a bygone age.

Dr. Evans was waiting on the veranda for the officers.

"Good old Dr. Evans—always on the spot," the sheriff said, stretching his fat legs as he crawled out of the car and got into the back seat to make way for the doctor in front.

"Hope we're not too early for you, Doctor," Colonel Livingston said.

Dr. Evans was already descending the long flight of steps.

"Too early?" he smiled. Despite his seventy-odd years the doctor was still sprightly. "John, I'm afraid you've forgotten your raising, You ought to remember that we country folks have our dinner early. I've been waiting for you at least half an hour."

"But when I was a young boy like you are, Doctor, I always had to wait for the second table," the Colonel countered.

Colonel Livingston was born and raised in Cooperville and, in fact, was Bob Lawson's first cousin. The two of them had often waited together impatiently while the adults lingered for an interminable time around the table before the way was cleared for them to be served.

As the car started off, the Colonel said, resuming his serious mood: "I particularly want to see Hendrix before he has a chance to read the papers tomorrow morning. There was nothing in the papers *this* morning about the murder, of course, for it was discovered too late."

"Don't kid yourself, Colonel, that he's gotta wait to get his news from a newspaper," the sheriff said.

"I know news travels fast," the Colonel admitted, "but I'm hoping we may get there first this time. Whether Hendrix is innocent or guilty of the crime, I'd like to talk with him before he sees the newspaper accounts or learns too much about the matter from other sources."

"That sounds like a good idea, John, but I'm not so sure it will matter much." Dr. Evans stroked his white Vandyke. "Walt Hendrix is a shrewd one. He's not likely to give himself away."

"Yes, I know. He's also quick-tempered. But, if we are tactful enough in our approach, we may be able to get something out of him."

"You mean that you're scared of him?" the sheriff barked.

"That's not the point, Joe," Colonel Livingston replied. "So far as I know Hendrix has never killed anyone. But he's a sensitive poor white brought up in the slums of Savannah and following a dangerous trade. One of his kind *may* suddenly go into a desperate frenzy. Right now, though, I'm thinking only of the best way to get the most out of him."

"Poor white! Humph!" the sheriff grunted. "I never seen one yet that had any guts. With all their boasts, they're damned cowards."

"You're wrong, Joe." Dr. Evans was emphatic. "I've known poor whites a long time, and I've had to be pretty intimate with them. You can't put them all in one category. Most of them are cowering and harmless, at least to a point; some, the type you have in mind, are mere blusterers. In general they will take an awful lot for a time; but there's a breaking point beyond which they'll fight a circular saw."

The sheriff was not squelched. "You think the bootlegger's our best bet, Colonel?"

"No, Joe, I don't. I think he's logically our *first* bet. But I think it's rather doubtful that he actually committed the murder. Walt Hendrix would surely know that his appointment with Bob Lawson would likely be known to others. And he'd be pretty sure that Bob hadn't made any secret of the fact that there have been words between them and that Bob had threatened to put him on the spot with the authorities in Savannah if he tried to palm off any more faked liquor. So, he'd know that suspicion would fall heavily upon him from the start. He'd have been taking an awful risk."

"My Lord, Colonel, I'll bet you that man could bump a feller off easier than he could spit out fresh chaw of tobacco," the sheriff said, apparently unaware of his inconsistency.

"Hold your horses, Joe. The fact that the man's a bootlegger and possibly a smuggler doesn't necessarily make him the killer type. Doubtless he would kill in a desperate situation, but I don't believe he ran into a situation with Bob Lawson last night that was desperate enough to make him commit murder—at a scheduled meeting in a solitary, unfrequented spot such as the old Lawson place."

"I'm not so sure, John, but that he *may* be our *best* bet." Dr. Evans adjusted his glasses and began fingering his watch chain as he weighed his words. "I grant you the fact that because the man's a bootlegger doesn't necessarily make him the killer type. And I grant also that if he had taken time to consider all the circumstantial evidence that there would be against him, he might have been deterred by it. But on the other hand, if these two had another run-in and if Bob hotly threatened to expose him to the enforcement agencies, or if Bob threatened to use his well-known influence in Savannah to have him sent up, I can see how it would be possible for Hendrix to fly into a passion and attack Bob."

"Now you're talkin' sense, Doctor," the sheriff interrupted. "That man ain't nobody's wallflower."

Dr. Evans continued: "The weight of the circumstantial evidence against him might well have been entirely out of his mind for the moment. Besides, if that were the only evidence against him, it would hardly convict him. He must have known this at the time, if he thought of that side at all."

Beyond Dover, they passed from a long causeway through the Ogeechee River swamp onto the dilapidated bridge across the river which separates Bulloch County from Screven. The bridge had long since been condemned as unsafe, but nothing had been done about it. The sheriff suddenly broke the trend of thought.

"Why the hell haven't they built a decent bridge here?"

"That's simple," Dr. Evans replied. "Sylvania politics. Many of the people in this part of Screven County are inclined to go over and trade in Statesboro, which is as near Cooperville as Sylvania is. You can imagine how the Sylvania merchants feel about that. A modern bridge would carry even more trade to Statesboro."

"Yeah, but how the devil they can make the highway people leave a rattletrap like this is more than I can see," the sheriff said.

"You know as will as I do, Joe," Dr. Evans answered, "that Sylvania controls the Screven County commissioners who in turn control the Screven Highway Commission. At least three out of five of the county commissioners are always Sylvania men. The Bulloch County commissioners have been more than willing to put up half the cost of a modern bridge. Not so the Screven boys. That's right, isn't it?"

"Hell no! It *ain't* right," said the sheriff, his eyes twinkling, his pot belly shaking as he nudged the Colonel. "It ain't *right,* but it's *true,* Doctor, perfectly true."

"As a matter of fact," Dr. Evans continued, "there's so much rivalry and prejudice between some of the people in Screven and some of those in Bulloch, that it might be pretty hard to give a bootlegger from Bulloch, being tried for murder of a prominent Screven man, a fair trial in Sylvania. I don't mean anything underhanded might happen, just that the jury might be subconsciously biased."

When the men reached Statesboro, they drove by the home of the Bulloch County sheriff and talked with him a few minutes about their mission. He was skeptical about Hendrix being guilty of the killing, but he quite agreed the circumstances warranted full investigation. He deferred to the officers from Screven to question Walt Hendrix.

They headed back toward Dover to the Hendrix Turpentine Distillery about eight miles north of Statesboro, on a side road. For several years it had been running only part time, because the turpentine industry in that region was on the wane. It had recently gone through bankruptcy; Hendrix had acquired a controlling interest, and had written his name large on the firm, to further camouflage his scheme. His actual work at the still, when he worked there at all, was that of cooper. His making, handling, and transporting of barrels served him well at times as a device for concealing his liquor. His bungalow was just across the roadway from his cooper's shop.

As the three men drove up to his house, they found him sprawled in a large armchair on the front porch.

"How do you do, Mr. Hendrix?" said Colonel Livingston as they walked onto the porch. "May we come in?"

"Looks to me like you're already in." Hendrix's powerful body and hard-boiled countenance bore a striking contrast to the small figure and delicate face of John Livingston.

"Even so, I hope we're not intruding."

"That depends on what your business is." Hendrix put his thumbs under his suspenders and reared his chair back against the wall. His baggy trousers hung sloppily about his waist and knees.

"We only want to ask you a few courteous questions about a matter on which you may be able to throw some light. And it would be the better part of wisdom for you to answer us with the same courtesy."

"I've heard that rot before, and I ain't answerin' no courteous questions unless I know what they're aimin' at."

"Listen. Hendrix, if you think we're after you on a bootleg charge, you're wrong. Bootlegging may or may not be concerned with the matter. But, I give you the assurance of a gentleman that nothing you may disclose now with reference to that particular avocation of yours will ever be used against you. Isn't that fair?"

"Well, Colonel"—Hendrix seemed more composed—"I know you got a mighty low opinion of me, but as for you, I know you're a man of your word. So the bars is down. Shoot the works."

"All right, Walt. We know that you had an appointment with Bob Lawson last night—never mind what about. Did you keep that appointment?"

"No, I didn't. I called it off." Hendrix spat his cud of tobacco over the porch railing and wiped his mouth with his hands.

"You called it off? He was expecting you when I saw him just a little before eleven last night," Dr. Evans said.

"I wrote him a letter Friday mornin', an' my son Charlie was goin' to Dover that day with his friends an' mailed it in plenty of time for Mr. Lawson to get it Saturday mornin'."

The Colonel continued the questioning: "Are you sure that the letter was mailed? We have seen Bob Lawson's Saturday mail and it contained no such letter."

"What the hell are you doin' pryin' into Bob Lawson's private mail?"

"Calm yourself, Walt, we'll come to that in a moment. We are not making any accusations, and it's best that we all keep our heads on our shoulders."

"God Almighty damn! What the hell are you drivin' at—'no accusations'?"

"Listen, Walt, this is a serious matter. I am compelled to ask you these questions—and more. You know that you are not compelled to answer them *at this time,* but if you are an innocent man, you will do far better to answer them in the manner of an innocent man. But under the law I must warn you that anything you say may be used against you."

This had a sobering effect upon Hendrix. The expression on his face now seemed one of bewilderment. Or had he gotten a grip on himself and assumed a disarming pose?

"Sure, I'm innocent, I ain't done nothin'! But if something's up . . . " He paused then shouted, "Charlie, come here!"

A strip of a boy came out, rubbing his eyes as though still half asleep.

"Did you mail that letter to Bob Lawson Friday?"

"Y-y-es, sir."

"Did you mail it in time to catch the Saturday mail?"

"I-I think I did." The boy was evidently confused and frightened.

"Well, the letter didn't go through yesterday *at all*. Are you sure you mailed it?"

"Yes, sir; but it might not have got in soon enough for yesterday mornin's mail."

Colonel Livingston broke in: "We might as well drop that question for the time being, Walt. If you didn't meet Bob Lawson, where were you last night?"

"I was here at home all night."

Colonel Livingston turned to Charlie: "Is that right, son?"

Hendrix interposed: "He wouldn't know. He was out gallivantin' till God knows how late."

"Think well, Walt. Are you sure you were at home *all night?*"

"Sure as hell, an' I can prove it. Mary! Come out here a minute!"

Mrs. Hendrix appeared with surprising promptness.

"I just told these gentlemen that I was home all last night. Wasn't I?"

"You sure was," she replied without hesitation.

"You see, gentlemen, my cards is on the table. Now, will you tell me what this is all about?" Hendrix's expression was still disarming.

"Bob Lawson went to keep his appointment with you last night about eleven o'clock, and this morning he was found dead on the grounds where you and he usually meet. His throat was slashed," Colonel Livingston told him.

"Bob Lawson murdered! My God! One o' my best—"

"Best what?"

"Friends."

"I know you mean *customers*, Hendrix, but we'll let that pass."

Dr. Evans spoke up: "As Colonel Livingston has said, we are making no accusations against you, Walt. But we will have to summon you to the inquest at my house tomorrow morning at ten o'clock."

"Well, if I gotta be there, I reckon I gotta be there."

The officers took their leave and drove on back to Screven County. As they entered Dover, Dr. Evans suggested that they stop by the railway station, which also served as the Post Office, to check on any mail that might have come for Bob that day.

There was still no letter for Bob Lawson from Hendrix.

Dr. Evans, his white Vandyke held tight in his hand, said absently, "That looks bad."

XI
Barren Ground

Late Sunday afternoon

The crowd that had gathered on and around the porch of Mason's General Store was discussing the tragic death of Bob Lawson.

By the time the officers appeared on their return from Hendrix's place, the news had spread all over the county. Multiparty telephone lines, radiating from Sylvania, linked up a goodly proportion of the farm houses thereabouts. On these lines, eavesdropping was an accepted custom. As a matter of fact, far from being annoyed by it, most people enjoyed having this means of social conversation. It was not infrequent, especially on Sundays, to have various people break in on a call and turn it into a friendly get-together over the wires. So, any news of particular interest quickly spread through the county and beyond.

The telephones had been alive all day; so, when the officers stopped at Dover for their fruitless check of Bob Lawson's mail they found the crowd unusually large for Sunday afternoon. As the three men came from the Post Office window in the station, the crowd drew around them and eagerly inquired whether they were on the trail of the killer.

"Nothing definite as yet," Colonel Livingston said. "Do any of you know anything that might help us?"

A wiry, little man with a long, droopy mustache squirted a stream of amber through his teeth and rubbed it into the floor with his shoe. "Doctor," he said through his nose, "I saw you meet the train last night; so I reckon you heard Will Sorrel lambastin' Bob Lawson."

"If he mentioned Bob Lawson's name any time, I never heard it," a bulky, stubble-faced man was quick to reply.

The little man came right back at him, "Well, you must of had your ears stopped up."

The two men sent scowling glints at each other.

"See here," the big fellow said with emphasis, "I ain't tryin' to take up for Will Sorrel, but I just want to give the devil his due. I know Will was cussin' and swearin' loud enough last night for a deaf man to hear—"

"But ye didn't hear him mention Bob Lawson, eh?" the little man interjected. "My God Almighty, man! How'd you miss it! Just as Bob came off the train Will cussed him to hell and said he's hopin' for him to burn in the hottest place down there. I heard him with both my ears and I can prove it."

Dr. Evans's mind went back. He had been vaguely aware of Sorrel's blustering as he stood talking with Bob for what proved to be the last time. But, he had ignored the rowdy, for he had heard the wind blow before. And since he had heard no specific reference to Bob, the doctor had not until now associated Will's bad temper with the tragedy.

"Did any of the rest of you hear Will make any threats last night?" he asked.

The others around who had been present the night before seemed to have paid little attention to Sorrel except to notice that he was in one of his foulest moods.

"Could someone tell us whether Will followed Bob as he walked toward home by the Old Dover Road?" Colonel Livingston asked.

There were a jumble of answers: "He rode off on a mule, but I don't recollect whether he took the Old Dover Road or the Sylvania Highway."

"I don't know exactly when he left, but I think he went by the Old Dover Road."

"Lordy, Colonel, we're so used to Will's runnin' off around here that we don't pay no more mind to him than we do the Ogeechee River running by over there. I doubt if anybody really noticed what became of him."

"Can any of you be sure whether he was walking or riding?" the Colonel pursued.

"I'm sure he was riding," a respectable-looking, middle-aged man volunteered without hesitation. "I wasn't here when he left, but I saw him when he came. I remember seeing him tie his mule to a sapling across the railroad, then give her a kick in the belly as he left her."

Dr. Evans drew the officers aside and suggested that they go at once to Sorrel's place.

"All right," Colonel Livingston agreed, looking at his watch. "It's only four-thirty, we'll have plenty of time."

"We'll have to drive by my house to pick up those casts," Dr. Evans added. "We'll want to compare them with the hoofs of Will's mule."

"The only trouble," the sheriff opined, "we ain't goin' to find that bird at home this time of the day."

"I think we will," Colonel Livingston said. "Whether he's guilty or not, he's doubtless aware of what has happened, and he'll know that suspicion will be heavy against him; so he'll be playing the good boy today."

As they drove through Cooperville they were aware of the deadly quiet. Behind those moss-hung groves whatever gossip was stirring was sequestered.

Returning to the Sylvania Highway, they had only about a mile to go until they reached the by-road that turned off by

Sorrel's farm. This road passed through alternating sand beds and clay gullies that led toward Sorrel's God-forsaken place. The men were so accustomed to such islands of scrubby land that dotted the otherwise fertile stretches of the county that they were scarcely aware of the barrenness around them.

They drove up to Will's dilapidated house with its slovenly surroundings, and hailed. When they had shouted his name several times, he slouched out.

He hadn't gotten around to his weekly shave, and his face was covered with a thick, red stubble. A dingy, gray undershirt and a pair of patched khaki pants were all the clothes he had on, and so meek was his demeanor that it was hard to believe he was the same person who had been so boisterous and defiant the night before.

"Will," the Colonel began as Sorrel came up to the car, "you were down at Dover last night weren't you?"

"Yes, sir."

"Were you drinking?"

"I might have had a dram or so, but I wasn't nowhere nigh drunk."

"And you weren't blustering or swearing either, I suppose?"

"I might have been talkin' loud like I do sometimes, but I wasn't really swearin'."

"Did you see Bob Lawson when he got off the train?"

"No, sir. I ain't seen Bob for several days."

"At least you must have had him in mind, for we understand you were saying ugly things about him."

"No sir, Colonel Livingston, I ain't said nothin' about Bob Lawson; I never even mentioned his name. And I swear that's the God's truth."

As Will talked he never lifted his eyes off the ground; he was digging a hole in the sand with the toes of his bare feet.

"All right, Will. Which road did you take when you left Dover?"

"I came by the Sylvania Highway."

"Do you mean that you *left Dover* on the Sylvania Highway?"

"Yes, sir, I swear I did."

"Have you heard anything about Bob Lawson since you saw him at Dover last night?"

"No sir, I ain't been off this here place since I came home last night. I ain't been feelin' good today; so I stayed home and rested."

"Then I assume that your mule is here. We are going to have to ask you to bring her out and let us take a look at her."

Though very nervous, Will had succeeded fairly well in holding himself together. He went readily to his stable and returned with the mule.

The men got out of the car with the casts and compared them to the mule's hoofs. The size matched, it seemed, but the casts showed practically new shoes, whereas it could be seen at a glance that those on the mule were badly worn.

"Thank you, Will. That's all for today," the Colonel said with a nod.

"Except," Dr. Evans added, "I'll have to summon you to an inquest at my house tomorrow morning at ten o'clock. Bob Lawson was found dead—murdered—on the old Lawson place this morning."

Will gave a gasp that puzzled the officers. They couldn't be sure whether it was one of genuine or feigned astonishment, but they could see he was greatly perturbed.

"Gentleman, for all my talkin' I ain't never had no mind to hurt Bob Lawson." Will's voice had become hollow.

"That's a point we'll have to talk with you about later, Will," Dr. Evans said.

The men watched Will's countenance pass through various contortions. Then, he made bold to say: "I ain't the only one that ain't had no use for Bob. There are plenty of folks that could have killed him . . . That nutty ole Mom Liza, livin' right there in his yard, and always prowlin' around, and you know how touchy she is."

"Come, come, Will," said Colonel Livingston; "you know Mom Liza wouldn't to do a thing like that."

"Maybe she wouldn't and maybe she would. She's mean enough . . . and what about that sassy nigger Chunky? He ain't had no more use for Bob than what I had, and I've heard him makin' threats against him—"

"When?"

"Heaps of times. I reckon as late as Saturday."

"You don't like Chunky, do you, Will?"

"No sir. That nigger's gettin' too big for his britches. . . . Then there's that old fool Sam Holloman. I've heard him rantin' about Bob and his gang poisionin' this area with citified sins. He'd love to get rid of him and all the city folks he fetches here."

"Will, have you ever heard Sam threaten anybody's life?"

"No sir."

"You don't like Sam either, do you, Will?"

"No sir; I'm sick an' tired of hearin' him holler."

"All right, Will," the Colonel concluded. "But I must warn you that you are not to leave the jurisdiction of this court without legal permission."

The officers were just about to head back to Cooperville when Colonel Livingston suggested, "While we're on this road, we might as well drive by Holloman's and sound him out."

The short by-road that had brought them to Sorrel's place was a local connection from the Sylvania Highway to the Cameron Road. The only other home on this by-road was Holloman's shack.

As the men drove toward Holloman's, Joe Satterfield's mind was still on Sorrel. "Them shoes don't prove nothin'. Even if them wasn't Will's mule's prints, he could have come 'round by the Sylvania Highway and still got to the old Lawson place in time to head Bob off before he got to his house."

"Joe, you may have something there," the Colonel said.

Dr. Evans was staring into space.

The car tugged along, straining through the deep sand beds or bumping through gullies.

"Still," said Dr. Evans as though he had pressed a button and brought himself back into their presence, "Will's motive was of such long standing that it seems to me it would have had to have some fresh agitation to bring him to the point of actual attack. He has been saying nasty things about Bob for years, and yet he has never lifted a finger to harm him. I had come to think of Will's ranting as a sort of obsession. I don't think Bob even looked over in Will's direction last night. I'm perfectly sure Bob didn't speak to him or about him while at Dover."

"That's just the point, Doctor: 'while at Dover'." The sheriff puffed as he pulled his big body forward on the back seat of the car. "But you don't know what sort of love scene went on between them if they met at the old Lawson place. A purty hot neckin'—"

"Have a heart, Joe," Colonel Livingston reproved.

Dr. Evans solemnly said nothing.

As the car stopped in front of Holloman's house, the Colonel said, "Dr. Evans, since you know this man better, being his doctor, suppose you lead off."

"All right, I'll break the ice."

The men got out of the car and walked toward the house. Chickens cackled and ran ahead of them across the fresh swept yard. Holloman was stretched on his front porch, evidently asleep. Once aroused, he yawned, rubbed his eyes, and blinked.

From behind his shaggy black hair and beard, he peered at the unaccustomed visitors. Then, he recognized Dr. Evans.

"Oh, it's you, Doctor," he drawled, bringing himself to a sitting position.

"Yes, Sam, and two of my friends, Colonel Livingston and Mr. Satterfield. We just happened to be over this way and thought we'd stop a minute."

Holloman had no chairs on the porch; so he motioned the men to the head of the steps. "You all set down, Doctor."

"Thank you, Sam. Have you been feeling all right lately?"

"I ain't been feelin' none too good. Them agues is tryin' to come back on me."

"Then you better take another round of quinine."

"Yes, sir, I've been takin' that."

"Do you sleep well?" the doctor pursued.

"Most of the time."

Colonel Livingston interjected, "Where were you last night?"

"I went fishing," Holloman replied.

"At night?" Dr. Evans queried.

"Late afternoon," Holloman said. "But I stayed down on the river until the clouds began to rise. Then I came home and went to bed."

"Did you see anyone when you were coming home?" the Colonel asked.

"I never seen anyone, but I had a feeling someone was follering me."

"And did you get home before the storm?" the Colonel continued.

"The storm broke while I was on the way home."

"Did you see or hear anything unusual?" the Colonel pursued.

"Just the storm."

"Perhaps you should know," Dr. Evans volunteered. "Mr. Lawson was murdered last night."

"Murdered?" Holloman asked, his face impassive.

"Yes," the Colonel confirmed. "And we thought you might know something that could lead us to the murderer."

"I'm powerful sorry to hear about Mr. Lawson," Holloman thought for a second. "I'm afraid I can't help you all. You know I always mind my own business. I don't have nothin' to do with them people over there."

"But we've heard you didn't approve of Bob Lawson's bringing his city friends down here. Is that true?" Colonel Livingston inquired.

"Well, there's been more runnin' around and liquor drinkin' since he came back."

"Did you ever say anything to Bob about that?"

"No, sir. I allowed it wasn't none of my business."

"Did Bob or any of his guests ever bother you?"

"No, sir. I ain't never give them no chance to."

The three looked at each other as though it was time to leave. "We thank you, Mr. Holloman," the Colonel said, and they turned back toward their car and headed for Linger-long.

Before they reached the grounds they could see that the crowd that had filled the house and yard all day had thinned out to a few small groups. Mr. Underhill was just preparing to leave. "Mind if I ride back to Sylvania with Mr. Underhill?" Sheriff Satterfield asked. "I need to do some paper work on these goin's on."

"We had probably all better get home pretty soon. But, if you want to go with Mr. Underhill, go ahead," Colonel Livingston told him. The sheriff hailed Mr. Underhill, and they drove off together.

Priscilla met Dr. Evans and Colonel Livingston in the driveway. "Who is Jake?" she inquired.

"Jake who?" Colonel Livingston asked.

"I'm sorry, but I don't know anything but *Jake*. I just happened to overhear some of the men who were talking this afternoon as they were standing about the lawn, and one of them said 'Jake says he knows who did the killing, but he's not going to tell.' "

The Colonel and the doctor looked at each other with questioning glances. They could not place Jake at the moment.

Priscilla continued: "Then somebody else said, 'Oh, you know how Jake is. Always trying to stick his nose in everybody's business. All he wants is to get attention directed toward himself. I wouldn't believe him on his oath.' "

"Oh, Jake Martin! That boy! I know who he is now." Dr. Evans's puzzled expression was gone. "He is just a poor boy trying to establish himself with his tongue. Can't be more than thirteen years old, but I've heard people say he's the most aggravating youngster in the county. Not mean, exactly, just nosey. Always roving, always gossiping. But, we'll have to see what he knows. I doubt really if he knows anything."

"Anyway," Colonel Livingston said, "we'll talk with him in the morning."

XII

Taft Is Deputized

Sunday evening

"Colonel Livingston, I ain't accusin' nobody of dis killin', but dey's one man dat I want to talk with you about." Taft said as the Colonel was getting into his car late Sunday afternoon to return to Sylvania for the night.

"All right, Taft, we're after stacking up all the evidence we can."

"You see, Colonel, dey's been lots of curious goin's-on in dis neighborhood lately; and Mister Bob did something that made a certain feller powerful mad."

"Do you mean that Bob Lawson had a misunderstanding with some of his neighbors?"

"No sir, Colonel Livingston, dat ain't it. It's about a man dat has come here lately and given us colored folks a lot of trouble. It's a long story, but I reckon I better give you de ins and outs of de case."

"Go ahead, Taft; let's hear all about it. Here, sit down," the Colonel said as he opened the door of the car and motioned Taft to get in.

Taft sat down by the Colonel and continued.

"Dere was a stranger to dese parts—a colored man by de name of Ezra Starkes—dat came here a month or so ago and said he was gonna start a college for all us colored people. Den he explain de plan. We were to give him as much money as we could and he would do de rest from an endowment fund that some rich Yankee had set up. He sent along a load of brick—about a thousand or so, maybe—and dumped dem down in de station yard at Dover, and said dem was de foundation. So de money start comin' in from all de little savin's—about six or seven hundred dollars, I reckon.

"Time pass and he ain't even start puttin' no college up. I didn't believe him from de first and I didn't give him a dime. But Br'er Frank Lovett, he drew out nearly all his money from de Post Office and gave it to him. By and by, Br'er Frank began askin' about when dat college will be ready."

"And what did he say?" Colonel Livingston queried.

"He told Br'er Frank dat dese things take time. Meantime, dis man built himself a sort of brush arbor dat he used for a meetin' house. It wasn't no more than a few saplin's nailed to de big water oaks with limbs and brushes piled on dem for de roof. De congregation had to sit on de ground or on pine slabs and boxes they brought in. He talk about a new kind of worship: you can sin all you want to, den get forgiveness, or, as he say, seek de Holy Ghost. Den he baptizes dem and say de sins are gone; go and sin some more."

"Were many of Bob Lawson's friends becoming followers of this man?" Colonel Livingston interrupted.

"Bob's people and lots of others were lettin' de crab grass ruin de crops while dey were sinnin' and seekin'. For miles around dey came and some stayed all day and all night.

"First dis man said he was a saint and called himself Saint Ezra. After dat it turns out dat he begins to call himself de divine healer; and he says he has power from on high to make de ailin' well without medicine. He established a hospital at Sister Lucindy Fawls's house and began practicin' his healing. But us men soon noticed dat he specializes on de women.

"All dis time Br'er Frank Lovett he was gettin' more and more uneasy about all dat money he had give for dat college.

So he went to talk it all over with Mister Bob and Mister Bob advised Br'er Frank to ask Br'er Burke to call a Lodge meeting and ask de healer to be honorary guest. Den Mister Bob advised Br'er Frank to tell de healer, in de presence of de brothers, to show some signs of action with dat college or else give us all our money back.

"But de healer told Br'er Frank he'd better be careful how he pesters with a *Dee*vine man. Before long we begin to hear talk about healer saying he's gonna set de spirits on Br'er Frank.

"Then, last Tuesday, Uncle Doctah died. Colonel, do you know who Uncle Doctah was?"

"Do you mean the negro herb doctor who lived across the railroad below Dover?"

"Yes, sir. I was de first one at his house after he died. I had intended to make a social call, but when I got dere it was too late. He was lyin' on his bed with his mouth open and his eyes rolled back. I could tell he was dead. And I knew I was the first one there, because de clocks were still runnin', and dere was no cover on de mirror, and ain't nobody turned de pictures to de wall. Well, Colonel, I was afraid to go in de house because I have a wife and eleven head of children. No way did I want any of dem to die this year because I had gone in the house with a dead man before de clocks had been stopped and everything."

Colonel Livingston was mildly amused by Taft's superstitious beliefs, but he didn't say anything and Taft went on talking.

"I was real lucky. About that time Br'er Frank Lovett come by and ask how Uncle Doctah was. I told him what had happened and why I was scared to go in de house. Br'er Frank said dat he didn't have no wife and children, so he would take care of what had to be done. After dat was all done, we started to lay Uncle Doctah out. Den I began to notice dat Br'er Frank was takin' advantage of Uncle Doctah's medical moonshine. I told him he'd better leave that alone or Uncle Doctah's spirit would sure come after him.

"Well, sometimes he left it alone and sometimes he didn't. But understand dat's just between you and me. I wouldn't want anybody else to know. We went about our business and got Uncle Doctah laid out. By dat time folks all around had heard about Uncle Doctah dyin', and dey began to come for the wake. The wake lasted all night, and then we buried Uncle Doctah the next day.

"But in the meantime Br'er Frank had a bad night. That divine healer followed him home from the wake and made like he was de ghost of Uncle Doctah. I think he might have killed Br'er Frank, if Br'er Frank hadn't jumped out of his window and gone to the house next door."

"What makes you say that? It's a pretty serious accusation," Colonel Livingston asked.

"Br'er Frank heard him messing with a knife and reaching for his throat."

"Are you sure about that, Taft?"

"I can't be sure, but it seemed dat way. Anyhow by now talk of de college was about given up, and de divine healer was buildin' himself up a fine business as a doctor. As I say, Sister Lucindy Fawls had turned her house into a hospital and her old man, Uncle Zede, was complainin' dat he had to sleep in de barn while de healer slept in his bed in de house.

"Mister Bob advised us to call another meetin' of de Lodge and talk over what was botherin' us, and what to do about Uncle Zede. We sent a committee in person to get the facts straight.

"Sure enough, we found out Uncle Zede out in de barn rubbin' his rheumatism with some liniment dat Uncle Doctah had given him. Uncle Zede told us how dey was acting. Dey frolicked, beat de drums, sang and danced most of the night. Not many men ever come, and when dey did come, de healer ain't cure dem much.

"He does his curin' by de layin' on of hands. If de pain's below de waist he rubs it out through de knees and legs, but if it's above de waist he rubs it out through de breasts. If anyone acts like dey is ashamed, he tells them de healer is holy and can't sin.

"I was elected spokesman for de committee from de Lodge, so I walked up to de door and knocked. Lucindy say, 'Who's dat?'

"I say, 'Some brothers. We have a sick man out here and he wants to see if de healer can heal him.'

"Den de healer, himself, come to de door and say through de keyhole, 'Bear with me, brothers, I have some sisters in here who is sufferin'. Please to wait until dey feel de power.'

"We heard Lucindy tell him not to open de door. Dat made me mad, and I say, 'Sister Lucindy, I and a committee from de Lodge is out here with your old man to talk with you about some of what's goin, on around here. Now you open dis door peaceable or we will bust it down, because *we are comin' in.*'

"She say, 'You are Mister Bob's uppity niggers, and if you don't get away from here I'm gonna fill you full of lead!'

"With dat we fell on de door and busted it down.

"I say, 'Ladies and gentlemen, dis committee is gonna read de law to dis man you call de divine healer.'

"With dat Lucindy say, 'How dare you speak disrespectful of de Reverend Doctor Starkes!' And she start for her pistol.

"One of de committee got de pistol and put it in his pocket. I start readin' de law. I say, 'Reverend Divine Healer Saint Ezra Starkes, whose righteousness belongs to de devil, you have stole money from almost every good brother around here. You have laid hands on our women and told dem dat you are holy and can't sin. You done follow Br'er Frank Lovett home from Uncle Doctah's house and brought de heart misery on him. You can't lie to me. I seen de tracks of your patent leather shoes with the heels in his yard. You would have cut his throat dat night if he hadn't been too quick for you. Now you confess dat to dis committee or else I might use dis rope on your neck tonight.'

"Br'er Burke spoke up, 'Make him tell it, Br'er Taft, we are all with you.'

"De healer made like he was tryin' to laugh and he said, 'Brothers, I was just tryin' to have a little innocent fun with Br'er Frank. If he hadn't run, I was gonna tell him not to worry about his money.'

"I say, 'You are lyin'. You heard dat Br'er Frank was de main leader in tryin' to figger some means of gettin' back de money dat he and de rest gave you on dat college. You aimed to kill Br'er Frank, you low-livered—'

"Lucindy butted in, 'Taft Cooper, I'll meet you in de court-house.'

"Br'er Burke say, 'Shut your mouth, Lucindy, or else I'll slam your teeth down your throat.'

"I kept on readin' de law. 'Dis has always been a respectable community, and we're gonna keep it dat way. Now your visitors are gonna sleep in de barn tonight and Uncle Zede is gonna sleep in his own bed. Sister Lucindy, you and dis divine healer are goin' somewhere else to do your whorin' from now on. We'll give him until midnight Saturday to get plumb out of dis neighborhood.'

"Den I say to my committee, 'You've heard de word of de law. Is dey a motion?' Br'er Burke say, 'I move de committee approve of de law as read.' When it was seconded I said, 'All in favor of de motion, say aye.' All de committee said 'aye.' Den I say, 'Uncle Zede it is decreed by de law of dis committee dat you sleep in your bed tonight.'"

"I happen already to know about this last experience with him," Colonel Livingston said. "The sheriff told me about it. The healer went to the sheriff in a terrible rage and tried to have your committee arrested for disturbing divine worship.

Sheriff Satterfield called Bob Lawson early Friday morning to find out what the ruckus was about. Bob agreed to stop by his office while he was in Sylvania and give him the word. Bob told him what he knew about the trouble Reverend Starkes was causing, and they agreed that if the healer tried to have anybody arrested that he could be prosecuted for practicing medicine without a license. I understand Reverend Starkes was still more furious when he heard that, but he felt that Bob had the dead wood on him; so he decided pretty quickly to not to have anyone arrested."

"Yes sir; dat was de last thing I talked about with Mister Bob. Dat healer was to clear out of here by Saturday night, but I don't know if he has gone or not yet. Some of dese women may be hidin' him out. But he ain't liable to stay around long. I've got my week's run in my pocket, and as soon as de funeral's over I'm gonna see can I find him. You know it takes a negro to catch a negro."

"Where would you go to find him?" Colonel Livingston asked.

"To Savannah. Dat's where most all de bad negroes from dese parts go to hide."

"Well, how would you go about finding him in Savannah?"

"If you wants to find a negro in Savannah, you look one of two places: one's out in Yamacraw and de other's de Union Station, generally between five o'clock in de evenin' and three o'clock in de mornin'. Dey seem to turn up dere sooner or later."

"Taft, I'm going to see that you have a chance to make that search," Colonel Livingston said. "But you won't have to spend your week's run. The law will pay your expenses. I'll see the sheriff and have him make you a special deputy and write a letter for you to take to Savannah to the sheriff of Chatham County to get his cooperation. You'd better go to him the first thing when you get there."

"Thank you, Colonel, thank you, sir," Taft said, his voice trembling. "But, don't you think we better keep all dis between ourselves, exceptin' of course Miss Prudence, because some of dese colored folks around here might put dat healer wise?"

"Quite right, Taft. You just keep your eyes and ears open. I think you may be a great help to us."

XIII
Dark Counsels

Sunday night

As the Colonel's car pulled away from Linger-long, Taft stood watching it until it disappeared in the trail of dust left in its wake. He was thinking that all the other deaths he had known had been so different; they had been the end of responsibility. Now, he felt that the tension about him would continue to tighten and that he would never again be at ease until the murderer was found. He looked at the tall sycamores in front of the house, their sleek trunks shining white in the twilight, and longed for life as it had been before Mister Bob was killed.

Taft noticed that the lights were turned on in Linger-long and that people were moving about in the house. Seeing Prudence on the south porch, he walked up close to where she stood and called a little above a whisper: "Miss Prudence, I want to talk with you a minute, please, ma'am."

"All right, Taft, I'll meet you in the porch office," said Prudence, sensing that his message was private.

On the end of the screened-in back porch, just off the rear entrance to the main hallway, Bob had arranged a sort of office where he could receive his colored friends, free from flies and mosquitoes. Bob's special chair was placed behind a rustic outdoor table, and other chairs were grouped informally.

Prudence sat down in Bob's chair and motioned Taft to be seated.

"I've just been talkin' with Colonel Livingston about dat divine healer. You know dat man got terrible mad with us in the Lodge for reading him de partin' law. And he went over to Sylvania to have us all arrested."

"Why, Taft, I didn't know *that!*"

"Yas, ma'am, dat's what de sheriff say to Mister Bob. Den Mister Bob told de sheriff to hold de healer for practicin' medicine without a license, if he don't leave us all alone. Then the sheriff had to call dat healer to his office and give him the word. And de sheriff say dat man was madder than a wet hen when he hear dat de law might be after him. But, he left de court house powerful quick after the sheriff give him de word."

"I knew that he'd been warned to leave, but I didn't know that there's been all that stir about him in Sylvania."

"Well, you see, Mister Bob went to see de sheriff Friday morning, and Mister Bob told me about it before he left for Savannah."

"Oh," Prudence sighed.

"What I want to tell you, Miss Prudence, is dat I want to find dat divine healer and pick a talk with him and see can I can find out if he knows who killed Mister Bob."

"But I thought he left before the tragedy."

"Ain't nobody seen him leave near as I can find out. Colonel Livingston just told me a little while ago dat he will give me de power of de law to investigate dat man wherever he is, dat is, if you're willin' for me to be gone for a day or so, Miss Prudence."

"Yes, Taft. But where on Earth would you begin to look for him?"

"I allow dat I should go to Savannah, like I'm goin' on one of dem business trips for Mister Bob; so nobody won't be suspecting what I'm up to. I expect he's down dere already, but if he ain't, he'll be down dere before long."

"Then you won't tell your friends where you're going?"

"No, ma'am. He might find out I'm after him and move on somewhere else."

"That's right, Taft. . . . You'll need some money, of course."

"No, thank you, ma'am. De law's gonna arrange about dat. . . . I'll tell Br'er Burke to do de feedin' an' such stuff for you."

Taft bowed himself out and walked alone in the deepening dusk to the Louisville Road. Turning onto this white line of sand, he trudged along automatically. Foremost in his mind were the last words that Colonel Livingston had said to him: "Keep your eyes and ears open, Taft; I think you may be a great help to us." This time tomorrow, he thought, he'd be on his way to Savannah where he hoped to find out what he wanted to know. He lifted his feet with renewed strength at this idea. Suddenly, he was aware of the low, rhythmic song of the insects coming from the wild hedges along the roadside. Above this droning, the solitary voice of Holloman rose in supplication to his God. Taft wondered why it was Mister Bob and not Sam Holloman that had been killed. *I guess God needed a good angel,* Taft told himself. He puzzled if Mister Bob as a spirit would continue to notice all these little things he used to enjoy. He imagined him with wings and maybe all his earthly interests would become like worn out clothes. He was thinking that angels always wore Sunday clothes and thought Sunday thoughts. Then Taft recalled pictures of angels he'd seen in the Sunday school books and he could not conceive of Mister Bob being happy with a dress on.

He quickened his steps along the old road. He was impatient for the hour of eight o'clock that evening, when the Lodge would hold its regular meeting. He knew that there were many ideas floating among his people, but they were not telling them to just anybody.

The Lodge held its regular meeting the first and third Sunday evening of every month in the Church of the Blessed Trinity. Regular church services, as customary among rural churches, were held only once a month, and the building was used at other times for various community gatherings. All negro men accepted as reputable citizens were eligible for membership to the Lodge. Most of the negro men around Cooperville belonged at one time or another. Bob Lawson was the only white man ever elected to the brotherhood.

The church, another landmark of the Louisville Road, was a most unpretentious building—unpainted, unadorned. As far back as anyone could remember, the small frame structure had crowned the hillock on which it stood. It had been there so long that it was accepted as a part of the natural scene. On each side of the building in front was a window, placed rather high, giving the suggestion of two big eyes. A prolific subtropical growth hugged its sides and at a distance looked like a Queen Elizabeth ruching. The small bell tower, perched on the roof like an Empress Eugenie hat, completed the suggestion of its being very human.

Before dark, groups of men had gathered and were standing here and there in the church yard, talking in undertones. As Taft came in sight of the groups, they slowly, as if without spirit, began sauntering into the building. Now that the hour for the meeting had arrived, Taft felt a deepending sense of responsibility. It was not a simple matter to say to his friends, "Who killed our friend and brother?"

"Brothers," Br'er Burke began, as he called the meeting to order, "as president of dis Lodge I'm gonna take de authority to dispense with all regular business and throw de meetin' open to discussion. We want to take up a matter dat has bent our hearts low. You all know dat dey ain't never been a day like dis in de Cooperville neighborhood. Some devil dat ain't good enough for Hell has shed de blood of de innocent. And somewhere dat devil is walkin' loose. We ain't knowin' who he, or maybe she is, but we sure know he's loose."

"Amen, brother," chanted the Lodge as in one voice.

"I could have told you last night dat death and de devil was keepin' company in dese woods. When I was walkin' home, I got de creepin'est feelin' a man ever has had. Look like sweat drops was freezin' all over me. Seem like all over I was plumb weighed down and couldn't lift my feet to make walk. I say to myself, 'I reckon I just has to lay down by de road and rest.'"

"Poor brother," responded the Lodge.

"Next thing I knew I saw my own tombstone walkin' to meet me up dat red clay hill by de Ole Mill Creek. On it waz written as plain as de letters on dis hymn book:

"'IN MEMORY OF ALONZO BURKE
IN GOD WE TRUST.'"

"Ummmmmmm," a knowing groan swept like a wave over the Lodge. The kerosene lamps were a-flicker, casting eerie shadows on the walls. The men looked about uneasily.

"About what time was it, Br'er Burke?" Taft found a sense of relief in the sound of his own voice.

"It was just before the thunderstorm."

"About de time Mister Bob was killed," Taft said solemnly.

"Br'er Burke," Br'er Frank Lovett was on his feet. "We are all liable to come across many a curious feelin' and experience with Mister Bob killed like he was. De devil is more than apt to get us all, if we don't stop him. Has anyone of you brothers heard of slack talk about Mister Bob around dese parts, from white or colored? Has anyone of you got a suspicion?"

Not a sound from the Lodge. The men seemed afraid to place the blame. Each was hoping another would break the silence.

"Br'er Burke," Uncle Jud Williams was slowly rising as with great effort, "on dis mournful occasion, I want to say dat I been workin' for Mister Bob nigh onto twenty years, and I ain't got no complaint against him. He's been my friend and he's been a friend to all of us. Of course, Mister Bob had his ways. We mighty soon learned not to ask him for nothin' when he walked lookin' at de ground. On de other hand, we knew when he say 'Good mornin', brother,' dat he would listen to us talk and take care of us."

"Aye, aye, brother," from the Lodge.

"I used to tell Mister Bob," Uncle Jud continued, "dat he got eyes in de back o' his head; dat he seen us comin' an' goin'. You all remember dat he told us not to burn up de litter in de fields, but to turn it under to make more land. One day he saw smoke in my corn patch. When he got down dere he found my boy, Chunky, pilin' on de corn stalks.

" 'Chunky,' he say, 'Who told you to burn dem stalks?'

"Chunky say, kind of sassy-like, 'My paw, de man what tends dis land!'

"Dat got Mister Bob's dander up and he say to Chunky, 'Look here, young man, I don't want any of your sass! You speak dat way again to me an' I'll feed your liver to de buzzards!'

"Before it was good an' dark dat same day, Mister Bob drove up to my house.

" 'How're you gettin' along, Uncle Jud?' he say.

"I told him I wasn't gettin' along none of de best on account of dis rheumatism in de knees."

Uncle Jud had been afflicted so long with rheumatism that his once strong, erect body was now drawn into bows and angles.

"'Well, Uncle Jud,' Mister Bob say, 'de Good Book say never let de sun go down on your wrath. It's a little *after* sundown, but I got here as soon as I could. De devil was walkin' in de fields today, and he was sort of rulin' things. He was rulin' Chunky and he was rulin' me.' He say, 'De Good Book say to keep the devil behind you, because when he gets in de front, you don't know where you're gonna land up at—exceptin' de devil always lands you up in trouble.' Dat's what Mister Bob say. And he put his hand on Chunky's shoulder.

"He say, 'Chunky gave me some back-talk today, and I've been ashamed of the things I told him. I want Chunky to know dat I am sorry. You know, Uncle Jud, de devil's catchin', and I want you to be careful and not let him get hold on you, and I want you to help Chunky shed him off so he won't get in more trouble.'

"Seems like dat sort of changed Chunky. He ain't made no more back talk. Seems like he is all de time in a deep study."

Of course Uncle Jud had no way of knowing all the things Chunky had said and done.

"De devil sure is catchin' all right. Mister Bob was right about dat," Taft responded.

"Umm-humm!" in chorus.

"Dat may be why he's spreadin' himself so big around here," Taft continued. "Dat divine healer has rubbed him out of so many of our women dat he might be lookin' for other places to stay. De devil sure must have gotten into somebody last night de way he went for Mister Bob."

Taft had purposely referred to the healer to see what the reaction would be. A titter of whispers swept over the Lodge. Something suddenly seemed to lessen the tensions of the gathering and all through the church the men were giving expression to their pent-up feelings:

"Ran poor old Brother Zede out of his house and made him sleep in de barn."

"He was more sinner dan saint."

"He brought de heart misery on Br'er Frank Lovett."

"He sure had plenty of sick women at his hospital."

Taft knew now that at least the majority of the men were with him. "Brothers, I say from de start dat man was phoney. I heard about all his healin's and I decided to bait him one night my own self. You all know dat I got about eleven head of children. So I went to de healer an' I say, 'Br'er Ezra, I've got a bad hurtin' under my left shoulder and if it keep up, I don't see how I'm gonna make feed for all my family.' He say, 'Brother, you better go to de doctor.'

"Of course now, I ain't accusin' nobody, because I ain't wantin' to put dis on nobody what ain't what done it. We ain't know yet who done it."

"Aye, Lord," burst from the Lodge.

"I think dis Lodge has a responsibility, and I want to know, are you all gonna help me find out who killed Mister Bob?"

"Amen, brother," filled the room.

"I want to say dat dis meetin' is for us brothers to resolve to get de man or woman who did dis awful thing. I don't want no brother to leave dis meetin' until he has sworn to his God to do all in his power from now on until de murderer is caught.

"Dat United States flag you see over dere is our property. You all remember it was give to dis Lodge by our deceased brother. He told us in his presentation dat he hope we would never do nothin' to dishonor it, and we ain't. My brothers, we would dishonor him, his maw an' paw, dat flag, an' everythin', if we didn't help de law find de murderer.

"Are you all ready to stand together? Are you ready to shed up blood? Is duty ahead of your life?"

"Amen, Br'er Taft."

"Den keep your eyes open," Taft continued, "and if you find out anything you want to report, take it to de law. If you ever get de murderer and you're sure dat's him, follow him and hang on to him until de law can get him.

"As soon as de funeral's over, I'm gonna be gone on a little business, but Br'er Burke, as president of dis Lodge, will be with you for all investigations.

"Now, let's us put our minds to work. You all has your suspicions, I has mine. You work your way, and I work mine. Amongst us we must find de murderer. Maybe we all are thinkin' about a different man. Maybe a woman. All right, let's us find out all we can about them all.

"Brothers, when I saw Mister Bob lyin' dead under de Ghost Oak it flashed across my mind: Whoever had de face to kill him? But you all know de killer ain't use no face. He slipped up on Mister Bob in de dark. A coward way, I call it, a coward way! I don't think de devil himself would have had a chance with Mister Bob if dey met up together man to man. But de devil don't want to play fair. All his rules are cheatin'. So he say to de killer, 'Slash him quick and give him hell before he gets a chance at you.' Yes, brothers, Mister Bob ain't had no chance to defend himself."

"Ummmmmm—" a wailing from the Lodge.

A black bat flew in through the window and darted aimlessly among the rafters, finally lighting up in the bell tower. The men who were seated under the tower rolled their eyes above them and moved stealthily over by the walls.

"Br'er Burke,—" all evening Dumplin had been trying to get up the nerve to speak—"last night down to Dover, I and Chunky were standin' by de store when Mister Bob got off of de train. Mister Sorrel, he was dere too, and feelin' de moonshine. When he seen Mister Bob, he say he was gonna do a little evenin' up with him. He say dey old men might have started it, but he would see to de finishin' up. He saw Mister Bob walkin' away on de Old Dover Road; he watched him until he was out of sight, den, he got on his old mule and followed after him."

"Sure looks bad, sure looks bad," several of the brothers said in succession.

"'A barkin' dog, a barkin' dog don't bite,' I told Dumplin when he got scared," said Chunky sneeringly. "Mister Sorrel, he's been talkin' dat way ever since before we were born. If he'd aimed at doin' anything to Mister Bob, he'd have done it before now."

"But if you all could have seen how mad he was!" Dumplin's round face looked even rounder in the uneven light.

"Now as for me," Taft said with a note of finality. "I can't understand why any man would to kill Mister Bob. And I don't want to put dis on nobody dat ain't done it. But I'm gonna see can I find out.

"Whatsoever any brother thinks about anybody dat might have done it, don't leave no stones unturned in dey tracks."

"Brother, we are with you."

"Amen, brother."

"I feel, brothers, dat Mister Bob is lookin' down on us dis very minute from his home on high. I guess he's sayin' to himself, 'I knew my brothers would look after me.' Maybe he's ridin' across de sky while de angels are singin' for joy when dey see him comin' through de pearly gates. I don't know, brothers. . . . I just don't know . . . how we all are gonna get on without him." Taft's voice had broken until he could say no more.

"Mr. President and brothers in dis Lodge." Parson Wilkes had come into the Church of the Blessed Trinity just in time to hear Taft's last words. "When de sun was settin' dis evenin', I was impressed with de heavy clouds dat rose in de West. Dey looked like dey was made of gold. I ain't never seen so many, and I ain't never seen dem look so grand like dat before. I say to myself, 'Dem clouds are gold and de good Lord is gettin' ready to pay Mister Bob off.' You all know, my brothers, de Lord will acknowledge all de good He see His children do.

"I reproach you not to weep." Parson Wilkes lifted his hands as if in supplication and slowly turned them over his audience in the gesture of a blessing as he spoke. "Mister Bob is where de one dat killed him will never be. But, where Mister Bob is, we will go. So, I reproach you again to wipe your eyes and ask de Lord to keep you in de path dat leads to de city of gold behind dem clouds dat I seen dis evenin'."

As their pastor finished speaking, the men reverently dropped their heads in prayer. From the silence that followed, there arose a soft humming which presently drifted into the singing with deep sincerity, *"Jesus, put your arms around me, and no evil thoughts can harm me; dear Lord, I'm in your care."*

XIV
He Talked Too Much

Early Monday morning

Dr. Evans was up early Monday morning. He took the cross path to the Lawsons' back yard, and, as was his habit at times, was looking everywhere and seeing nothing. A moving object suddenly caught his eye. He came to himself with a start. It was Wormser emerging from the old Lawson back yard. Coming nearer he said: "I see that both of us are up early this morning, Mr. Wormser."

"Yes... that's right, yes.... I woke up early, was restless, and decided to begin my morning walk. You are a doctor; so I am sure you recognize the value of exercise." Wormser seemed rather agitated. "I have wanted from the first to explore the old Lawson place, but there have been too many distractions.

"It was fortunate that I took this occasion to do so. I have just discovered the lifeless body of a boy, lying in practically the same spot where Bob Lawson was found."

"No!" Dr. Evans's face was a puzzle. *"Two murders in two days!* in Cooperville... Incredible!"

Together, they walked to the place where the body lay.

"Jake Martin!" Dr. Evans shook his head and stroked his Vandyke. "Poor boy! He talked too much."

Both men approached the body cautiously and scrutinized it without disturbing it. The throat was slashed in the same ghastly way that Bob's had been.

Neither spoke for a moment.

Presently Dr. Evans said, "We must call Colonel Livingston and Sheriff Satterfield. But meanwhile the place must be kept clear."

Dr. Evans walked on to the road toward Linger-long where he saw Br'er Burke busily engaged in washing the Lincoln. He called him over, told him what had happened, and instructed him to assist Mr. Wormser in keeping the place clear.

Br'er Burke stared wide-eyed. Then bowing a polite, "Yes, sir" to Dr. Evans, he took his place as guard but was careful to remain some distance from the body.

It was not until Dr. Evans turned again toward the Lawson residence that he recalled, with some effort, his reason for being over there so early in the morning. He wanted to have a private talk with Prudence. Ruby saw him coming and informally invited him in through the back entrance. "I think Miss Prudence is dressin' now; I'll see if she can come," she said, and started toward Mrs. Morris's room.

"May I use your phone?" the doctor asked.

"Yes, sir, Doctor, go right ahead."

He called Colonel Livingston and notified him of the new developments.

Prudence greeted him in the hall as he was leaving the telephone and invited him into the library. She felt intuitively that he wanted to talk with her alone.

"There are several things I want to talk to you about," he began, "but first I must tell you of what we found this morning. . . ." Dr. Evans could hardly bring himself to tell her of another violent death, the body lying, at that moment, where Bob's had lain.

"I want you to feel perfectly free, Dr. Evans, to discuss matters with me or ask me any questions you wish."

Dr. Evans had always admired Prudence's frankness and sincerity. He had often thought what a pity it was that Lester had not inherited some of his mother's sterling qualities.

"Prudence, you're always so understanding," he said, "you may have heard me ring Sylvania a while ago. It was to notify Colonel Livingstone that Jake Martin was found dead at the old place this morning."

"Murdered?" Prudence gasped.

"Yes."

"I somehow felt afraid for the boy when I heard about what he had been saying yesterday afternoon. . . . I feel so sorry for his poor mother. Does she know about it yet?"

"No, I thought I'd better tell you first, and someone might be able to go from here."

"If you'll excuse me a minute, Doctor, I'll call Mary and Martha Singleton and ask them to go on and tell her."

Dr. Evans looked at the library about him. He was surprised at the size of Bob's collection of poetry and psychology. He was fingering through a book on abnormal psychology when Prudence returned from the telephone.

"I want to ask a few questions about some of your guests," the Doctor said. "Please understand that we have no specific evidence against any of them, but some hints have been dropped that seem to call for clarification. How seriously do you think Mr. Harvey regarded Bob's attentions to Mrs. Harvey?"

"I can't believe for a moment that Allen would ever have thought in terms of violence toward Bob, if that's what you mean. They have been such close friends and have had so many pleasant associations. As I see it, and as Allen may have seen it, Bob and Priscilla were not altogether discreet, and they did not consider such matters in the same way that we do—and that Allen does. No, Dr. Evans, Allen could never have done that."

"Well, do you know anything definite about this business affair that has recently come between Bob and Mr. Tyler?"

"Nothing definite. You know Bob never told me much about his business affairs. Of course, I sensed that there was something in the air. I know that Gordon has, in the last few years, become over-ambitious to gain wealth and power. It may be partly Irene's influence. He is not as companionable as he used to be. But what differences there may have been between him and Bob, I feel sure they were still the best of friends."

"Well, about Mr. Wormser—is he connected with Mr. Tyler's business?"

"I don't know, Doctor. I asked Bob about him when he first came down, and you know how Bob was, 'Now don't go worrying your pretty head about him, Prude,' he said. 'He's all right. He's a friend of a friend of mine and I thought a little outing in God's Country would be good for him.' He's evidently a friend of the Tylers."

"It's all so baffling," Dr. Evans said.

On his way to rejoin Wormser, Dr. Evans ran across Gordon and Irene in the yard. "Have you heard about the other tragedy over there?" he asked, his eyes fixed on the Ghost Oak.

"Yes, we've just been talking with Albert Wormser about it," Gordon said.

"I thought this place was so placid." Irene flicked away the remains of her cigarette.

"Well, I assure you, Mrs. Tyler, that this is most extraordinary," Dr. Evans countered.

Their attention was drawn to Colonel Livingston's car as it drew up alongside of the old Lawson place. Dr. Evans excused himself and joined the Colonel and Sheriff Satterfield.

"Strange that there's no blood on the grass," was Colonel Livingston's first remark on seeing the corpse—"A gash like that should have brought plenty of blood, wouldn't it, Doctor?"

"Hell yes," Satterfield countered. "Like a fountain."

"Certainly, I had thought of that," the doctor affirmed.

He and the sheriff examined the body more closely but found no clues.

Colonel Livingston said with decision: "There's no question that the crime was not committed here; it was done somewhere else, and the dead body was brought here, probably in the night.... But, from where?"

"Who found the body?" Colonel Livingston asked.

"I did," Wormser said. "As I told Dr. Evans, I was out for a walk. I consider the early morning down here the best part of your day."

The Colonel turned to Dr. Evans: "I suppose you have found no traces about the grounds."

"I've canvassed that situation pretty thoroughly," the doctor answered, "and I don't believe it holds any promise. As you can see, the grounds here are well covered with grass and undergrowth and the road has been too much stirred up since the Saturday night's storm to hold foot prints. I walked for some distance along both sides of the road, looking for any promising marks in the little patches of firmer soil here and there, but the murderer was too canny this time to leave such traces. But I haven't had time to make a thorough search."

From Colonel Livingston's expression he was struggling with a painful thought. "I should have investigated that boy and his story last night. I might possibly have prevented this. Probably not."

Dr. Evans was consoling. "You would not have been able to find that boy. And if by any chance you had, he would have told you nothing. In a matter like this he would have avoided law enforcement officials until confronted with the compulsion of testifying on the stand."

The sheriff added, "That boy would run off his mouth just to hear himself talk. You know he would have clammed up if he seen law men around. He really was nobody's fool."

Colonel Livingston's eyes were drawn to the dirty hands of the dead boy. He noticed the contrast between them and the clean well-groomed hands of Bob Lawson and felt that here was symbolized the difference in their upbringing—the boy's mother, who had been widowed in his infancy, was a good hearted woman, but she had been so weighted with responsibilities that she had been unable to give him the attention he should have had.

The sheriff was knocking out his pipe on the heel of his shoe. He was growing impatient. "We must talk to his mother; has anyone notified her yet?"

"Yes," from Dr. Evans.

"Well, shouldn't we see her next?"

Colonel Livingston agreed. "But, I want to come back here and make a more thorough investigation of the boy's clothing and this surrounding area. Has anyone called the funeral home?"

"Actually, I felt we should talk with Mrs. Martin first," Dr. Evans observed.

The three men drove across the creek to the Martins' house. Mrs. Martin came out of the house, red-eyed and sobbing.

After the men had expressed their condolences and Mrs. Martin had assumed her best air of composure, they were seated on the porch. Colonel Livingston inquired: "Mrs. Martin, have you any idea who could have done this deed?"

"None in the least, Colonel Livingston. I know that poor Jake"—she almost broke down again but recovered—"was mischievous and inclined to run around as boys will. He may have bothered folks sometimes, but he never done nothin' really bad, and I can't *imagine* anybody wantin' to *kill* him."

"Do you know where he was yesterday, evening and last night?"

"He come in about the middle of the afternoon, got him somethin' to eat, and went out again. He said he was goin' over to Cooperville, that he might go to meetin' last night.

"He often stayed out later than he ought to have, especially on Sunday nights. So, I didn't know until this mornin' that he hadn't come home. I was sort of worried when I found out that he hadn't."

"Thank you, Mrs. Martin. We'll let you know as soon as we find out anything definite," Colonel Livingston said as they turned to go.

"Thank you, gentlemen, I *do* hope you'll find who killed my poor boy," Mrs. Martin sadly responded. As they drove away, Dr. Evans remarked: "There's little enough evidence that seems definite in the case of Bob Lawson, in this case there seems to be none. As I see it, we are bound to concentrate on the question as to who committed the first crime, for if we solve that, we'll have solved the other also."

"In all probability," Colonel Livingston replied, "that is certainly the natural inference. But, it is barely possible that we have two separate crimes to investigate. Even so, quite likely they are related in some way."

When they returned to Linger-long, the knots of people conversing here and there in the yard, gathered around the car. But, they were more in quest of information than they were able to contribute any clues.

"Any news?" came a voice from the crowd.

Dr. Evans shook his head and looked at his watch. "Nine-forty," he said. "Remember the inquest is at ten."

XV

The Coroner Presides

Monday morning

If a man as many-sided as Dr. Evans could be said to have had a hobby, it was the spacious lawn to the rear of his house. Around it he had grown a thick bamboo hedge, which afforded him privacy when he wanted it. Overspreading it were huge water oaks draped with Spanish moss. Scattered about were numbers of benches and outdoor chairs, for here he often had informal gatherings of his friends from near and far.

He was by nature a very sociable person despite the fact that he sometimes preferred solitude when he might enjoy to the fullest those meditations, which often gave him the appearance of absent-mindedness.

As was previously arranged, the inquest on the killing of Bob Lawson was to be held on his lawn. Dr. Evans, as coroner, had decided to defer the inquest on Jake Martin because of lack of evidence at the time.

Before opening the proceedings, the coroner turned to Colonel Livingston and said in an undertone: "John, I want you to sit with me and ask any questions that may occur to you. By the way, you have your notes with you, don't you?"

"Thank you, Doctor. Yes, I have."

The two men seated themselves behind a table on the flagstone terrace at the rear of the house and looked out over the gathering of people that filled the enclosure.

After the oath had been administered to all those who were be questioned, Taft was called as the first witness. The coroner obtained from him the necessary testimony as to the finding of the body and the condition in which it was found. Taft was then dismissed.

Dr. Evans then addressed the group: "As painful as it was for me, I performed a careful autopsy on Bob's body. I found no bruises or scratches that might have indicated a struggle. It looks as though someone had slipped up on him from behind and plunged a sharp knife into his left jugular vein and slid it across his throat. His death was probably instantaneous, and he was left lying in a pool of his own blood."

There was a shocked silence among those gathered for the inquest. Dr. Evans added, "So far, we have no trace of the weapon." He then paused for people to regain their composure.

Hardly knowing where to begin next, he noticed Mom Liza trying to slip away from the assembled group. "Just a minute, Mom Liza," he called. Mom Liza turned around and faced Dr. Evans.

"Mom Liza," Dr. Evans began, "you walk around a good deal at night, don't you?"

"Yes sir, Dr. Evans, you know I do," Mom Liza replied sulkily. "Why have you got me mixed up with this killin' mess. You know I ain't never harmed a fly."

"Now, Mom Liza," Dr. Evans's tone was mollifying, "we're not accusing anyone. We're simply trying to find out who *is* to blame. We thought you might have seen someone. Will you tell us whether you saw anyone about the grounds of the old Lawson place last Saturday night?"

"I didn't go out of my house Saturday night. I ain't been feelin' good, so I took a physic; den I ain't had no wakin' sickness dat night."

"Well, if you didn't see anyone, did you hear anything that might in any way have to do with the murder of Bob Lawson?"

"I told you, Doctor, dat I wasn't out dat night."

"All right, Mom Liza, that's all for today—unless Colonel Livingston has something to ask."

The Colonel shook his head. The old woman walked away mumbling. Dr. Evans had already talked with Prudence privately, and had mercifully excused her from the ordeal of the inquest. So, Lester Morris was the next to testify.

"Lester, where were you last Saturday night between ten-thirty and twelve o'clock?"

"I was in bed. I thought Mother told you I had a headache that evening, and she gave me an aspirin tablet about ten-thirty, and I went straight to bed."

"Did you hear any unusual noise or noises around eleven o'clock or later that might possibly be associated with this case?"

"No, sir. I slept like a log after that aspirin and didn't wake up until I heard the commotion at the house the next morning."

"Do you know of any person who might have had a grudge against your Uncle Bob, or who for any reason might have wanted to murder him?"

"I've seen Uncle Bob get mad enough with a good many people to want to kill them at the time, and I guess a good many people have got just as mad with him. But, for all that, everybody knows he meant well, and I can't see why anybody would actually have killed him."

"Thank you, Lester."

Allen Harvey was then called.

"I must say that it pains me greatly to subject the guests of my late friend to embarrassing questions, but I have to fulfill my duties under the law," Dr. Evans said apologetically. "Mr. Harvey, I believe you told us that you came in from Sylvania after the storm Saturday night. Did you go immediately to your room?"

"No, Dr. Evans, you must have misunderstood me with reference to the time I reached Linger-long. I said I drove in from Sylvania and went to my room after the storm. As a matter of fact, I actually drove into the garage just as the rain was beginning; so I waited there until it was over and then went to my room."

The doctor turned to the Colonel: "Is that right, John?"

Colonel Livingston referred to his notes and found that there was no essential conflict with what Allen had said about this before. He simply had omitted to say just when he reached Linger-long, and that he had remained in the garage during the storm.

"Substantially correct, Doctor," the Colonel said.

"Mr. Harvey, did you see or hear anything about the place or its environs that night that might have been in any way associated with the murder of Bob Lawson?"

"Nothing at all. I was enjoying watching the spectacular storm; such phenomena have always greatly interested me. After the storm, I went to my room."

"Mr. Harvey, as I recall, you told us yesterday that you saw Mr. Wormser in the library playing solitaire when you came into the house Saturday night. Do you think you might have been mistaken as to the person you saw?"

"I am sure, Dr. Evans, that it was Mr. Wormser."

To protect those directly concerned from the idle gossip that might have spread through the crowds, Dr. Evans refrained from raising any question regarding the love triangle. He felt that was a matter that could be taken care of through private hearings and, if necessary, in court later on.

When Mr. Wormser had taken the stand and the testimony he had given privately the day before had been reviewed, Dr. Evans asked in the same matter of fact tone: "I believe you said that you went directly from my home to your room and retired for the night."

"Sorry, Doctor, if I gave you that impression; it is not entirely a correct one. I did go to bed at once, as I said, but I was unable to sleep because of the unusually brilliant lightning and crashing thunder. The storm had disturbed me, so I threw on my bathrobe and went down to the library and played solitaire until the storm was over."

"Did you see Mr. Harvey when he came in?"

"I was aware of doors opening and closing and of stirring in the hallways, but I hardly looked up. I was intent upon my game."

Wormser was dismissed, and Allen was called again to the stand.

"Sorry to trouble you again, Mr. Harvey, but I wish to ask you another question or two. When you saw Mr. Wormser playing solitaire on the occasion in question, how was he dressed?"

"He was in a light summer bathrobe."

"Did he look up, or give any sign of recognizing you as you came in?"

"I believe not."

"Thank you, Mr. Harvey. That's all."

Gordon, Irene, and Priscilla were called in turn, but none of them could—or would—give information to lead anywhere. Their alleged alibis were the same as they had given the day before.

The doctor then asked for Will Sorrel.

Colonel Livingston turned to the coroner and said, "Doctor, if you don't mind, I'd like to question Will."

"By all means."

"Mr. Sorrell," the Colonel began, "I understand that you were down at Dover on Saturday night?"

"Yes, sir."

"You were drinking, swearing, and talking rather boisterously, I hear."

"Yes, sir, but I wasn't drunk."

"When you saw Mr. Lawson among the group by the train, did you make any reference to him?"

"No, sir, I never paid no special attention to him. I don't recollect even callin' his name."

"You told us yesterday," Colonel Livingston looked at his notes, "that you were *not swearing* and that *you did not see Mr. Lawson at all.* You have, at least by clear implication, contradicted yourself twice."

"Well, about the swearin', Colonel, you know a man gets so his swearin' is sort of like his swallerin'; he don't particularly notice when he does it. I must have forgot. And as for Bob, maybe I did see him and forgot that too."

"Will Sorrel!" the Colonel shouted with exasperation. "No more of your lying! We have witnesses that you were in a frightfully nasty mood on Saturday night, and that with the vilest of oaths, you made murderous threats against Bob Lawson."

Sorrel was completely cowed. He could not at once bring himself to reply.

"Whatever I said, I never meant no harm by it, Colonel. I sure ain't had a mind to kill nobody. I know I spout off my mouth when I've had a dram or two. But I ain't never hurt nobody."

"You told us that you came out from Dover by the Sylvania Highway. Think carefully, are you quite sure—remember you were drinking and may not have been thinking clearly—are you certain that you did not take the Old Dover Road?"

"Yes sir, Colonel. I'd been drinkin', but I wasn't so far gone but that I knew what I was doin'. I'm sure I came by the Sylvania Highway."

"That'll do, for the present."

The next witness was called. "You go ahead, John," Dr. Evans said.

"Mr. Hendrix," the Colonel turned his eyes rigidly upon the witness. "I understand that you had an appointment with Mr. Lawson for Saturday night about eleven o'clock, and that you wrote him a letter canceling the appointment. When was that letter mailed?"

"I done told you that I sent that letter to Dover on Friday in time for the Saturday morning mail. I gave it to my boy to mail, but he forgot or something and it didn't get mailed until the next day, or so he says."

"Now, Mr. Hendrix, you will recall that your boy told you in our presence yesterday that he had mailed that letter Friday. When the letter finally came it bore a Dover postmark for several hours later than our visit to you Sunday. How do you account for that? Did you write that letter after we left?"

"No, by God! I tell you I sent that letter to Dover on Friday." Hendrix studied a minute. "Maybe that boy of mine was more careless than he owned up to. Must have had it in his pocket when he was talkin' about it. He did go off to Dover directly after you all left."

"Is your boy in the habit of telling lies?"

Hendrix dropped his head and considered his answer. "Yes, sir, he lies once in a while," he said.

"Is this a case of like father, like son, Mr. Hendrix?"

"Yes sir—I mean, no sir. Colonel Livingston, I'm sure that I ain't never lied to *you.*"

When Hendrix was dismissed, the coroner inquired whether anyone in the audience could furnish any additional information. There was no response.

Mr. Wormser broke the silence by speaking out cautiously, "Not exactly additional information, but I have a question. Wasn't Mr. Lawson's body robbed? If robbery was the motive for the murder, wouldn't that eliminate Mr. Lawson's guests as suspects?"

Dr. Evans considered his answer carefully: "I had thought about that, Mr. Wormser. It seemed obvious to me that the robbery may have taken place after the murder. If someone who is not likely to be suspected of robbery killed Bob, he might have taken the valuables to avert suspicion. On the other hand, it is possible, of course, that robbing the body was done later by someone other than the murderer."

Mr. Wormser said no more.

Then came the expected verdict: "... by person or persons unknown."

When the inquest was over and most of the crowd had left, Br'er Burke made his way to the officers.

"I reckon dis ain't got nothin' to do with Mister Bob's murder," he said, "but it might have something to do with de killin' of dat boy, Jake. On my way to dis meetin' I took a short cut through Mister Bob's fruit orchard, and about half way across de orchard—I reckon about two or three hundred yards from de house—all of a sudden I come across a passel of blood on de grass."

"*Blood*? Did you notice any other clues?" Colonel asked.

"No sir, Colonel, I looked all around good, but I ain't seen nothin' else dat look out of de way, exceptin' de grass by de blood was kind of messed up like. But dey wasn't no tracks as I could see."

Colonel Livingston turned to the Doctor: "We'd better investigate that right away."

Dr. Evans's eyes looked glassy. "In Bob's fruit orchard! That close to his house!" He noticeably shuddered. "Yes, John."

XVI
Blood on the Grass

Late Monday morning

Br'er Burke led the doctor and the Colonel directly to the spot where he had seen the blood. There it was on a stretch of grass that separated the fruit orchard from the pecan grove. There it was, within two hundred yards of Linger-long—within fifty yards of the Old Dover Road! A clotted mass of blood upon the trampled sod, and flecks of dried blood on the upright blades of grass.

"How long has it been there, Doctor?" the Colonel asked.

Dr. Evans probed the clotted mass with a twig. "Can't say with any exactness," he said, "but something like twelve to fifteen hours, more or less."

"Beastly!" Colonel Livingston's face was ashen.

"Trapped as he was raiding the peach orchard," Dr. Evans said meditatively, still staring at the blood. "The boy probably thought no one would notice him while the focus of attention was directed toward Bob."

"That's about it, Doctor." Colonel Livingston was looking across the orchard. "I can see a number of ripening peaches."

"Uuumph!" Br'er Burke's face was drawn into a frown. "He sure was de beatin'est youngun I ever seen. Ain't no fruit dat ever get ripe without he knew about it."

"Now let's see . . ." Dr. Evans pondered. "Anyone could have come down the Old Dover Road to where this strip of grass begins, knowing his tracks would be lost on the trampled sand. The murderer might have run into Jake accidentally. Or he might have been looking for the boy. Br'er Burke's right. Wherever there were ripening peaches Jake was likely to appear sooner or later."

"That's right," Colonel Livingston agreed. "It was a sort of game with him—quite honest as long as he wasn't caught at it."

"Yes," the doctor said. "And with the trees as bushy and thick as they are around here, the murderer would have run practically no risk of being seen. It would have taken only a few seconds actually to do the deed. The body could have been moved later."

Colonel Livingston thoughtfully stepped over the bare ground around the nearest trees. He shook his head and said: "Just as I had feared—a jumble of tracks. We'll never be able to single Jake's tracks out, much less his murderer's."

"I never thought of lookin' for footprints dat far away from the blood," Br'er Burke said apologetically.

Dr. Evans was stroking his Vandyke. "It has just occurred to me that Bob's guests wouldn't have known Jake's habits well enough to fall in with him in that way. That would sort of eliminate—"

"Oh, no, Doctor." The Colonel was emphatic. "You forget how these city folks are. They don't have the summer-porch rocking-chair minds that they say we country people have. Didn't you notice that Mrs. Harvey identified the boy to us by things she'd overheard about him? A city slicker could pick up all he'd need from apparently naive questions or from casual eavesdropping on a crowd like that big crowd around Linger-long yesterday afternoon. It seems to me that a person staying at Linger-long would have had the most likely opportunity."

"You may have a point there," the doctor admitted. "We'd better get them all together right away and spring this new evidence on them and watch for reactions. Br'er Burke, it's a good thing you took this short cut this morning. It may serve as a key to the whole mystery."

"Yes sir, Doctor, I sure hope so," Br'er Burke said as the two officers turned toward Linger-long. Then he walked on to the Old Dover Road and headed for home.

"The more I think about it, Doctor, the more it looks like a crime committed by someone right here on the scene," Livingston remarked as they walked along.

Dr. Evans was not watching where he was walking, and his body was bobbing up and down as his feet struck turf and bare depressions along the ground.

"Hold on, Doctor!" Colonel Livingston grabbed Dr. Evans's arm. "What's this?"

"More hoof prints!" the doctor panted. "On the near side of the road this time."

The ground in the orchard was fairly clean and, emerging from the stretch of grass less than a hundred feet beyond the blood, a line of hoof tracks heading toward the old Lawson place went zigzagging around the peach trees. They passed across the orchard and were lost on the Old Dover Road.

"You wait here, John, while I go for some plaster." The Doctor was off almost in a run.

There had been many rains since the soil had been plowed and the ground was so well settled over most of the orchard that the path of prints was clearly marked. Colonel Livingston walked alongside the tracks. He was searching for another set of tracks leading to the blood on the grass, but he never found them.

Dr. Evans, accompanied by Taft, was returning with the plaster.

"Dem ain't no mule tracks dis time, Doctor," Taft said the moment he laid eyes on the prints. "Dey is too big for any mule. Some horse made dem tracks."

"You're right, Taft. They're entirely too large to have been made by a mule."

"Doctor, dis old horse ain't had on no shoes. He was barefoot as de day he was born. You can see dat as plain as daylight," Taft said, rolling his eyes at the two men.

The doctor and the Colonel squatted down by the tracks and looked at them more closely.

"Taft's right," the doctor said.

"This may be easier than we think." Colonel Livingston seemed to have had an inspiration. "Let's prepare the casts and get over to the house."

When the plaster had been poured, and Taft had been asked to look after it, the officers continued their way toward Linger-long. Colonel Livingston told the doctor all the things he'd thought of while he'd been waiting. "I don't really think it's much use to question the folks at the house," he said.

"That's true," Dr. Evans replied between short breaths, "if they were all around the house all evening and night. But I'd like to know what kind of alibis they have to offer."

"I wonder, after all, if Hendrix isn't our man. He could have worked that trick as slick as boiled okra," Colonel Livingston said. "That was pretty shrewd—using a horse without shoes. Makes it lots harder to get a clear-cut cast."

"Yes," Dr. Evans assented, "on the other hand there are relatively few horses unshod. It will be much easier to check on them."

"If we'll sort of hurry up we might have time to run over toward Statesboro and see Hendrix again before the funeral," Colonel Livingston suggested just as they reached the Linger-long yard.

"Not a bad idea, John."

The men went to the back entrance so as to avoid callers. Ruby answered their knock and led them around to the south porch. Her face was beaming with curiosity.

"Have you all seen de fruit orchard blood?" she asked.

"How did you know about that?" There was disappointment in Dr. Evans's voice.

"Br'er Burke told me so I could tell Miss Prudence to pass on de new evidence."

"Damn!" the Colonel said under his breath.

Prudence joined the men at once and volunteered that she had not told anyone about the blood. "I have been waiting," she said, "to talk with you first."

"Prudence, we want to talk with all the Linger-long group together right away," Dr. Evans said and added, "here on this porch if it's all right with you."

"Whatever you think best, Doctor," Prudence replied without hesitation and excused herself to have Ruby invite the others out.

Colonel Livingston had been watching Prudence closely, and from the look on her face when she spoke he felt sure she had understood why the south porch had been chosen—it overlooked the old Lawson house, the Ghost Oak, and the fruit orchard.

One by one Prudence and her guests came onto the porch. *It is the same way it was Friday night when they were going into the old Lawson house,* she thought, *none of them would admit it, but each was affected, more or less, by a sense of fear.* Prudence could not bring herself to think that any one of them was guilty. And yet she was tormented with the consciousness that she might at that very minute be facing the criminal. And she thought what a risk they all might be running, living, as they were, under the same roof. Then, she thought she wished she could quit thinking.

Ruby appeared at the screen door. "Miss Prudence, I found everybody exceptin' Mister Lester, but I can't find hide nor hair of him nowhere."

"Oh, I'm sorry, Ruby. I forgot I'd sent him to Dover on an errand. He'll be back before long. Ask him to come right out when he comes."

"All right, ma'am."

"I apologize for having to question you all over again so soon," Dr. Evans began, "but we need to know where each of you were last night."

What a pity, Priscilla thought, *to smear the tragedy all over the house.* She would never again be able to go into the library without thinking of the questioning yesterday; and now they were ruining the south porch for her—the beautiful south porch, so cool and summery-looking in its fresh green and white. If Bob's house could only be left free, untouched, for him to live on in their memories. *But, they would never think of that,* she thought. *Kill him again in the library! Kill him again on the south porch! Where would this killing ever end?*

"Mrs. Harvey."

Priscilla jumped. "Yes, Dr. Evans."

"Did you hear Jake Martin say he knew who the murderer was?" Dr. Evans asked.

"No, sir. I had wandered to the back porch for a minute and just happened to overhear a group of men in the back yard talking about it," Priscilla replied.

"Do you know who they were?"

"No, sir, I never saw any of them before."

"Would you recognize them if you saw them?"

"I—I'm afraid not. You see, as soon as I heard what they were saying I went to the living room to get Allen. But by the time we got back to the porch the men were lost in the crowd. And when we asked about what I had heard, several people said yes, they'd heard what Jake had said too; but no one seemed to have paid any attention to it. They replied pretty much the same as you did, Dr. Evans, that the boy was just talking—that he really didn't know anything. Isn't that right, Allen?"

Allen nodded his head. "Yes."

"So Allen and I dismissed it for the time, as the others had," Priscilla continued. "But when I saw you coming back later in the afternoon I thought I'd better tell you."

"Did you leave this house from the time I left late yesterday afternoon until early this morning, Mrs. Harvey?"

"Let me think. . . . Yes, Allen and I walked out together, I should say from nine to ten. But, we didn't go outside the yard. We were in the rose garden most of the time."

"Were there other people around while you were out?"

"I didn't see anyone."

"Or hear anyone or anything out of the ordinary then or later? I understand your room overlooks the grounds around here." Dr. Evans made a semi-circle with his hands.

"The room, yes, but I saw nothing from it, Dr. Evans."

"Mr. Harvey, did you leave this house from the time I talked with you late yesterday afternoon until you walked out with Mrs. Harvey?"

"No, Dr. Evans, I didn't; I came into the house as she did and didn't leave it again all night." Allen shifted uneasily in his chair.

"Did you go immediately to your room?"

"Yes, and went to bed."

"Mr. Wormser, did you get in on any of this talk about Jake yesterday afternoon?"

"I'm sorry; I missed that, Doctor. I stayed around a while to be polite to all those people. But enough of strangers is enough. You know I'm given to wanderlust; so I took my car and drove as far away as the law allows. Got back about suppertime; after that I played chess with Mr. Tyler until about ten, and then went to my room for the rest of the night."

"About your drive—was anyone with you?"

"No."

"Where did you go?"

"I went to Dover and had a Coke and, after that, in and out of the country roads around—just wandering."

"Did you by any chance happen to see Jake Martin on your drive?"

"No, Dr. Evans. I had never laid eyes on the boy until this morning."

"Mrs. Tyler—"

Irene sighed with an appearance of boredom. She spoke rapidly as if anxious to have it over with. "I was in the living room until nine o'clock, assisting with the callers. After all of them had left, I went out on the back porch where Gordon and Mr. Wormser were playing chess and had a whisky and soda with them. Then I went up to Prudence's room. She was tired and so was I, so we decided to take sleeping tablets and try to get some rest. I left her room and went immediately to mine."

"Had you noticed the absence of anyone of this group up to this time—except in cases already accounted for?"

"I'm sure that I'd seen everyone of them at intervals during the evening."

"At intervals?"

"Well, you could hardly expect us all to be together all the time."

"Mr. Tyler, was your wife asleep when you went to your room?"

Irene moved quickly and uneasily in her chair and looked scornfully at Dr. Evans.

"From her deep breathing I thought so, Doctor. I didn't speak to her."

"What time did you go to your room?"

"Must have been twelve, maybe one—I didn't notice."

"And from ten—when Mr. Wormser left you?"

"It may look bad, Doctor, but, before God, I didn't move from that chess table all that time. I was thinking, thinking, thinking. . . ." Gordon was pulling at his mustache. "I have been more closely associated with Bob than any other man in all my life. And all our associations together kept flashing across my mind. I don't know when I went to bed, but I do know that I didn't leave this house."

Lester had come up to the screen door while Gordon was talking.

"Come in, Son," Prudence said.

Lester opened the door, eased in, and stood against the screen.

"Where were you last night, my boy?" Dr. Evans asked.

Lester seemed quite composed. "I was in Mother's room with her, until Mrs. Tyler came in. Then I went to my room and listened to the radio until it signed off at one. After that, I remember thinkin' what a mess all this is, and wonderin' how it would all end. I must dropped off to sleep then, for that's all I remember."

The eyes of the officers were intent upon the group as Dr. Evans announced: "We have discovered a mass of blood in the fruit orchard, and it appears that Jake was murdered there and afterward carried to the Ghost Oak. We also found the tracks of a horse going across the orchard in the general direction of the Ghost Oak. The horse, we presume, was used to carry Jake's body."

The silence that followed was trying. The shock on the face of everyone was so evident that no single expression stood out particularly above the others. Gordon stood up and began pacing the floor.

Irene was the first to speak. She lit a cigarette, flipped the match into an ashtray, and said: "Of all the dumb things for a human being to do."

But no one seemed to notice what she said, for at this moment Taft sprang a new sensation. No one had noticed him come up, but he was standing just inside the door. "Dr. Evans," he called.

"What is it, Taft?"

"Dem tracks, sir, belong to Balaam. I matched dem up with his old feet."

"No, no, not Balaam!" Priscilla cried. Allen gave her a puzzled look.

"You're sure, Taft?" Colonel Livingston asked.

"Yes, sir, I'm sure; but you better see for your own self."

The Colonel and the doctor excused themselves and followed Taft to the stable. The barn in which Balaam was kept stood west of the driveway that led from the garage to the Old Dover Road. A high, untrimmed, privet hedge ran the length of this driveway, almost hiding the barns and other outhouses.

The two men needed only a glance at the casts against Balaam's hoofs to know that Taft was right.

"Is Balaam's stable kept locked?" the Colonel asked.

Taft could not hide his amusement. "No, sir; he'd be good riddance. Ain't nobody want to waste feed on a poor old horse like dat, except Mister Bob."

"We're just going around in circles, Doctor," the Colonel said with a note impatience. "It looks again like the murderer is right here on the scene. The only alibis that all of them could give for last night would be that they were in the house all or nearly all the time—some asleep, some awake. We may have just listened to some tall lying—from somebody."

"I hate to think about such a thing, John."

"Now, Doctor, we can't afford to get sentimental. Did you notice that Mrs. Harvey said nothing about where she was after ten o'clock? And *she* didn't say Mr. Harvey was in his bed. Who said he was? He did! Who knew where anybody else was after ten o'clock? Nobody! And they all knew Balaam was in his stable."

Dr. Evans thought he'd never seen Colonel Livingston so obdurate.

Taft walked away, sorry he had spoken lightly of the old horse—since Mister Bob was unable to defend Balaam.

"You know, John, the more I think about it the more I doubt whether anyone at Linger-long could have committed the murder and moved the body into the old yard and gotten by with it."

"I don't see why you say that, Doctor. Everyone was free to go where he pleased so long as he stayed within the jurisdiction of the court. That left them free to go about in the neighborhood. When Jake was leaving yesterday afternoon any one of them could have walked off with him—nobody was noticing every move that was made. Then, when they were safely away from the house the murderer could easily have knocked Jake unconscious, slashed his throat, and left him right there between the orchards until everything was quiet about the place. A body, lying in grass as deep as that between the orchards, would never have been noticed unless someone accidentally stumbled across it. Then, after it was dark the criminal could have taken Balaam out and carried the body across to the Ghost Oak."

"Yes," the doctor said dubiously, "that could be. But I'm thinking that Jake wouldn't have walked away with anyone who he thought was the murderer."

"But, Doctor, it was your own idea that Jake didn't know who the murderer was—that he was just talking."

"I guess I am thinking a little inconsistently," the doctor admitted. "There are so many angles to be considered. But when I pin myself down, I really don't think Jake knew what he was talking about."

"Then wouldn't the boy have felt flattered at any attention from an Atlantan?" the Colonel asked. "And wouldn't he have proudly walked off with any of them? After all, wasn't attention just what he was after?"

"Probably."

"You know, Doctor, these city folks are shrewd; some of them would stop at nothing if the motive were strong enough."

"But, John, these people are not gangsters—they're Bob's friends."

"Now look here, Doctor, Bob Lawson has been murdered in cold blood. Somebody did it. And from what we've discovered this morning it appears likely—to me, at least—that someone right here on the scene did it."

"Perhaps. But I'd like to talk with Walt Hendrix again." The doctor looked at his watch. "Twelve o'clock," he said. "It's too late to go to Statesboro this morning, and I have to perform the autopsy on Jake's body after the funeral. We'll have to talk with Hendrix later. He might give something away that would enable us to corner him. He could have taken Balaam out as easily as anybody else."

"Sure. Anybody could have taken the old horse. But there we go in circles again. Suppose we go over and talk with Mom Liza and see if she knows anything about Jake or Balaam."

On their way they encountered Wormser. "I'm glad that I met you two together," he said with less reserve than usual. "I want to explain something."

"By all means," Dr. Evans said, "go ahead."

"I want to explain that a great many people know me when they see me, but only Mr. Lawson knew me for what I am."

"How long had Bob known you?" Colonel Livingston asked.

"Fifteen years, I'd say. We met at a convention. Mr. Lawson liked my ideas about insurance. Briefly, I believe that a constant study of living conditions in the territory that a company covers, with planned approaches for regional differences, makes a good insurance background. Selling insurance is more than carrying a pad and pencil in your pocket. For the last ten years I've been working privately on this for Mr. Lawson, making aptitude tests of his employees, gathering statistical information on the people and on the economic conditions—"

"That's news to me—" Colonel Livingston broke in.

Dr. Evans gravely said nothing.

"As you can see, my work has exposed me to all types of life. I've even had some experience in criminal cases. I have no definite information to offer you on this particular case, but I've found a few things I'd like to follow up," Wormser said and then asked: "May I get away for a day or two?"

The officers looked at each other in complete surprise at this request. Dr. Evans cautiously answered, "Suppose we let you know about this later."

"Thank you," Wormser replied and turned toward Linger-long.

The doctor and the Colonel were already near Mom Liza's cabin and they could see her sitting outside on an old log doorstep, stringing green beans. Colonel Livingston was reminded of an experience he had had with her when he was a small boy. He had been impressed with the woman's large ears that stuck out at right angles from her head. Childlike, the little fellow could not keep his eyes off of them. So, one day he had asked her about them. She had told him that they had grown that way because she always slept with them folded forward and tied down to her head so as to close the openings. And when he had looked at her in bewilderment, she had told him further that she did this to keep the earwigs out.

These little bugs, she had explained, might crawl into her ears while she was asleep. If they once got in, they could never be gotten out; they would eat the brains out. Everybody knows that, she had assured him. For years afterward he had slept with his ears folded over too, childishly praying that an earwig would never get to his brains.

"Hope you're feeling well today, Mom Liza." The Colonel was almost overcordial.

"Humph!" Mom Liza grunted and said nothing.

"We have reason to believe, Mom Liza," Dr. Evans said, "that someone slipped old Balaam from his stable last night to bring the body of Jake to the Ghost Oak. Do you know anything that might help us find out who it was?"

"I ain't tellin' nothin'. I ain't botherin' nobody, and I ain't wantin' nobody botherin' me." Mom Liza kept stringing beans, never looking up.

"But, Mom Liza," Dr. Evans urged, "you've had two dead bodies lying right here in your yard within the last two days! Surely you want to help us find anybody who is mean enough—"

Mom Liza's lower lip was hanging over her chin in a frown. With a note of impatience she said: "How come you white folks always keep pesterin' us poor colored people? We ain't know nothin'."

"Come—come, now, Mom Liza," Colonel Livingston picked up a handful of beans and began stringing them. "You sort of sleep with one eye open, don't you? Or maybe you were out walking with both eyes open last night."

Mom Liza was amused at the Colonel and his beans. She stopped working herself to watch his maneuvering. "Well," she mumbled, "maybe I did see someone leadin' dat old horse in the barn last night, but dat ain't nothin'."

Colonel Livingston dropped his beans and began writing in his notebook. "Could you tell who it was?"

"No sir; I was way down de road and couldn't make out."

"Was he coming from the direction of the Ghost Oak?"

"How'd I know where he was comin' from? I just seen him leadin' de old horse in de barn, and I ain't seen no more."

"Do you have any idea what time it was when you saw him?"

"I done told you all dat it was last night."

That was everything the officers were able to pry out of the elderly woman, but they had a feeling that she had not told them all she knew.

XVII
Dust to Dust

Monday afternoon

In the living room of the Lawson home the quiet was oppressive. Misses Mary and Martha Singleton sat on a large sofa with funereal solemnity. They had come to Linger-long as they returned from Mrs. Martin's that morning, and had remained to receive guests for Prudence. The stream of people coming to offer their personal condolences had kept the two ladies constantly engaged until now.

But, as the hour for the funeral was drawing near, friends had ceased to call; the gravity of sorrow was soon to be shifted to the church. The two elderly ladies, already behatted and looking like second editions of Queen Mary, were waiting for the family and the house guests to assemble.

Wormser appeared from somewhere in the rear and softly tip-toed up the stairs.

"Did you ever see anybody as quiet moving as that man?" Miss Martha whispered.

"Never!" Miss Mary emphatically whispered back. "When he's around I feel just like I have soft, green worms crawling on my neck."

Miss Martha shivered. "Oh, Mary!" she said. "Well, I feel that whichever way I turn my back, long claws may reach out and grab me."

"You're tired, Marty, too tired."

"Who's that?" Miss Martha jumped nervously and clutched Miss Mary's arm.

Irene Tyler's high heels clacked as she came down the stairway and walked into the room. "Oh, you're still here," she said, half-whimpering, half-sighing.

Miss Mary held her body erect and spoke with quiet dignity. "Prudence asked us to ride with the family and guests."

"It will be a relief to get away from this house and grounds under any circumstances, even for one hour, where we'll be free from the incessant ringing of the telephone. I feel that I'll lose my mind if it rings another time." Irene put her hands over her ears. "There it goes again! Before the old sound dies out it's ringing a new one in."

"We like it that way," Miss Martha said, welcoming a fresh topic of conversation. "It's so much company."

"But I would go *crazy* listening to two longs, one short; one long, three shorts; and a thousand other combinations, and never knowing when it's ringing for me." Irene was still standing as though impatient to be off.

"Oh, you'd soon get used to it—just like you got used to breathing. You'd never know it was ringing unless you stopped and made yourself listen. But when *your number* would ring, it would stand out just as if that were the first and only time the bell had sounded that day," Miss Martha replied, trying to make the guest more comfortable.

Miss Mary's attention had been distracted from the conversation; she was listening to Prudence and Lester down the hallway.

"Oh, Son," Prudence was pleading in undertones, *"please* won't you wear it for Mother's sake if you won't for your Uncle Bob's?"

"Ah, ballyhoo! Mom, I can feel just as sad without that black crepe on my sleeve. I don't want to go around advertising my sorrow." Lester's tone was impatient, but somewhat sobered.

"But I'm afraid people will talk about you if you don't wear it, and I couldn't bear that." The tenderness in Prudence's voice was appealing.

"Okay, pin it on if it will make you feel any better. But I'm against all this funeral paraphernalia."

Allen and Priscilla came down the steps together and stopped in the doorway of the living room. Grief had painted dark circles about Priscilla's eyes; and her trim, black outfit, in striking contrast to her fair skin and hair, made her very impressive.

She was carrying a glass of water and a prescription box. She turned to Irene. "Won't you take this, dear? It's the simplest sort of sedative. It'll make you feel much better."

Irene took the glass and lifted it as if offering a toast. "A bromide to quiet my nerves in placid Cooperville!"

Allen stepped over toward the Misses Singleton and spoke to them. "You've made life easier for all of us today. When I see the interest and devotion of people like you, it renews my faith in human nature.

"Thank you, Mr. Harvey," Miss Mary responded graciously.

"Thank you very, very much," Miss Martha added, obviously flattered by Allen's attention.

Gordon and Wormser appeared quietly in the hall and stood looking out the front door. Presently Gordon turned to the group.

"The family cars are waiting for us," he said. "I'll get Prudence and Lester. I think it's time we were going."

When Prudence came out, she maintained her usual stoical expression. She glanced briefly at everyone as she was slipping her hands into her black gloves, and it seemed for an instant as if she were going to speak. But no words came. Lester, looking taller and thinner than ever, held out his arm, and Prudence took it as they turned toward the waiting cars. Miss Mary and Miss Martha followed immediately behind them. Then came Allen and Priscilla, and Irene, Gordon, and Wormser.

As far down the Louisville Road as one could see were cars filled with relatives and friends, waiting for the hearse to lead them.

Dr. Evans and Colonel Livingston had gone earlier to Wormser's room to see what he had found. The collection had seemed of such little consequence—a few animal hairs, Wormser's soiled handkerchief, and a little wad of dusty threads—that they were afraid he was making up an excuse to get away with a good start. His conversation had become too free as compared with his former reticence, they thought. "All this can wait a little while," Colonel Livingston had told him. "You'd better stay around until we can see how some of these other leads come out."

The officers had then gone to the church in advance of the funeral procession. The crowd had been gathering since noon; and when the two men had reached the grounds, they found the building already filled, except for the reserved pews. Large numbers were standing around in the grove outside. The negroes were gathered in almost as large numbers as the whites. It seemed that everyone who had known Bob Lawson for miles around was present.

Such a large attendance was doubtless because of the devotion of Bob's wide circle of friends. But from the talk about the tragedy that went on in the mingling groups and the speculation as to who committed the crime and why, it seemed that curiosity and love of excitement also played an important part. One strolling around the churchyard that early afternoon would have absorbed a wide diversion of reactions:

"It's going to seem mighty lonesome around here, now that we're used to Bob and all his friends roaming around here."

"Why in the hell don't they arrest some of the people they know could have done it and put 'em through the third degree? Like as not some of 'em would come across."

"It seems such a pity to be cut down that-a-way when he's just now got his new house all fixed up so nice and all was settled down so peaceful-like."

"I don't believe anyone brought up around Cooperville would stoop to such a low down crime."

"I feel so sorry for Prudence. She was so optimistic about having Bob here to help get Lester straightened out."

"Maybe Lester'll turn over a new leaf now that he's the only man left in the Lawson family. I've know responsibility to bring many a boy to his senses."

"Will Sorrel sure has put his foot in it. I reckon if he ever gets out of this, it'll learn him a lesson to keep his big mouth shut."

"If that man Harvey *is* guilty, a feller can't very much blame him. I'll be doggone if I'd stand by and watch any man take my wife—especially a pretty little thing like Miz Harvey."

"What about that Tyler woman? They say she hasn't said a pleasant word since she's been down here. They say she's plain money-mad and thinks we're a bunch of simpletons. But then I guess she'd never bend her fine self enough to do a job of killing. That *would* be work!"

"Hendrix was the last person Bob had an appointment with, and you heard at the inquest how weak his alibi was. A bootlegger that was hatched in the slums of Savannah as he was can lie easier than he can tell the truth if it will save his face, and I wouldn't put it past him to slash a man's throat."

"I want to know more about them folks that's down here from Atlanta. I've heard that in them big cities you can't trust nobody nowadays. Them that sits in the highest places are just as apt to be the meanest of any, if things are the way I've heard they are. And they study up on how to hide their meanness. Of course, now, if Bob was here, he could out-brain any of 'em."

"I'm worried about Georgia Life. I'm afraid Gordon Tyler'll suck it into his empire now that Bob's out of the way."

"What about one of them hoggish men Bob saw in Savannah that day? If one of them knew about how much swag he had on him, he might have shadowed him all the way to Dover and done it. He could have took the mornin' train back again. I've heard that Bob had nigh onto four thousand on him that night. That's no small pickin's for one of them Savannah guys to bump a man off for."

"Lordy, ain't this the awfullest thing you ever heard of. What would poor old Miz Lawson say if she could know it? Like as not she'd turn over in her grave, for she sure set a heap of store by that boy."

"That shark, Tyler, was trying to rob Georgia Life to the tune of millions, and Bob stood in his way. I think Mr. Wormser was his hit man."

"No. I think Mr. Wormser's all right. Bob probably felt sorry for him and thought maybe he'd enjoy a little vacation in the country. Seems like he does enjoy driving around."

"I believe Mom Liza's holdin' out on the officers. That woman has always known every detail about what goes on around, but she says she knows nothin' about this biggest Cooperville happenin'."

"Hush your mouth, black boy. You're liable to get yourself shut up in de calaboose for falsifyin'. You know no ghost could have made no gash like dat. Besides, ghosts ain't carry no knives. Dey chokes folks to death with dey hands."

"I'd sure hate to be in Ruby's shoes, havin' to cook over dere where we all know dere are ghosts."

"You worryin' about ghosts at the Lawson place. What about dat ghost chasin' Br'er Frank?"

"Shh! Here comes Sister Lucindy Fawls puttin' on all dem uppity ways. Is you notice dat gold tooth she just growed in de front of her big mouth?"

"I was just thinkin' how Mister Bob'd like to be here at his own buryin' himself and see all dese people here."

Jake, who was to be buried next day in a country church yard several miles away, was scarcely mentioned, except for his roving, gossiping habits, his uncanny way of knowing what was going on, and the relation which his murder might have had to that of Bob Lawson. It was the general sentiment that Jake had been killed to stop his tongue. Who killed Jake? To know that would probably unravel the whole mystery.

The funeral procession was approaching the spacious church grounds through the moss-hung canopy that was the Louisville Road. The old church, like the homes, stood well back from the road, in the most picturesque setting of that pridefully picturesque village. Massive live oaks said to have been old when De Soto passed that way; pink-flowering crepe myrtles and mimosas, reaching up for the sunlight through the sprawling limbs of surrounding oaks; and tall magnolias, glistening in their regal splendor, all lent their beauty to emphasize the solemnity of the occasion.

As the procession arrived, the crowds respectfully fell back on either side of the entrance way. Heads were bared and tongues were silent in deference to the dead as the flower-laden silver casket was borne down the avenue into the church.

Of the solemn service within little could be heard by the crowd outside except the music, for the pastor's voice was moderated as befitted the occasion. Toward the end of the service, a group of Bob's negro friends were called upon to sing his favorite spiritual. "Swing Low, Sweet Chariot," and Taft's family sang, "When the Roll Is Called Up Yonder."

When times came for viewing the remains for the last time, long columns of people, white and colored, passed down the aisle by the casket and out the rear door toward the cemetery.

At the grave, after the masonry had closed over the casket and the pastor had repeated his solemn "dust to dust," the dull thud of the first spadefuls of dirt echoed hollowly.

No one present was more deeply stirred than Taft, but he had gained an iron grip on his emotions. He quietly swore: "I'm goin' after de man what done dis thing to you, Mister Bob, and before God, I ain't gonna stop 'til I get him."

Late Monday afternoon

With thoughts of Bob still uppermost in his mind, Dr. Evans drove to the mortuary in Sylvania to perform the autopsy on Jake. The first thing the doctor noticed when Jake was laid out on the slab was a fresh wound on the knee. Further examination showed that the other knee and the elbows were scraped raw as though Jake had slid on the ground. There was dirt in all the wounds. "That child was running from someone and fell down," Dr. Evans said to himself. "But who was chasing him? That person could have been the murderer." The doctor also noticed that there were grass stains on Jake's clothes as he removed them. There was nothing on the body to indicate the cause of death, except the slash in the throat. It was almost six o'clock when he was able to leave the mortuary and walk down to the Sylvan Café. He ordered a ham sandwich and a cup of coffee and then went to the telephone while his meal was being prepared. First he called Colonel Livingston at home. "Colonel," he began, "I'm really glad to find you home. I discovered some things in the autopsy that you and the sheriff should know about. No. I don't want to talk about them on the phone. Could you and Joe meet me at the Sylvan Café? Well, bring him right over if you can. I haven't had a bite to eat since I left you right after noon, so I'll wait here for you."

Dr. Evans went back to his table and began to sip his coffee as he waited for his sandwich. He wished his sandwich would come soon, because he wanted to get back to the peach orchard before dark.

He was about halfway finished with his sandwich when Colonel Livingston and Sheriff Satterfield came into the café. He rose to greet them and motioned for them to sit down. A waitress came over to take their orders. "May I order something for you?" Dr. Evans asked. The Colonel declined.

"Better make mine black coffee," the sheriff requested. "It looks like we're going to have a stay-awake night."

"As a matter of fact, I do want to go back to the peach orchard before dark if we can make it," Dr. Evans replied. "When I was examining Jake's body, I was sure he had died of the gash in his throat. But I noticed his knees and elbows had been recently skinned as though he had fallen and skidded on his knees. He could have been running from someone and slipped or tripped and fallen."

"Son of a gun!" the sheriff exclaimed. "I reckon Jake's luck ran out on him."

Colonel Livingston was less emotional. "Doctor, do you think that Jake was being chased and fell just before he was caught and murdered?"

"It appears that way," Dr. Evans replied. "At least I think we should go back to the orchard and see if the samples of dirt I have from Jake's clothes match the dirt in the orchard . . . and see if there is any evidence of a body sliding on the ground."

The sheriff gulped down his coffee while Dr. Evans finished his sandwich. It was still light outside when the three men left the café.

"I'll take my car," the Colonel volunteered, "so that you don't have to come back to Sylvania."

"I prefer not to go to Linger-long because there is not much daylight left," the doctor instructed. "We can park in my driveway." They parked in Dr. Evans's driveway and hurried over to the place where they had seen the blood on the grass.

"I can see signs of scuffling in the grass. It's trampled down around here," the Colonel observed.

Dr. Evans lifted a handful of dirt and held it close to the sample of Jake's torn pants he had brought with him. He studied it a minute and said, "This could be the place that Jake fell. The dirt is the same color and texture."

"Dirt is dirt," the sheriff spoke up. "It's either dirty dirt or red clay or sand. Around here it looks like dirty dirt."

"It's beginning to look like someone chased Jake in the orchard," the Colonel observed. "But no one would kill him for stealing peaches. The killer must have had another motive. Do you suppose Jake really knew who killed Bob Lawson?"

Dr. Evans was still looking at the dirt in his hand. "There's no doubt that wherever Jake fell and skinned his knees, it was in dirt like this, but the sheriff's right. There's dirt like this all over this area. I was hoping to find a more definite clue—like skid marks."

The three men studied the area carefully but could find no skid marks. "Well, Colonel," the sheriff finally said, "we've chased enough wild gooses for one day. Are you ready to go back to Sylvania?"

"I don't think we'll find any more evidence here," the Colonel replied. "It's been a long day. We might as well wait and see what tomorrow brings."

XVIII
An Alibi Upset

Tuesday morning

On Monday large rewards were offered for information that would lead to the arrest of the person or persons responsible for the deaths of Bob Lawson and of Jake Martin. Whether mainly in hope of reward, or of interest in the case, numbers of people came to the authorities with all sorts of stories, most of which were implausible or so slim as merely to be filed for possible future reference. But, early Tuesday morning, some information came to Dr. Evans that was not to be set aside.

First, a brawny, rather grimy, young man, evidently a mechanic, appeared on the porch of Dr. Evans's home.

"Reckon you don't know me, Dr. Evans, but I know you all right. I'm Ed Blitch; my father was Squire Blitch over in Bulloch. I run a little garage and blacksmith shop just off the Statesboro Road, across the river."

"Be seated, Mr. Blitch." Dr. Evans motioned him to a chair. "I'm glad to see you. I knew your father quite well, and your grandfather."

The young man paused, nervously fumbling with his hat, as though reluctant to speak his mind.

"They were both fine men," the doctor continued. "I remember hearing my father say that your grandfather was the best carriage builder in South Georgia. You seem to have inherited his mechanical turn."

"Well, I don't know so much about that," said young Blitch modestly. "I still keep the old shop open, but it's mostly a filling station and garage now. But I do some blacksmith work, and that's really what I want to see you about.

"I don't like to get mixed up in a murder case, but I happen to know something I feel I ought to tell. I read in the paper that when you tried to match Will Sorrel's mule hoofs with the tracks, you found they wouldn't match because his mule's shoes were much worn, and the tracks showed new shoes."

"That's right."

"I remembered right away that I'd shod his mule a few weeks ago. Will must of *changed* them shoes."

"What!" Dr. Evans exclaimed.

"Of course he may have more than one mule, but I know I shod one for him."

Dr. Evans seemed in a quandary. He was thinking to what length a man will stretch his brain to save his neck. If Will *had* changed the shoes, the doctor was wondering whether they would ever be able to prove it. Unless they could find the new ones, it might be a case of one man's word against another's. Finally he said, "Will has only one mule. I'm sure of that. Was anyone else present when you were changing those shoes?"

"No sir, Doctor, but I thought it might help you to know that the mule has been fresh shod."

"I hope it may help a great deal, Mr. Blitch. I appreciate your coming to me with this, and I shall treat it as confidential unless something important comes out of it. We shall certainly investigate it right away."

Blitch bowed himself away.

Dr. Evans rang Sylvania, called Colonel Livingston and Sheriff Satterfield in turn, and asked them to come out at once.

A little later, as the coroner was pouring a pail of water into the leaky radiator of his dilapidated Model T, Sam Holloman came up. He was dressed in faded bib overalls, looking tall and muscular, with serious eyes and an untrimmed black beard.

"Mornin', Dr. Evans. Can you spare a minute?"

"Certainly, Sam, always. Hope that last round of quinine did the work. You are looking better."

"Yes sir, I'm feelin' a heap better. At least I ain't had no more agues lately."

"Well, is there something I can do for you this morning?"

"Doctor, you know I don't want to get myself into nothin' that ain't my business."

"That's right, Sam, I know you always sweep around your own doors."

"But there's been somethin' weighin' mighty heavy on my mind. When you all was at my house Sunday evening, you asked if I'd seen or heard anythin'. I hadn't paid no 'tention to it 'til I got to studyin' after you left. I went to the Lord in prayer. I prayed and prayed over it. Then I recollected Saturday night, about the middle of the night, I heard a mule or a horse galopin' by my place, and it was goin' in the direction of Will Sorrel's house."

"You don't suppose it was a loose mule?"

"No, sir, Doctor, I could hear somebody sayin', 'giddap, giddap.' "

"I'm wondering, Sam, if that *were* Will, why he came by your house when his house is nearer the highway?"

"I don't know, sir, and I can't be sure who it was, but couldn't he of come around by the Cameron Road and cut across by my house?"

Dr. Evans pondered. "That's right, he wouldn't have been nearly so likely to be seen at that hour going that way. He could have turned off, of course, at the Mills Place. . . . Your place and Will's are the only ones that are on that connecting stretch between the Mills Place and the Sylvania Highway.

"Sam, what you've told me may prove to be very valuable. If you learn anything else, please feel free to come to me, and I'll keep it as quiet as possible."

As Holloman disappeared down the driveway, Dr. Evans suddenly remembered that he had not gotten the casts. He hurried up the long flight of steps leading into the house. Presently he emerged through the front door with a medical kit in one hand, and the casts in the other. He was just putting them into his car when the officers from Sylvania drove up.

"What's up?" Colonel Livingston questioned without waiting for a formal greeting.

"I never would have guessed that Sorrel had it in him. Before we went to his place Sunday he had *changed the shoes on his mule.*" Dr. Evans then told the men what he had learned that morning from Blitch and Holloman.

"Well, get in, Doctor, we'll lose no time," the Colonel said.

"Thanks, John, I'll take my own car so it won't be necessary for you and Joe to come back to Cooperville."

At Dr. Evans's suggestion they drove around by the Mills Place to make inquiries. There they found that more than one person had heard the galloping steed go by sometime after the storm had passed over on Saturday night. But none of them had any ideas as to the identity of the rider.

The officers drove on to Sorrel's place. There seemed to be no one at home; so they straightway began exploring the premises, with special attention to the stable, tool shed, and other outhouses. But in time they wearied of this fruitless search.

"Looks like we're gettin' nowhere fast." the sheriff said. "You know I don't think that geek would risk hidin' them things here at his own house. I believe he'd have throwed 'em in the river."

"You don't know Will Sorrel, Joe," said Dr. Evans. "He wouldn't have thrown something like that away. He would have hidden them where he could get his hands on them for later use, if and when the storm blows over. He probably buried them somewhere around here in the field or over in the woods."

"Good idea, Doctor," the Colonel said, and stepped into the tool shed. "Here, Joe, take this shovel; the doctor and I will take these hoes and we'll look around a bit on our own."

Joe Satterfield was wading waist deep through broom sedge and blackberry briars, occasionally stopping and poking among matted clumps of grass, when he suddenly lunged forward and yelled: *"Doctor! Oh, Jesus, Doctor. I'm snake-bit!"*

The doctor and the Colonel both came in a run.

"What kind of snake?" Dr. Evans called breathlessly as he tore through the briars.

"Don't know. Got away too quick."

"Where'd he strike you?"

"On my fanny, Doctor, on my fanny!"

The doctor looked and saw an ugly tear in the seat of Joe's trousers.

"Let's get to the car as quick as we can."

The two men hurried away, leaving Colonel Livingston, armed with a hoe, searching for the snake. They all knew that it was important to know what kind it was.

"How do you feel, Joe?" Dr. Evans asked as they hastened toward his car. He was worried. To save his soul he could not remember whether he had the drugs he needed in his kit.

"Don't know, Doctor. Kind of numb, I guess."

"How'd it happen?"

"I was squattin' down lookin' amongst the grass. Must have almost sat down on the dumb thing," the sheriff panted.

When they came into Sorrel's yard where they had parked the cars, Dr. Evans noticed that Will's mule was there.

"Will! Will!" he called commandingly.

Will appeared in the doorway of the house.

"Bring me a pan of water and some soap, quick. Joe's had a snake bite."

"Serves him right for messin' around my place," Will said sourly and went for the water.

"In here, Joe." The doctor swung open the back door of the Colonel's car, and Joe stumbled in. "Lucky thing I have my medicine kit in my car." The doctor got his kit in a minute and began looking for the wound while waiting for Will to bring the water. "Where is the bite, Joe? I don't see it."

"Here—there, right at the end of my finger."

"There's no abrasion at all."

"But it bit me, Doctor, I tell you, it bit me."

As Dr. Evans examined the sheriff's trousers more closely, he noticed the tear was over the hip pocket. He pulled a wallet from the pocket and saw the fang prints on the lower corner of the leather. "Joe, I'm afraid your bite was vicarious."

"My God, Doctor, how bad is that?"

"Not bad at all. What I meant was that your wallet got the bite, not you. All you have is a slight bruise to show for it."

"You mean I ain't bit?"

"That's what I mean."

"I sort of wondered why it didn't hurt no more than it did. Then, I allowed the poison was killin' the pain."

"So that's why you thought you felt numb?" the doctor was smiling.

Colonel Livingston, the sweat literally streaming down his neck, came trotting across the yard. "How is he, Doctor?"

"He'll live."

"I'll say I will. And besides, Colonel, I've just had a lesson in high finance—a new way how a man's money can save him." The sheriff had sprung from the car as he finished fastening his trousers.. He held up his wallet. "See them prints? Them's the bite."

"Humph!" the Colonel was both relieved and amused. "At that, Joe, you have nothing on me. I've had a lesson, too, a lesson in sleuthing techniques." He drew horseshoes from his pocket.

"Well, God Almighty, man!" Joe bleated. "Where'd you find them?"

"The snake led me to them. I was looking around for it and I came across a hollow log. I poked my hoe into it; but instead of a hiss, I heard a clink., And these are what I dug out."

Sorrel, who had appeared in the meantime, almost dropped his pan of water as he set it down.

They got the casts from Dr. Evans's car and compared them with the shoes.

"A perfect match," the doctor said.

Colonel Livingston examined them more carefully with a magnifying glass. "You're right, Doctor."

"Will," the Colonel began. "Why did you change the shoes on that mule?"

Will sat down on the running board of the car, buried his face in his hands, and shook his head dejectedly. Terrified as he was, he did the fastest thinking he ever did in his life. Guilty or innocent, he must have realized he would have to acknowledge the evidence they had against him and try to account for it.

"I see now I done the wrong thing.... I shouldn't have changed them shoes," he managed to say remorsefully. "I should have gone and told y'all the truth about what I'd done as soon as you asked on Sunday."

"Why didn't you, Will?" Dr. Evans asked.

"Because I knew I didn't kill Bob Lawson—God knows I didn't—but I knew I was sure to be suspected. There were a heap of things against me. I've known of men to hang on circumstantial evidence and it turned out they weren't guilty. I just got in such a state Sunday that I reckon I didn't know what I was doing. I knew my old mule might have left tracks; and if she did, I knew you'd find them sooner or later. I'd saved them old shoes, thinkin' they'd come in handy sometime for a pitchin' game. So I just changed them."

"Didn't you stop to think how bad that would look if anybody found out about it?" the Colonel asked.

"I see now that it's the worst thing I could have done with folks like you trackin' me." Still shaking his head, Will pulled a soiled handkerchief from his pocket, wiped his eyes, and blew his nose noisily.

"According to the evidence, Will, you could not have been far from the spot at the time it is presumed that Bob Lawson was killed. What do you have to say about that?" The Colonel continued his questioning.

"Of course there is no need to deny no more than I came home by the Old Dover Road, but I came straight on home. I never stopped nowhere and I didn't see nothin'."

"Will, you're the damndest liar God ever made!" Colonel Livingston could not hide his impatience. "You said just a few minutes ago that you ought to have told us the truth from the beginning. And already, you're lying again. These shoes are proof you stopped not far from the spot where Bob was murdered that night."

Will's face revealed fresh alarm. He gulped as though about to speak, but the words would not come.

Colonel Livingston went on: "You mule's hoofprints leading up to the scene were unmistakably dented by raindrops. A little beyond we found that the tracks were undoubtedly made after the storm had passed. Can you account for that?"

At this point Will seemed to pull himself together as though a new idea had occurred to him. "Well, Colonel, I see you've got me again. I swear I'm goin' to tell you the truth this time. I ran into that thunderstorm, and it started to rain just as I got to the other end of the old Lawson place. So, I pulled up under one of them big oaks until the storm passed over."

"Under the one that is called the Ghost Oak?" Colonel Livingston asked.

"No sir. I must have been a hundred yards on the other side of that tree. The storm didn't last long, and as soon as it was over I came on home."

"From Cooperville on how did you come?"

"By the Sylvania highway."

The officers looked at each other. They doubted what Will had just said, but they had no way to prove he was lying; so they let the matter rest temporarily. However, Colonel Livingston warned Will again not to leave the neighborhood until the investigations were completed.

As the officers were getting into their cars, Dr. Evans called over: "John, I think it might be a good idea for you to come on out to my house this afternoon, and we'll invite the Lingerlong group over and talk about this whole thing—informally, you know."

"Okay, Doctor."

When Dr. Evans reached home, he drove his car around to the shade of his back yard. As he was getting out, he noticed a negro boy sitting on his back steps, evidently in the deepest dejection.

"Why, Dumplin, what's the matter?" he asked in surprise.

"I'm scared them ghosts are goin' to get after me." Dumplin's bare feet, showing below his overalls, were squirming like two big fighting bugs. "I promise, Doctor, before God, I promise I had nothin' to do with Jake." Dumplin was wiping his dripping eyes and nose with the back of his hand and then on to his sleeve.

"What are you talking about, Dumplin? You're not sick, are you?"

"I don't know, Doctor. Dey say if I don't tell you what I know, dat Mister Bob's spirit will get me before morning."

Dr. Evans sat down by the boy and spoke more calmly. "Dumplin, have you done something that you wouldn't want Mister Bob to know?"

Dumplin nodded and sobbed convulsively.

"In that case, I think you had better tell me. Maybe I can help you."

"I didn't mean no harm to nobody, but dey say—"

"Whom do you mean by 'they say'?"

"De Lodge, sir. Br'er Burke and Uncle Spode and the rest of them. Dey say if I ain't told you de ghosts might get after me."

"What have you done, Dumplin?"

"I took old Balaam out of the barn Sunday evenin' and rode him over to see my gal. I was passin' his stable comin' home from de Lodge meetin' and de notion just struck me. I allowed nobody would be noticin' dat old horse." Dumplin almost gained control of himself now that the story was out.

"So you rode across Bob's fruit orchard on Balaam?"

"Yes, sir. I took a short cut across the fields and across the orchard. But I ain't seen nobody around dere." Dumplin looked up at Dr. Evans for the first time, his big brown eyes looking like white disks on his round black face.

"Is that all?"

"Yes sir." Dumplin rubbed his ragged shirt sleeve over his face.

"You'd better be careful how you use other people's things. You might get into serious trouble sometime. But, I am glad to know what happened. Don't worry too much about it this time. Just be more careful in the future." Dr. Evans thought that was not what he should have said to the boy, tut it had come out involuntarily. He felt flustered and wanted to get quickly inside his house where he could think alone. He noticed Dumplin walk away with a relieved, skipping step.

But, inside, Prudence was waiting for him with some more news, "Oh, Doctor, I'm glad you're back," she greeted before he had time to get his breath. "I believe Mr. Wormser has run away from us."

"Don't tell me."

"He was not around at supper time last night, but no one was particularly concerned, for he has been rather irregular about coming to meals ever since he came down here. But, when Ruby went to tidy up his room about nine this morning, she found his bed had not been slept in."

"What time did he leave yesterday? Did anyone see him go?"

"Apparently not. So far as I have learned, no one has seen him since yesterday afternoon."

Dr. Evans studied for a moment. "I wonder if we should have that Atlanta detective come down here. I'll talk with John about that this afternoon. . . . Oh, by the way, John and I had decided to invite your Linger-long group over here for an informal conference at about four o'clock. Would you mind passing the word along?"

"I'll be glad to, Doctor. Perhaps Mr. Wormser will show up by then."

XIX
Grapevine Gossip

Tuesday noon

All the vines of neighborhood gossip led to the doors of the Singleton home. The elderly mistresses of the house, Miss Mary and Miss Martha, were awakened to a new alertness by the same incidents that roused Cooperville into a whispering hive of excitement.

Two days after Bob Lawson's body had been found, Miss Mary and Miss Martha were seated at their dinner table absorbed in the same animated discussions that had held their attention since the fateful day. But the animation of the two old ladies did not disturb the quiet dignity of their surroundings—a dignity built by their forefathers, which the sisters still sought to preserve in their own modest way. Oil portraits of their ancestors looked down upon them from the walls. The ancient banquet table had been shortened, to be sure, and the number of chairs had shrunk from a dozen or so to only two. Of course, there were no longer servants in the livery; but the faithful Queenie, with her kindly face, was on hand, always ready to serve.

Queenie was born the year of the Diamond Jubilee, and her mother had named her in honor of the sedate old Queen and her vaunted love of peace: Queen Victoria Jubilee Peace McGuire. She was descended from Ethiopian ancestry and was proud of her position as maid in the home of the Misses Singleton. She kept the house immaculate, and took great pride in serving the meals with dignity. However, she did keep an open ear for gossip, both in the Singleton home and among her friends on the outside. She seemed to enjoy this two-way street: passing on to her mistresses the gossip which she gathered among the negroes, and sharing the chitchat of the Singleton ladies with her friends. And the Singleton sisters, though aware that much of what they said would not be kept confidential, were much interested in whatever news and rumors she could bring them.

Queenie had just begun to clear away the dishes from the main course, when Miss Martha made clear her beliefs for the seventeenth time.

"You know, Mary, I can't help but think that contemptible Will Sorrel killed Bob Lawson." She clucked her lips and spoke with derision. She was usually prompt in her judgements, and not always incorrect. If she gave the appearance of being dogmatic, she was nevertheless wiling, as a rule, to consider other points of view.

"I still can't see why you keep saying that," Miss Mary said crisply.

"Because Will's the meanest man I know, and because he hated Bob with a frightful vengeance and had often threatened to kill him. You remember how they used to fight when they were boys. Why, I, myself, saw Will take some terrible beatings from Bob. That would be a reason enough for a man like Will." Miss Martha sat up straight in her chair and closed her lips firmly.

"Perhaps," Miss Mary said calmly. "But, don't you think that underneath Will's bluster, he's too cowardly to kill anybody?"

"I'm not so sure about that," Miss Martha replied. "Ever since his father was killed by Bob's father, Will's sworn he'd get his revenge. To my certain knowledge he's made threats against Bob. And I believe he killed him—and then killed Jake for fear the boy really did know something."

"Yes, ma'am, Miss Martha, dat's what some of de colored folks say," Queenie volunteered, without interrupting her serving. "Dem dat were down to Dover Saturday night say dey heard Mister Sorrel cussin' and swearin', and some say he threatened to get even with Mister Bob den."

"Queenie, do most of your friends think Will Sorrel killed Bob?" Miss Martha questioned eagerly.

"Some does. But some of dem are wonderin' about Mister Hendrix. Chunky say he seen Mister Hendrix down to Dover Sunday evenin' about an hour by sun. Chunky say he looked like he was kind of snoopin' around. He called some of de men together an dey rode off in his car a piece and den came back. I reckon he was sellin' dem some moonshine."

"Do you know whether he had anything to say about the murder?"

"No ma'am, nothin' dat I know of. Chunky say Mister Hendrix was standin' around dere with his hands in his pockets, den out, and in and out, and in and out. Dere was some talk about Jake sayin' he knew who done de killin'. Wasn't long before Mister Hendrix slipped out like a eel. And some believe he decided den and dere to shut dat boy's mouth."

"That's very interesting, Queenie." Miss Mary spoke kindly, for she didn't want to discourage the maid's frankness. "Will you go to the basement and see if there's another jar of those Bartlett pears? I think I prefer them for my dessert. Look carefully, and don't come back without them."

As the two ladies thus sat, Miss Mary at the head and Miss Martha at the foot of the table, they might very well have been a picture clipped from some rare old book. All their lives, they had followed a set custom as to their manner of dress. Miss Mary always wore a suggestion of blue, Miss Martha of red, their color combinations being carefully harmonized. Their hair, now completely white, was brushed back into neat French coiffures. But any telltale marks of age were quickly belied by the sparkle in their eyes.

Miss Martha gave her sister a puzzled look as Queenie left the room. "Mary, surely you haven't forgotten that there are no more pears?"

"Oh, yes, I know. But that'll keep her busy for a while. Queenie might tell her friends what we say; so I'd rather not discuss Will Sorrel and Walt Hendrix when she's around," Miss Mary said. She was the older of the two, and inclined to be more discreet.

"I certainly don't agree with you, Marty, about Will Sorrel," Miss Mary continued. "He didn't kill Bob. He wouldn't have had the nerve to kill."

"You mean *openly*, Mary. Of course he is not the kind to pick a deadly fight in the open, as his father did years ago in Sylvania. Oh, Will fought when he was a boy, but he wouldn't do that now. He's too degenerate. He still has his father's bluster, but has no more stamina that a jellyfish. He's the kind that might very well have crept up in the dark and struck Bob before he had a chance to defend himself."

"I don't even believe he'd have done that," Miss Mary argued. "In fact, I don't believe anyone in the vicinity of Cooperville would have killed Bob Lawson. The people around here aren't the kind that kill. You know well enough that nothing like this has happened in Cooperville as far back as we can remember. Of course, there was the tragedy of Will's father, but that happened in Sylvania under the abnormal influences of court week. I believe these murders were the work of an outsider. It might possibly have been Walt Hendrix, but I doubt it. I suspect one of those men from Atlanta."

"Well, I don't believe it was Walt Hendrix," Miss Martha replied. "He may have been on the scene, but he didn't have any motive—at least not a sufficient one."

The Misses Singleton were great readers of detective fiction. They were the chief patrons of the rent collection at the Screven Drug Store. In fact, it was largely through their influence that such a "library" had been established there.

"You're right on that point, Marty. Bob would never have let a quarrel over liquor reach the point of a fight. He had too much pride for that. Suppose he was angry with Hendrix and suppose the man was nasty about it. Bob would have been too tactful to let anything like that lead to serious trouble. He'd have just waited and had the authorities deal with Walt later."

"Even so, I think we should tell Dr. Evans what Queenie has told us about Walt," Miss Martha said.

"Oh, by all means," Miss Mary agreed, then quickly added: "Still, I can't get away from the idea that it was the work of one of those people from Atlanta."

"No, Sister, they are old friends of Bob's, and were his guests. They wouldn't have killed him. Besides, if any of them had done the killing, he'd have used a pistol."

"I'm not so sure," Miss Mary said with an air of wisdom. "Just because Bob's guests are from the big city doesn't mean they are pistol packing gangsters."

"But, Mary! Remember Bob was robbed as well as murdered. Surely none of his guests would be a robber."

"Look at it this way, my dear. Suppose the killer had assumed that the authorities would reason just as you do. Then, wouldn't he likely have committed the robbery to throw them off?" Miss Mary said complacently.

"That's something to consider," Miss Martha admitted doubtfully. "But the officers went over the house and grounds thoroughly before anybody had a chance to leave the premises. And they couldn't find a thing."

"Of course they didn't. Any of those people would have seen to it that Bob's watch and things were hidden away before his body was found."

"Well, there's a detective in Atlanta investigating Mr. Harvey, Mr. Tyler and Mr. Wormser. But I'm quite sure that none of them killed Bob." Miss Martha was dogmatic.

"You know as well as I do, Marty, that every one of them had both motive and opportunity. Not one of them has an alibi that is thicker than a sieve. If I had to single out the one I least suspect, though, it'd be Mr. Harvey."

"Why?" Miss Martha asked eagerly.

"Well, from all I can gather he is the most decent of them. He's bound to be decent to be able to run such a successful business. And, I don't think he was bothered that much with Bob's flirtations with Priscilla."

"I'm not surprised that Bob was attracted to her. It is most unusual that a young woman is so beautiful and charming, and yet so sensible and well-poised."

" 'Beautiful', 'charming', 'poised'," Miss Mary repeated in staccato tones. "Yes but I question 'sensible'. I doubt the stability of her newfangled notion about the freedom of certain relationships."

"Well, Mary, I regret to admit that nothing shocks me any more," Miss Martha said with a sigh of ennui. "People have become so bold with all their secret sins that they must have almost destroyed the joy of sinning."

"Marty! I'm surprised at you!" Miss Mary took a sip of water and swallowed with effort. "Mr. Harvey seems like such a nice man."

"Oh, I would never suspect him," Miss Martha spoke quickly as though relieved on this point. "Besides, his motive wasn't strong enough. If he knew that Bob was a born bachelor and never meant anything serious by his flirtations—and he must have known that—why would he kill Bob? No, I'm sure he would never have done such a thing."

"But, Mr. Tyler!" Miss Mary shook her head darkly. "You know what he was up to. And you know how Bob stood in his way. I believe he's the kind that would do anything if big money were involved. And his wife appears to be one who would screw his courage to the sticking place."

"I don't suspect Mr. Tyler at all." Miss Martha pulled her chair up closer and rested her elbows on the table.

Miss Mary frowned disapprovingly but said nothing.

"Even though I don't believe that the crime was committed by anyone at Linger-long," Miss Martha continued, "Mr. Wormser is the only one of that group that I could ever bring myself to consider. Nobody except Mr. Tyler seems to know anything about him. He's a puzzle even to Prudence. They say that Mr. Tyler asked him down here of his own accord, without an invitation from Bob. Some believe that he's Tyler's Man Friday."

"Bob told Prudence that Mr. Wormser was a friend of his, but then, Bob was a great spoofer," Miss Mary said with a sharp tilt of her head. "We certainly know that Mr. Tyler had a motive, and if what we hear is true, Mr. Wormser had one too, even if it was what one might call collusive. And, neither of them has a substantial alibi."

"I declare, Miss Mary," Queenie said as she came back into the room, "I looked through all dem jars of fruit in de basement, and dey just ain't no more pears down dere."

"Then just serve us some applesauce from the icebox." Miss Mary ordered.

"De colored people are all powerful down in de mouth because nobody ain't found de killer," Queenie said as she finished clearing the table for dessert. "Br'er Taft has had to take care of some business for Miss Prudence, but soon as he comes back dey all are goin' to take more action. Dey say if Mister Bob was here and some of dem were killed, he would have found out before now how to find de one what done de killin'."

"Bob *was* very clever that way." Miss Mary was thinking of the many stories she had heard of how Bob had worked with, and had drawn out the colored people, especially the ones who lived on his place. "I cannot imagine Bob Lawson as dead. Everything about him was so very much alive."

"Yes, ma'am, Mister Bob always knew all de goin's-on. I remember dat time when Railroad Lawson stole a hog. Mister Bob came around our way de very next mornin' and told us dat he seen in a dream de one what done de stealin'. And, when he found Railroad, he took him right down by de Ole Mill Creek where de hog was tied. I'm telling you, Mister Bob could *see* things."

"You all weren't afraid of Bob, were you?" Miss Mary asked.

"Lordy, no! You see, Mister Bob say he wasn't born with a caul, but he say he was born with a six-sense. Dat's how he found out about some more of Railroad's doin's. Railroad, he made himself a liquor still down in de swamp. Mister Bob dreamed he saw dat still, and de next morning he told Railroad exactly where it was. Railroad said, 'No sir, Mister Bob, I ain't got any still.' It wasn't a week before Railroad was down dere running off a charge when Mister Bob walked up and caught him red handed. Yes, ma'am, if Mister Bob was here, dere wouldn't be all dis huntin' around. He'd go to sleep tonight, wake up in de morning, and take de law right to de man what done de killin'."

"Have your people been trying very hard to find the killer?" Miss Martha already knew how seriously they had taken the matter, but she wanted to get Queenie's version of it.

"We all is just like a covey of scared partridges." Queenie's eyes were wide with excitement. "We know dey's somethin' awful to be scared of, but we don't know exactly what it is, and we don't know how to find it. But we all is a committee dat ain't rest night or day since Mister Bob's been killed. Yet and still we ain't for certain found de killer yet."

"Queenie, what became of that colored preacher who was holding a revival meeting down the road?"

"You mean, Miss Martha, dat divine healer?"

"Yes."

"Lordy, Ma'am, they drove dat man out of here. He had what dey call de magic touch. All us what ain't fall for him sure kept our doorstep sprinkled good with salt so if he step over dat salt he wouldn't never come back no more. We were scared he'd put a spell on us. Dey say he sure had it in for Mister Bob for sickin' de Lodge on him."

"Do you know where he went?" Miss Martha pursued.

"I don't know for certain, ma'am, but dere's somethin' about dat man I ain't told you yet."

Queenie related to the Misses Singleton all that she had heard about the preacher's conduct and how it had culminated in Bob Lawson and some of his colored friends having given him until midnight Saturday to leave the community.

As Queenie talked, the minds of the old ladies went back to the evening about two weeks before when they had gone with Dr. Evans, Bob, and Prudence to the brush arbor meeting place to hear the man. There had been so much talk among the negroes about the divine healer, pro and con, that this group wished to observe him in action in order that they might be able to form their own opinions.

On one point they were all agreed: the healer had a most remarkable magnetism. His well-proportioned body was flashily groomed in a checkered coat and white flannel trousers, an outfit that he habitually wore and that was very flattering to the mulatto. He spoke rapidly and with an enthusiasm that elicited from his followers emotional responses of exceptional fervor even for negroes. One of his tricks for getting response was to follow almost every statement by the question, always fervidly and dexterously put: "Ain't-dat-right?" It was like one word.

On this occasion he had taken "Roads" as his subject.

"Take a highway map of dese United States, and you'll see you can start from anywhere in de country and if you make de right turns you'll land up in New York. Ain't-dat-right?"

"Dat's right."

"Sure enough."

"Give us more!"

"But any way you go, you bound to have *dee*tours. Ain't-dat-right?"

"Dat's right!"

"Praise de Lord!"

"Amen, brother, amen!"

"Well, so's de road to heaven. You can start from anywhere, and if you make de right turns you'll get dere. Ain't-dat-right?"

"Sure is!"

"You're talkin', brother!"

"Bless God!"

"Glory be!!"

"And dere are always *dee*-tours on dat road too. You're bound to git off de straight and narrow path now and den. Ain't-dat-right?"

"Sure is."

"Blessed Jesus!"

"You said it, brother!"

"Praise God!"

"It seems to me that some of you are on a dee-tour now," the healer continued. "Some of you ain't given as much as you can for buildin' a college for your children. You know the Lord Jesus said to take care of children, 'for of such is the kingdom of Heaven.'"

"Oh Lordy."

"Bless my soul."

"It don't matter so much if you stray—just so you *always get right again.* Ain't-dat-right?"

The healer had struck a soul-piercing chord. Before the evening was over, the meeting had become almost pandemonium. Some were shouting; some were in trances; and some were singing "The Holy Ghost Special." The visitors quietly withdrew from the scene.

"From what we saw at the brush arbor meeting place, and what Queenie has just told us," Miss Mary said as the ladies went out onto the front porch, "I would say that the mulatto preacher must be regarded as one of the likely suspects."

"Perhaps." Miss Martha's voice implied doubt.

"I am not at all convinced in my own mind that both murders were committed by the same person. You know how these crime waves will get started. Somebody who was tired of Jake might have seized this opportunity to stop his pilfering and gossiping while attention was centered on the murder of Bob."

"Well, if we suppose that, for the sake of the argument," Miss Martha granted as the two fastidiously arranged themselves on pillowed gliders for their siesta, "the second murderer certainly had the right idea. With the exception of that blood in the fruit orchard, I don't believe there's a single clue to Jake's murderer. And unless it does turn out that there is a link-up between the two crimes, I doubt if we'll ever know who killed Jake."

"You know, I feel more and more as the negroes do; if Bob were here, he'd find out who the murderers are," Miss Mary said with a note of finality.

"Well, I go back to my original opinion; I maintain that Will Sorrel is suspect number one." Miss Martha spoke with an air of satisfaction.

"But, you know, Marty, from all our reading about such cases, the most obvious suspect is usually not the one that's guilty."

"Yes, usually—in detective fiction, Sister. But, that's not so widely true in real life. If this were a mystery story most readers would suspect every one around here—except Bob and Jake—*at one time or another* and whomever it turned out to be, they would rationalize that they suspected that person all along."

"Oh, yes," Miss Mary agreed; "if this were a detective story some readers would even suspect Prudence."

"Yes. Some of those improbable stories might end up with Prudence having done it."

XX
The Checkered Coat

Monday and Tuesday

As Taft walked away from the cemetery he felt in his pockets to make sure that the all-important documents were still there: the letter from Sheriff Satterfield to Sheriff Walters in Savannah; his own commission as a special deputy; and the two warrants for the healer, one on a charge of fraud, another—to be used only in case sufficient evidence developed—for murder.

He hurried on home, threw a few clothes into his family valise, and walked down the Old Dover Road to catch a train for Savannah, as he had often done before when he had gone on plantation business.

Taft had slept very little the night before; his nerves had been so taut with resentment and his mind so full of his prospective man hunt that he could not relax. And both Sunday and Monday had been strenuous days for him. So, finding a seat to himself, he stretched out on the plush cushion and was soon lulled to sleep by the monotonous clatter of the moving train. He did not wake until the porter touched him on the shoulder and called, "All out for Savannah!"

On previous trips to the city Taft had stayed in Yamacraw with Miss Sissy Blake, a cordial and respectable negress who kept a small rooming house. He caught the first street car to Yamacraw.

"Well, shade my eyes, if it ain't Mr. Taft himself, or is it his ghost?" Miss Sissy greeted him with outstretched hands. "Whatever brought you to Savannah on a Monday evenin'?"

"I come to look after a little business about Mr. Lawson." Taft had purposely said "about" instead of "for." He was conscientious about lying, especially in connection with a dead man. "I'm liable to take two or three days to wind up my business," Taft continued, "so I hope you have a place for me to sleep."

"Now you know, Mr. Taft, there's always room for one more." Miss Sissy smiled, her white teeth shining in the dim light. "Come right in and make yourself at home." She led him to a vacant room on the second floor.

It was evident that Miss Sissy did not know about Bob's death. Taft was relieved not to have to discuss the matter with her, for that might cause conjectures as to the purpose of his mission. After arrangements had been completed for the room, he was free to go about his business.

He went to the nearest telephone booth. It was well after dark—after nine o'clock—so, presuming that Sheriff Waters would be at home, he called his residence.

"I want to talk with Sheriff Waters, please," Taft began. "Oh, you're the sheriff? Well, I'm Taft Cooper from Cooperville. I'm down here about de murder of Mister Bob Lawson." Taft paused to listen to Sheriff Waters.

"Well, dere's a heap dat you can do for me, please, sir," Taft said in reply. "Sheriff Satterfield of Screven County has deputized me to try to catch a certain feller, and he's written you a letter askin' if you'll please, sir, help me to catch dat man if he's down here." Taft listened again.

"Oh, Sheriff Satterfield already called you up? Yes sir, I'm de man he meant. . . . Yes sir, I have de papers in my pocket. . . . You mean your office in de courthouse? Yes, sir, I'll find it all right. I'll be right over dere. Are you sure you want me to come tonight? Yes sir, I think it's important too, so I'll come right on over."

Going directly to the office of Sheriff Waters, Taft introduced himself and presented the letter and credentials that Sheriff Satterfield had sent with him. Sheriff Waters in turn authorized Taft to arrest his man, if he found him, in that county, and told him to call upon any policeman or other officer for aid if necessary. The search, however, must be conducted as quietly as possible; for if it leaked out that the healer was being sought, there were people who might try to hide the suspect.

Taft walked out of the sheriff's office with fresh hope. He had come to Savannah to find Ezra Starkes, the divine healer, and at the moment he felt it was going to be an easy thing to do. He went straight back to Yamacraw, determined first to comb the squalid, crowded slum for his prey.

Yamacraw, one of the oldest parts of Savannah, was quite the most dilapidated and least reputable. It had long been largely a negro quarter, though interspersed with poor whites and foreign elements. Its narrow streets and alleys—some paved with cobblestones, some not paved at all—were either muddy or dusty according to the weather. The old tenements of dingy clapboards or eroded brick were in various stages of disrepair. What with its poverty, overcrowding, and all manner of maladjustments, its reputation for law and order was none too good. Yet, a goodly part of its mixed population was normally law-abiding. Many of the crimes that had darkened its record had been connected in some way with transients and fugitives from justice.

For several hours, Taft walked the littered streets and alleys of Yamacraw, peering through the windows of pool rooms, dance halls, and public eating and drinking places. All along, he kept shifting his eyes among the faces in the streets. But there was no sign of the healer. He then made his way toward the Union Railroad Station. This building stood at the edge of the city, in a locality just a little removed from Yamacraw. The main body of the city's fixed population, which had to get on and off trains at this station, arrived or departed by private car or taxi. But to transients and loafers, it was a sort of social center. Taft looked about until he found a secluded seat in the waiting room and continued his vigil. Of course there was no certainty that the healer had gone to Savannah. He might possibly have stopped in some smaller place, such as Guyton or Matlow. Taft knew only that in this region, Savannah was the goal of all adventurers.

As he sat and watched people coming and going, he felt a strange consciousness that, for once in his life, he actually represented the law. He wondered just what he would do or say if he saw his man. He felt a little sick at the thought. So, he stepped across the street to Jay's Place and bought a hot dog to settle his stomach.

"Feelin' good, brother?" the waiter in charge of the stand asked in an over-friendly manner.

"Yes and no," Taft replied, longing for conversation, yet skeptical as to the wisdom of talking with a stranger.

"Are you a travelin' man?" the waiter persisted.

"I travel down here once in a while." Taft decided the man was too friendly, so, turning his eyes to the sign above the counter—JAY'S PLACE—he gulped the remainder of his sandwich and walked back into the station.

The clock in the waiting room pointed to one-thirty. The throbbing crowds of an hour or so earlier had thinned down to occasional groups. Taft sauntered in and out, around and about, with an indiffernt gait, but with a keen eye upon every passer-by. At three o'clock he decided to abandon his search for the night.

One thing Taft had never been able to do was to go to bed on an empty stomach. He disliked the idea of being quizzed by the hot dog vendor, but Jay's Place was the only stand he knew of that was open; so, he decided to buy a sandwich as if in great haste and return to his room to eat it. And that is what he would have done if he had not seen a familiar-looking checkered coat slip into a car and drive away from Jay's Place just as he started toward the stand.

"Shades of dem Red Coats!" Taft swallowed a lump in his throat. "I sure have seen a checkered coat like that plenty of times. Yet and still, it might not be the same man wearin' it."

There was not a taxi in sight; so Taft couldn't follow the car. The street light was too dim and the man vanished too quickly for his features to be distinguishable. All Taft had to go by was the checkered coat and the general appearance of the person. He thought rapidly. Then he walked calmly up to Jay's Place and sat down on a stool in front of the hot plate.

"I'm hungry enough to eat a whole cow, brother. Will you please to fry me your biggest steak?" The change in Taft's manner was quite noticeable to the waiter.

"You must have found a gold mine, brother," the waiter said in a questioning voice.

Taft looked about to be sure the two men were alone, then eased a liquor flask from his pocket and winked across the counter. "Do you think a gullup of this might tough *your* spirits up a little bit, too?"

"Well, I'm a son-of-a-gun, you sure can't tell what a body's like by the way he acts. When you first came by this evenin', you were as shut-up as a clam." The waiter was pouring generous drinks into half-filled glasses of crushed ice.

Taft sipped at his drink slowly until the steak was ready, then passed it over to the waiter to finish. The waiter became more and more talkative and Taft more and more evasive as he sat eating. Presently, Taft turned the volley of questions.

"How long have you been workin' here?" he asked.

"About a year, I reckon," the waiter answered without hesitation.

"Are you acquainted with most of de folks around here?" Taft lingered over his food as he talked.

"With all I've ever seen. I don't forget many people, once I've had a good look at 'em." The waiter leaned across the counter, his hot breath befouling the air before him, and talked into Taft's face. "If I was to meet you in the middle of the Okefenokee Swamp ten years from now I reckon I'd still be rememberin' you."

"Rememberin' folks dataways makes for good business," Taft said.

"Seems like it does help." The waiter sloshed a rag around in a pail of water, squeezed it, and wiped off the counter.

"Is your business commonly as slow as it is tonight?"

"Now that's one for you! The gentleman here just before you asked me that. I told him about this time of night they ain't many people hungry." The waiter was back in Taft's face, the wet rag oozing beside his plate.

"He a stranger here?" It was difficult for Taft to control his voice.

"You're right. He's a travelin' man. Says he travels so much and is in so many crowds that he likes a peaceable place to eat at."

"What's he travel at?"

"He takes orders for things."

"Orders for what kind of things?" Taft's blood was boiling. It was so like the man he was after to give an evasive answer.

"Now you got me. He never said—just things. He's a good-lookin' man, the kind that makes you like him from the first. He said I sure could fry a good hot dog." The waiter stood up his full height, pride running the length of his body.

"Would you be knowin' *him* ten years from now, if you were to meet him in the middle of O-ke-fen-o-kee?"

"I just told you so."

Somewhere in the distance Taft could hear the clink of milk bottles as the delivery boy made his morning rounds. But there was no one to be seen as he stood looking from Jay's Place. "Well, your place sure is peaceable enough dis time of de night. . . . But, I reckon I better be gittin' along else it might be sun-up before I get to bed."

Taft felt more confident that his guess was right—that the healer was in Savannah. If the man had been to Jay's Place once and found it to his taste, he would probably go back there again, in the dead hours of the night. Taft decided to go to his room and rest until day.

Some five hours later he made his way to the office of Sheriff Waters and reported the incidents of the night before with emphasis upon the checkered coat, its connections, and what the waiter had told about its wearer: "a travelin' man . . . takin' orders . . . orders for what? Just orders . . . a good-lookin' man—de kind dat make you like him from de first." Taft didn't mention *magnetism* or *hypnotic influence,* but he sensed the idea and somehow conveyed it.

The sheriff was impressed but not too confident. The man in the checkered coat might have been the healer; but Savannah was a big place with lots of hideouts, and it would probably be difficult to find the particular checkered coat. Of course, there was a chance that he might go back to Jay's Place. It seemed worth posting a plain clothes officer there for a night or two with a car near at hand. He would send a deputy who was good at such jobs. He would also have the night waiter at Jay's Place quietly informed of the circumstances and the reward being offered.

Taft was cautioned to avoid Jay's Place, to go to the Union Station only after dark, and then to keep in the shadows. Otherwise, he was free to continue his search as he pleased.

It was a tedious search—a lonesome search. He met very few people that he knew, and he did not feel free to talk with those whom he did not know. So completely were his interests concentrated on the one objective, that it wearied him even to think of anything else. This one interest drove him along, but he could not ignore his surroundings. He passed by eating places, their dingy walls filled with odors and noise; by laborers, singing, joking, and laughing in spite of the burning sun; by lovers, their hands happily clasped as they stepped along the cobblestones; by frolicking children, their sweaty faces encircled by swarming gnats and flies. But none of these was talking about the murder, none seemed even aware of it. That was something Taft could not understand. He had somehow pictured Savannah as being almost as much upset as Cooperville and Screven County. He had felt that all the world would be stirred by such a crime. Yet, no one he had seen in Savannah, except the sheriff and his deputies, had appeared to know or care anything about it. He failed to consider, of course, Bob's wide circle of friends in the city whom he had no opportunity to contact.

When darkness finally came, Taft eagerly made his way toward the Union Station. He intended only to say "Howdy" as he passed Jay's Place and to move on to the station. That is what he intended to do, and would have done, had not the waiter beckoned him to come in.

"Well, the travelin' man's been here again," the waiter whispered through the corner of his mouth.

"What did you say? Explain yourself!" Taft gasped.

"It's like this. As soon as I came to work this evenin' the man that the sheriff sent came in—you know what I mean," the waiter said with a wink. "Well, me and him laid out exactly what we'd do. He was to park his car a little ways from the stand so he could see me give him the high sign and so he'd be ready to follow any car that drove up in front of here for service. Then he set by to wait. He aimed to get the man here, if he could, but if he couldn't, then follow him."

"Where's de officer now?" Taft asked, seeing that there was no car parked in the block.

"Maybe out lookin' for you. Your man took us by surprise. We weren't exactly expectin' him before dark, and then not the way he came."

"He's already *been* here? You sure?"

"Sure as I am that you're here. He came up in a taxi on the other side of the street about sundown and had the driver come across and get a passel of hot dogs and doughnuts. I figured the driver was gettin' 'em for himself and ain't paid him much mind. Then I looked across and seen him handin' 'em to a fellow on the back seat. I saw right away that fellow was your man." The waiter continued to talk in hoarse whispers through one side of his mouth.

The story was interrupted while he served a customer. Ordinarily that should have taken only a minute. But, the waiter was excited and put Georgia cane syrup on the hog dog instead of mustard. But, he made it all right by washing off the hog dog, getting a fresh roll, and generously applying the mustard. The customer walked off, munching his sandwich.

"As I was saying," the waiter continued, his face close to Taft's, "I saw right away that the fellow was your man."

"Did he have on de same checkered coat?"

"I ain't particular notice the coat, but he sure had on the same face. Well, I gave the officer the high sign. But, you see we were expectin' him to drive up on this side of the street like he did last night; so our car was on the wrong side of the street and had to turn around before the officer could follow him. By that time the taxi was turnin' the corner."

"And de officer *lost* him?" Taft took a paper napkin from the counter and wiped great drops of sweat from his face.

"He lost the taxi for a while, then spotted it again and followed it about six blocks before he could get it stopped. But there wasn't a soul in the car but the driver, and the driver said his passenger got out just after he turned the corner beyond the station; said the man threw him a dollar and jumped out amongst a crowd of people. The officer drove back by here and told me what had happened and went off."

"Did de taxi driver know de man he was haulin' around?"

"Not from Adam's house cat! I sure hate it that we missed him so slick. Maybe he'll get hungry again tomorrow." The waiter was so close that the moisture from his mouth sprayed Taft's face.

Taft turned his head and coughed, then patted the waiter's shoulder. "Well, good night, brother, you done your best."

"Son of de devil." Taft gritted his teeth and muttered as he walked away. He reasoned that no good could come from hanging around the station all night. The man must have known that he was being followed and would, almost certainly, avoid that locality for a while.

But, when he talked with Sheriff Waters, Taft changed his mind. The sheriff advised him to return to his watch at the station. There was no certainty that the suspect who had visited Jay's Place was their man; there might be other men in checkered coats who had reasons to avoid pursuit. As a matter of fact the healer had no particular reason to think he was being sought; there had been no mention of him in the newspapers. As to the man who had left the taxi so hurriedly, whether he was the healer or not, he may suddenly have spied someone in the crowd whom he wanted to see, and may not have been fleeing at all.

Taft went back to the station and continued his vigil until the sky showed signs of day.

XXI
Confidences

Tuesday afternoon

"Heaven, heaven; everybody talkin' about heaven ain't goin' dere..."

Priscilla Harvey was awakened by the rhythmical strains that floated through her windows. She rubbed her eyes and sat up in bed with her arms about her knees like a child. She hadn't meant to go to sleep at all; she had gone to her room to think—to see if she *could* think to a conclusion—to any sort of satisfactory conclusion.

"I got shoes, you got shoes, all God's children got shoes..."

Priscilla got up and went to the window. In the rose garden she could see Br'er Burke alternately digging and carefully pulling out grass with his forefinger and thumb. His strong body was slowly weaving back and forth in accompaniment to his task and to the music that was born within him.

"I'm goin' to walk all over God's heaven..."

If there was a special show place at Linger-long, it was the rose garden. Prudence had designed it and consistently looked after its cultivation. Somehow roses and Prudence belonged together—when you looked at her you thought of roses, and when you looked at roses you thought of her. The same meticulous care that went into her personal grooming she extended into this plot. From its entrance, through an arch of ramblers, to the trellised arbors on its sides, it displayed only specimens that were an honor to their setting. A large square, across which ran white sand paths in the design of a Jerusalem cross, it made an attractive picture as Priscilla looked down upon it from the second floor window.

Priscilla glanced from the garden to her watch. "Ye Gods! It's almost five o'clock. How could I ever have slept like that!"

She felt ashamed that she could drop into such a sound sleep while working out a problem of such importance. Then she felt as if the walls of the room were closing in upon her. She grabbed a pale blue dress from the closet, hurried into it, and ran down the steps out onto the lawn. Her hair, uncombed, fell in soft curls about her face and down the back of her neck. Her sea-blue eyes looked wild for a moment in her dilemma.

"*Heaven . . . ahh . . . heaven . . .*" Priscilla walked in the direction of the singing.

Br'er Burke jumped at the suddenness of her approach. He was startled both that she was there at all, and that there could be anything so lovely.

"I suppose these rose bushes are afraid not to grow when you get after them, eh, Br'er Burke?" Priscilla was faintly smiling.

"Yes ma'am, Miss Harvey, I reckon dat's about de way it is," Br'er Burke answered, a line of blue gums showing above his gold-filled teeth.

"I'm going over and sit in one of your attractive arbors. I've a feeling there might be a breath of air stirring out here."

"Yes, ma'am, go right ahead, go right ahead. Miss Prudence is liable to be out here pretty soon now. Most generally she comes out dis way late every evenin'. She says dis here garden's her golf." Br'er Burke slapped his thigh and bent double with amusement.

Through side glances, he watched Priscilla as she walked across the garden. He remembered the only time he ever heard Bob Lawson mention her.

It was in the early spring. Bob and Taft had been standing in front of the garage. Br'er Burke had been mowing the lawn and just happened to stop for a minute's rest alongside them when he overheard what they were saying.

". . . And all de help say you must of got de Holy Ghost. Dey say in all de time dey's known you, you ain't never spoke to dem so pleasant," Taft had said.

"I don't know that it's the Holy Ghost as some of your folks have found it," Bob had replied, "but a new spirit has come into my life, the eternal spirit of love, love of everything and everybody."

"Mister Bob, I want to ask you dis," Taft had ventured. "Are you in love with Jesus, or are you in love with a woman?"

"Taft, your question would take a lot of explaining to answer, but briefly, it took a woman to bring about the change."

"Are you aimin' at gettin' married?" Taft had then been more concerned; he had wondered how this would affect Prudence and Lester.

"Not now, maybe never," Bob had said and added thoughtfully; "She has a man already."

"Ummm," Taft had grunted, making crosses on the ground with the toe of his shoe.

"Wonderful Priscilla," Bob had said in an undertone, looking up through the tops of the white-limbed sycamores.

Br'er Burke was brought back to the present by the cawing of a crow overhead. "Dat might have been a puzzlement to me den, but it sure ain't a puzzlement to me now . . . now that I've seen her," he mumbled as he pulled the weeds from around a Red Radiance.

"Were you saying something to me?" Prudence was standing over Br'er Burke.

He wondered how long she had been there? How on earth she got there? "No, ma'am, no, ma'am; I—I was just amusementin' for my own enjoyment," Br'er Burke said, embarrassed at being caught talking to himself.

Prudence was carrying a pail half full of water. That was as much a part of cutting roses to her as were the shears. She cut the stems very carefully, slant-wise just above a bud, and plunged them into water. She saw Priscilla coming down the path and went to meet her.

"Why, dear, I didn't know you were out here," Prudence said as they both turned back toward the arbor.

"I came out hoping for a late afternoon breeze. But when I found there was no breeze I just stayed on anyway." Priscilla wondered if Prudence could tell she was worried.

"The heat is a little trying," Prudence admitted.

It was one of those dry, hot South Georgia days—so still that you could hear a stray leaf fall. Across the stillness came echoes of Holloman's evening prayer. The sun shone raggedly through the trees, and the long, clinging sprays of moss caught up the beams and hung like a delicate, opalescent fringe about the garden.

"I had never noticed these delicate touches of color in the gray moss before," Priscilla said with a rather poor attempt to make her voice sound enthusiastic.

Prudence changed the subject. She was one of those thin-skinned people who ache in the presence of intense beauty, and she was hardly in the mood to discuss a thing so ethereal. "I'm glad that we women decided not to go to Dr. Evans's with the men this afternoon," she said. "There are times when either sex is better alone."

"Where's Irene?" Priscilla asked.

"She's on the north porch reading a volume of Mencken's *Prejudices.* I had a limeade with her just before I came out. But she's so absorbed in the book that I decided to leave her alone."

"Imagine reading such a book at a time like this!" Priscilla was off her guard. She regretted what she'd said the minute she'd said it.

Prudence made no reply.

Another dead end, Priscilla thought, looking at the moss hanging as still as stalactites above them. Starvation sauntered up and eased himself down at their feet. Priscilla turned to Prudence, and suddenly the cloak of reserve fell from her.

"There are times, Prudence," she began, "when one simply has to confide in somebody. And, frankly, there is no one that I know in whom I feel more confidence than I do in you."

"I appreciate that greatly, Priscilla."

"I want to talk to you about Allen—and Bob. As you know, Allen is suspected. I'm perfectly sure that he's innocent, but he's placed in such an ugly position.... In fact it's uglier than has yet come out."

"I feel perfectly sure that Allen could never have done such a thing," Prudence said, "and I don't think the authorities really suspect him."

"I wish I could feel that they don't. But I know from things that have come to me that they do suspect him, probably more than you realize."

"Why do you think so?" Prudence seemed surprised.

"Because of me. As you know, I was very fond of Bob. And, as I have reflected upon the matter, I have come to realize that I permitted myself to love him more than—I mean I was perhaps more open with my feelings for him than was altogether wise. When Allen decided to postpone his visit here, I came on down because I wanted to be with Bob. Allen seemed to think nothing about it at the time, but apparently suspicions began to arise after I left. That's why he quickly disposed of his business and came on down here Friday."

"But Allen—"

"Prudence, I'm going to talk to you frankly. I am of a very affectionate temperament and crave more attention than Allen has given me. I am thoroughly devoted to him and I know he is to me. But, he makes me feel that I am just a part of his business. Of course, we go places and do things together, but his business is always foremost in his thoughts. Not only has he forgotten how to have a good time, he doesn't even miss it."

"It's very easy, Priscilla, for an idle woman to misunderstand a busy man," Prudence replied thoughtfully. "I am inclined to think that the undemonstrative men are often the most sincere."

"Allen has been wonderfully good to me. Too good, I suppose. But I'm left alone so much of the time that I become restless. I must confess that is why I decided to come on down here by train when Allen let his business detain him in Atlanta. I didn't expect him until the next day. I was really surprised to see him, and I suspect he came down earlier because of Bob. He didn't like it at all when Bob and I came in from the swimming hole as we did Friday afternoon."

"I noticed that he seemed rather quiet, almost moody, that evening," Prudence said, "but I thought he was tired. Of course, I had sensed that you and Bob were fond of each other, but Bob was always so generous with his affections that I had thought little about it, and didn't know that Allen had taken it that seriously."

"He hadn't, until this visit. But, he became quite angry Friday night, and didn't conceal the fact after he and I were alone in our room.

"And, Prudence, this is the point that troubles me most." Priscilla's voice was low and troubled. "Allen made an ugly threat against Bob that night; he was very much agitated and unstrung about something. I don't know what, but I'm sure it was—was something irrelevant. However, if the officers should get onto this, it might go hard for Allen. I wouldn't tell them for anything in the world if I could help it, and yet, if they asked me, I couldn't lie."

"Oh, they'd never ask you," Prudence reassured her. "A woman can't be compelled under the law to testify against her husband."

"Not outright, I suppose, but under such circumstances as these, one doesn't always have complete self-control. I am not sure that I could conduct myself even in a casual conversation with them but that they would detect I was hiding something. And even if I couldn't be forced to talk, my concealment might weigh as heavily against Allen as if I told the whole truth. Imaginations can easily run wild in a situation like this."

"Do you think Bob knew how Allen felt about you and him?"

"No; I feel sure he did not. He had only known Allen as a good sport. Bob knew that nowadays people are not as narrow as they once were with reference to marital relations. He probably thought Allen was as tolerant in such matters as he and I."

Prudence understood what Priscilla was saying, though she didn't accept that point of view. She had often thought that Bob was too modern in his attitude toward women. She felt definitely that there was a right and wrong in this particular case and, much as she loved Bob and Priscilla, her sympathy was with Allen.

"Neither of you would have hurt Allen consciously," she said in a questioning voice.

"I don't think so. We never talked about Allen. We were so completely happy together that we let it go at that."

"Then Bob was not trying to take you away from Allen?"

"He never talked to me about that. I don't suppose everyone could understand Bob and me. Our love increased our love for others. My relationship with Bob made me more appreciative of Allen. But when I told Allen that, he felt that I was just playing up to him to keep him calm."

"It was a most perplexing situation."

"I know it was. And I tried to explain it to Allen, but he couldn't see it. But can't you see, Prudence? Haven't you felt at times that there were parts of yourself that had never had a response?"

"Yes," Prudence answered. She almost felt that she understood Priscilla.

"Then suddenly to live all those unlived parts—" Priscilla continued, "and even to live parts of which you had no consciousness before. Well, it made life wonderful. And when I knew that it was contributing to Allen, instead of taking from him, I couldn't see why all of a sudden he objected."

"I understand Allen. It's disturbing to any man to see his wife love another man."

"But I loved Bob differently from the way I loved Allen. Do try to understand me, Prudence. Allen had been satisfied with me like I was. And, being satisfied, I can't see why he should be upset if I found some new joy outside of him so long as it didn't interfere with my relationship with him. I don't feel that love can be held to any set formula. It just evolves like all life. And is just a varied. It can't be marked off in feet or yards or miles. It's boundless."

Prudence was looking down at Starvation, and Priscilla wondered what was going on in her mind.

Priscilla hesitated briefly then went on: "It seems perfectly natural to me for people to love in different ways. It was meant to be that way. Individual traits just naturally stimulate individual responses. And that makes life so much more interesting. If men were like peas in a pod they'd be very monotonous. But, I don't have to tell you, Prudence, that men are different and that some women appreciate their differences."

"I see," Prudence said in a tone admitting that Priscilla was almost convincing.

"I believe in marriage, but I don't believe that it should cut men or women off from all the other inspirations they may find," Priscilla added. "I think if husbands and wives would accept this view they'd find more joy in each other. It would nourish love, and romance wouldn't die so soon."

"Well, you may be right," Prudence acknowledged meditatively.

"Allen didn't see things that way. Of course, I know that he never thought of Bob in terms of violence. He was just talking Friday night to get it out of his system; or perhaps to impress me with the devotion he has for me. Allen is not an artist, you know; he's a practical man."

"No, Allen couldn't have—any more than you could." Prudence spoke positively. "He just isn't made that way."

"But I feel sorry for him—oh, so sorry. Think of him having to bear the embarrassment of being suspected on account of me. You simply can't imagine how miserable I am for having placed him in such a position."

"But you know, dear," Prudence consoled, "you never had any intention of hurting Allen. You shouldn't blame yourself so much."

Priscilla was biting her lips.

"I think we'd better go in now," Prudence suggested as she stood up and absently pulled off a faded rose. "The mosquitoes sometimes become rather annoying at this time of day."

When they reached the house Allen greeted them. "Oh, hello! I've been wondering where you two were."

"We've been out in Prudence's beautiful rose garden," Priscilla answered with remarkable calmness.

"Prudence, has Mr. Wormser shown up yet?" Allen asked.

"No, Allen, and I'm afraid now that he's not going to."

XXII

In Yamacraw

Wednesday morning

When Taft left the Union Railroad Station at dawn Wednesday, he went directly to his room at Miss Sissy's and went to bed. But, he could not sleep. Pictures of Mister Bob, of little incidents and experiences in their lives, kept passing through his mind like a succession of moving pictures. One particular incident that had occurred a few weeks before stood out. He could just see Mister Bob as he had told this story:

There was an awful confusion over at Railroad Lawson's house, and Bob went over to see about it. When he got there, he found Railroad going the rounds, whipping his wife and all his children.

"Railroad, what's the meaning of all this ruckus?" Bob had asked.

" 'Twixt you and me, Mister Bob, I'm just obliged to sweep out once in a while," Railroad replied with a sheepish grin.

"But what's the trouble? Why are you taking this particular morning to sweep out?"

"To get at de truth, Mister Bob, de old woman got de devil in her. She won't get up and fix my breakfast after I've been plowin' for nigh half de mornin', and I'm hungry."

"Well, Railroad," Bob said solemnly, "it looks like the devil gets in everything. I saw you trying to beat him out of the mules this morning. I tell you, *the devil's catchin'*. If he gets in one, he's liable to get in all. Sometimes he gets in the pump or the furnace or the light plant. And when we go to fix them, he sometimes gets in us. Now, Br'er Railroad, you're a good Christian, and I don't want you to let the devil get in you just because he got in the old woman."

"*De devil's catchin'*," Taft said out loud, coming back to the immediate situation. He was thinking: If that *was* the healer in the taxi, he would be using all his powers as a good-looking man who makes people like him. He would be using these powers to build up a protective following—a following that could help him to hide or furnish alibis if necessary. The man must have that "college money" with him to spend freely. Taft thought: *it's especially easy for the devil to get followers when he is flush.*

"But supposin' Sheriff Waters was right," Taft muttered to himself reluctantly; "supposin' dat man wasn't de healer. Supposin' de healer ain't in Savannah. Or supposin' dat man was him and he decide to lie low from now on and is aimin' to have all his vittles fetched to him." Taft's mind was a bewilderment of disjointed questions. He might as well not try to sleep. He could think more clearly if he were up and dressed and out in the open.

He stretched his tired body to the full length of the bed, then brought himself to a sitting position. Blended odors of coffee and bacon floated into his room. *That is one thing that Savannah has in common with Cooperville,* he thought. *Cooperville—good old Cooperville—would it ever be the same again?*

Above the mingled noises in the street Taft heard the city clock strike eight. Already Miss Sissy was up and at her morning cleaning. The broom and dustpan clicked in the hall as she swept alongside his door. He rose and began dressing.

From across the street, he could hear a woman calling to Miss Sissy to come over to her house right away, saying in a jubilant voice, "I've got somethin' *wonderful* to tell you."

Miss Sissy called back with all her good humor, "It'd take six strong horses to hold me over here." She plumped down the stairs and across the cobblestones.

Presently, the woman raised her voice excitedly, and Taft heard her say, "Oh, Sissy, I've never been so charmed; he's so *very* good-lookin' and so *manly*!"

"And where all is it you and him are goin' to?" Miss Sissy asked enthusiastically.

"Oh, everywhere—Savannah Beach, boating on the river, and—we may be gone 'til night, or—or," she said exuberantly, "we may *never* come back."

Taft strained his ears to hear more, but the woman had gone inside. "Help my soul to get right!" he said, reaching absently for his hat. "I believe dat woman is in with dat healer!"

When he came into the hall, Taft noticed the dustpan and broom sprawled where Miss Sissy had left them in the doorway of the room opposite his. The door was partly open, displaying a half-made bed. He was consciously prying when he cast his glances about the room—until suddenly his eyes popped wide, and his heart bounded to his brain as he spied a checkered coat.

"Son of de devil!" he muttered behind gritted teeth. "If dat ain't dat healer's coat I sure am powerful fooled. Umh!"

He crept stealthily to the door, eased it slowly wider, and looked about. There was no one in sight. He slipped into the room and hastily examined the coat. The pockets were empty. Then more carefully he plowed through the dresser drawers, hoping to find Bob Lawson's watch and ring. But if they were there, his search of the room did not reveal them. With taut muscles and unsteady hands Taft was trying to put a pair of trousers back on a hanger when he pricked his finger on a pin.

"Hold on! What's dis?"

Taking out the pin, he found that the cuff of the trousers had been ripped, and there, inserted in the fold were two pawn tickets.

"As easy as dat! Br'er divine healer, I'm gonna to borrow dese tickets for a few minutes, if you don't mind." Taft smiled as he tucked them into his pocket.

He had seen the name of the pawnshop many times in patrolling the streets, so he made his way directly to the place. Laying the tickets on the counter he said, "I want to redeem dese, please, sir."

When the pawnbroker produced Bob Lawson's watch and ring, Taft could hardly contain himself. When told what it would cost to redeem them, he fumbled through his pockets and managed to reply, "You're askin' a little more dan I've got in my pocket right away, but I'll see can I raise it." The broker arched his brows, shrugged his shoulders, and handed the tickets back. Leaving the pawnshop, Taft hurried to the drug store that was almost opposite Miss Sissy's, and entered a telephone booth. Through the door of the booth and a window of the store he could keep an eye on her entrance way. He called Sheriff Waters and told him what he had discovered. The sheriff promised to send a Mr. Turner, the same deputy who had chased the taxi the evening before, to help shadow the healer.

While waiting for Turner, Taft decided to step back over to Miss Sissy's. He felt that he had to know whether the healer had already returned to his room. He hurried along, mumbling to himself, "I sure can't let Miss Sissy get wind of dis. Dat healer has rubbed some powerful pains out of our women and like as not, he been workin' on her. She might help him give me de jump."

At the top of the stairs Taft found everything just as he had left it—the broom and dustpan, the door, the half-made bed, and the checkered coat. "Thank you, Jesus, for helpin' me," he murmured reverently.

Taft went back to the drug store to wait for Turner. He could hardly conceal his elation as he selected a stool that afforded a view of Miss Sissy's front door; then he ordered coffee and doughnuts. As he sipped and munched, he prayed that his helper would come quickly. He felt sure that the healer had only gone out for breakfast and would soon return to the cover of his room. But no! It was not necessary for him to return to his room before going out for the night—that is, if he were the "charming" man in question. He evidently had all his money on his person and could just as easily meet the woman somewhere else.

"A package of Luckies," said a voice at the tobacco counter. Taft rolled his eyes and breathed deeply to hold his heart in place. It was the man the sheriff had sent; Taft knew from the description. He knew too, from the man's knowing glance and slight nod, that the recognition was mutual.

"Mister Turner?" Taft asked in an undertone as soon as the clerk moved on to serve other customers.

Turner nodded. "Taft?"

"Dat's me, and I sure am glad you're here."

"You've been doin' a mighty good job accordin' to what de sheriff says, and we sure can't let dat man get away dis time."

"You're right about dat, Mr. Turner."

The two men sauntered on out, and Taft indicated Miss Sissy's house and the window of his room overlooking the street. It was agreed that Taft would go back into the rooming house while Turner watched along the street. And as soon as the healer returned to his room, Taft would signal from his window.

Back in his room Taft walked over to the window and surveyed the surroundings below. There was Turner, seated in the front of the drug store, sipping a Coca-Cola and apparently browsing over a copy of the *Savannah Morning News*. No sign of the healer.

Taft paced the floor, talking to himself. "Suposin' dat healer ain't comin' back here today. Supposin' he ain't never comin' back—goin' to meet dat woman somewhere else.... No! He might leave dat checkered coat, but he ain't goin' to leave dem pawn tickets. Yet and still, he might have come in while I was at de pawnshop and found out dem tickets were gone and decided to skip on out while de skippin' was good."

He pulled a chair over by the window and sat watching the street below as he listened for footsteps in the hall. Shrieks of laughter bounded up to him. A group of children had come into the street and were playing tag. He remembered how he and Bob Lawson had loved to play that game when they were small boys. Only their game was different, for they had such wide places in which to run that sometimes it would be hours before he was caught. Once Bob had chased him off and on all day before he had caught him. An involuntary smile passed over Taft's face as he thought of that particular chase.

He would never be able to think of Bob Lawson as dead. They had been too much alive together. Always, he would feel, in spite of the fact that he knew it could never be, that Bob would suddenly, just naturally be around Cooperville again. And even though Taft knew there would always be the disappointment of not having him really turn up, it seemed better to him to feel that way.

A black cloud was rising. Taft could see it and feel the wind from it as it blew the flimsy curtains against his face. A zigzag streak of lightening shot across the sky. He momentarily covered his eyes. But, through his eyelids and heavy hand, he could feel the lightning repeat itself, and soon to the accompaniment of thunder. The children forgot their game of tag and began playing in the huge drops of rain that heralded the shower. Taft remembered how he and Bob as small boys had dared each other to run out into the rain until they were wet to the skin. It was the first time it had rained since that fatal night.

There were steps on the stairs—masculine steps and bold ones. Just another roomer perhaps, for the healer would hardly feel that safe anywhere, Taft thought as he slipped over and peeped through his slightly opened door.

"Son of de devil!" Taft's heart was pounding all over his body and his muscles were taut as iron girders as he watched the healer stamp through the hall, enter his room, and slam the door.

Turner had seen the man go into Miss Sissy's and was already walking in that direction and was watching for Taft when he gave the signal.

A moment later, when the men burst into the healer's room, they found that he had piled into bed with his clothes on and was feigning sleep.

"Is dat your man?" Turner asked.

"Dat's him all right," Taft answered, then loosed his wrath against the presumptive murderer: *"You nasty, low-down devil!* You—!"

"What—?" The healer sprang up, but his courage wilted when he recognized Taft.

"You hell-fired killer!" Taft shouted, his eyes glowering through the man. "We're arrestin' you now in the name of de law for de murder of Mister Bob Lawson! And, you're goin' to hang by your neck until you are dead; den you're goin' to go to Hell where you belong. You—"

"Hold on, brother, no use losin' your temper," the healer said as he crawled out of bed. "You can't do dis to me! I ain't killed Mister Bob! I swear to God I ain't!"

As the healer moved nearer, Taft placed himself against the door, drew his gun, and continued: "You says you ain't done it; maybe you ain't, but one thing sure, you're goin' to have to tell it to de court."

Turner stepped forward and took a pair of handcuffs from his pocket. "Easy, Taft," he said. "We'll have to take him in. He's got a lot of explaining to do."

"But I ain't killed Mister Bob," the healer protested again as Mr. Turner closed the handcuffs on him.

"See dese pawn tickets what I got out of your britches?" Taft waved the tickets in the healer's face. "Dem's for Mister Bob's jewelry. Now what you—?"

"Wa-ait a minute, brother!" The healer was struggling with his handcuffs. "Dat don't prove nothin'; I got dem tickets from a white man; them tickets don't prove I killed Mister Bob; dem tickets are perfectly legitimate; and—and—what's more, you ain't got no right to come into my room."

"I ain't, eh?" Taft used his free hand to draw from his pocket his warrants and his commission as a deputy and shook them in the face of the man. "See dese papers? Dey's your doom, Mister Divine healer; dey's your doom!"

"Come on, Taft," Mr. Turner urged. "We've got to get this man down to the police station."

XXIII
"A Pretty Kettle of Fish"

Wednesday afternoon

Coopervile had spent a restless night. Wormser had undoubtedly disappeared. Since he had first arrived at Linger-long, he had been driving around, apparently out of pure appreciation of "God's Country." When he had not shown up by the time of the stag conference at Dr. Evans's on Tuesday afternoon, the men began wondering where he was. But, everyone hoped that he would turn up that night; for he had casually driven away in his car late Monday, leaving everything in his room in perfect order.

But Wormser had not returned Tuesday night. Or Wednesday morning. The officers had decided that all his driving around had been a cover-up for his actual get-away. They had concluded that the situation demanded more outside aid, and had sent out a search order for him through state and federal authorities.

In the mid-afternoon the doctor had come onto his front veranda and was watching every car that approached on the Louisville Road. He was expecting Colonel Livingston, who had called from Sylvania to say that he was coming out with some news that he preferred not to discuss over the telephone.

Strolling alone in the grove at Linger-long, Priscilla had noticed the doctor sitting on his porch and had decided to pay him an informal call. She had become a great admirer of the old gentleman. She was attracted by his penetrating mind, his unaffected gentility, his unselfish devotion to his community; and she was more than a little amused by his occasional absent-mindedness. As she walked toward his house she was hoping that she might be able to draw him out on the all-important question as to the possible identity of the criminal. She was praying that he might absently drop some hints as to whether he seriously suspected Allen.

The doctor received her with his usual cordiality—perhaps more than usual, for no man could fail to be attracted by Priscilla's feminine charm.

"You know, Dr. Evans, this is my first experience in a truly rural community in the plantation area," she said.

"And you, a native Georgian!"

"Well, I've lived in Atlanta all my life and my vacations have been spent at resorts. But you know resorts—they're usually set in an artificial atmosphere and filled with a lot of city people who are trying to kill time. It's so refreshing to be here where everything seems natural and easygoing."

"Such sentiments, Mrs. Harvey, had much to do with Bob's coming back here to live."

"The more I see of this place the better I understand why he came back. The people I have met here seem so wholesome—so unhurried and friendly."

"Cooperville has long prided itself on those characteristics."

Priscilla wanted to ask Dr. Evans what new light there was on the tragedy, but was afraid this question would be too pointed. Instead she remarked, "By the way, where is Taft? I haven't seen him around for several days."

"Why," Dr. Evans paused to think of an evasive reply, "he's probably off looking after some of Bob's affairs."

"I've wondered and wondered and wondered who on Earth could have wanted to kill Bob," Priscilla said in sincerity and yet, with the hope that her concern might lead Dr. Evans to throw some light on the matter.

"These murders are most perplexing to all of us, Mrs. Harvey. In my long experience as coroner this is the most baffling case I have ever encountered. We have gathered a lot of evidence; or, rather traces of evidence, but in no instance have we found the linchpin. Colonel Livingston is on his way out here now with what he says is very important news."

"I thought murders had been unknown in these parts," Priscilla said.

"Oh, we have held that as a tradition in this particular community. But, you see, my jurisdiction covers the entire county. Even so, murder cases are rather uncommon. And yet I have served on some pretty difficult ones in my time, but I have never known one in which there were so many suspects and so much inconclusive evidence."

"Whoever did this, I can't believe it could have been anyone of Bob's circle of friends." Priscilla was so intent that she was not aware that Colonel Livingston had driven up and was on his way into the house before Dr. Evans framed a reply.

"Glad to see you, John. Come in." The doctor rose and clasped the Colonel's hand cordially.

"I see you are in charming company, Doctor. How do you do, Mrs. Harvey?"

"It's the other way around, Colonel Livingston; *I* am the one who is in charming company," Priscilla countered and gracefully excused herself.

As soon as she was out of hearing, the Colonel said abruptly: "Taft and a deputy from Savannah got in about an hour ago with Ezra Starkes, the healer. He has confessed to the robbery, but not to the murder of Bob or the boy. His story seems plausible, but I'm not at all sure that it's true."

"Good old Taft!" The doctor's face was radiant. "I knew Taft would get him!"

"The healer admits that Bob had met with Sheriff Satterfield about the trouble the healer and his healing methods were causing. He also admits that Bob had told him that the sheriff would have him charged with practicing medicine without a license if he caused any more trouble. The Lodge had set Saturday midnight as the deadline for him to get out of the community. He says that he intended to catch the Saturday evening train for Savannah but that Lucindy Fawls persuaded him to stay over Saturday night. She kept him hidden out until time to catch the early train Sunday morning. On his way to the station, according to his story, he took a short cut across the old Lawson grounds, keeping as well hidden as possible. Suddenly, he came across Bob's body. His eyes were caught by the glitter of the diamond in the early morning sunlight and he said to himself Mister Bob wasn't going to need that ring any more. It was the case of 'finders keepers,' so he took the ring. And then, he took the wallet and wrist watch too. The watch was still running and he saw that he had time to make it three more miles down to the Cameron Station, and he thought that would be safer than going to Dover, so he went down there and caught the train for Savannah. He swears that is what he did."

"You know I have thought from the first, John, that it is possible that the robbery might not have been committed by the murderer. So the healer's story may be true."

"Yes, Doctor; it *may* be, and *may* not."

"Well, how did Taft ever run him down?"

"By using plain common sense and his knowledge of human nature." The Colonel explained Taft's strategy, then returned to the story of the healer.

"The man claims that he didn't sleep Sunday night for fear of being robbed. But, by Monday, he had became so tired that he pawned the jewelry and went to Miss Sissy's and got a room. Then he folded the pawn tickets and pinned them in one of the cuffs of his trousers, thinking nobody would ever think about looking there for anything. The money he wrapped in a handkerchief and attached to the inside of his underwear which he wore night and day.... At least we know the last part of his story is true."

"Oh, well," said the Doctor, "he'd have to make those points fit with the known facts."

"Certainly. We'll have to see if we can check on whether he really went to Savannah Sunday morning and was there Sunday night. If he was, he could not have murdered Jake. And it's practically certain that whoever murdered Jake murdered Bob."

"Yes, practically certain. But there is still a bare possibility that the two crimes may have been unrelated."

"A bare one, Doctor, but extremely bare."

Colonel Livingston was staring at the bamboo hedge that bordered Dr. Evans's yard. "There's someone trying to eavesdrop on us, Doctor. See there—peeping through that hedge."

Dr. Evans turned and saw who it was. "Come on around, Mom Liza," he called in a mollifying voice.

As the old woman approached the veranda the doctor asked, "Is there anything I can do for you?"

"Dere was; dat is, dere is; but I'm willin' to wait, seein' as how you're busy."

"Aren't you feeling well, Mom Liza?"

"'Tain't dat, Doctor. It's something dat's wearin' on my mind."

"About yourself?"

"No sir, Doctor. It's about Mister Bob."

"You wouldn't mind talking before Colonel Livingston, would you?"

"No sir, I reckon it's about as much his business as yours."

She came up and sprawled her large frame on the steps. "Doctor, when you asked me dem questions at dat inquest, I wasn't tellin' all I knew. I never lied, because I didn't stir 'round none dat night. But I did see one of dem white men goin' from de ol' place."

"Do you know who it was?"

"Yes sir, but I wasn't goin' to say nothin' about it, because I ain't wantin' to get mixed up with dese white folks, but de Lodge brothers have been pesterin' de very life out of me. Dey're after almost everybody. Dey's been tormentin' Chunky, and poor Chunky don't know nothin'. Dey say dat we all are obliged to tell all we know."

Mom Liza paused and seemed in a great mental struggle, but the men did not press her. Presently she continued: "Well, with dat thunderin' and lightnin' and all I was awakened. When dat storm busted, I got up to shut my window, because it was blowin' in. Den after de storm passed, I got up again and opened de window. About dat time de lightnin' flashed across de sky and I saw a man walkin' fast like nearly runnin' close up behind dat hedge what runs up by Mister Bob's garage."

"Do you mean on the back side of the hedge—the side toward your house?"

"Yes sir."

"Did you see him clearly?"

"Yes sir, you remember it was lightin' fast dat night. Dat first flash when I saw him wasn't hardly passed before dey was more lightin', so I saw him good and plain."

Colonel Livingston was becoming anxious. "Mom Liza," he said, "you know it's your duty under the law and before God to tell us who that man was."

"Yes, sir; dat's what I know. And dat's what's been eatin' on me."

"Now, Mom Liza," Dr. Evans coaxed, "you know that you can trust us, and if you tell us who this man was, we'll see that no harm comes to you from what you say. Won't we, Colonel Livingston?"

"We certainly will. You can rest easy about that, Mom Liza."

She drew her long legs up and hugged her knees in deliberation. "Gentlemen, it was de one dey call Mister Allen."

Colonel Livingston sprang to his feet. "Good for you, Mom Liza." He patted her on the back and gave her a package of chewing gum.

The old woman was as pleased as a child. She unwrapped a stick and carefully refolded the tin foil wrapping, stuck it back in place, and walked away mumbling, "Save all things, save all things."

Dr. Evans went to the telephone and called Linger-long and asked that Allen come over at once.

"It seems that the Lodge is on the job," he said as he returned to the veranda.

"Yes," the Colonel replied, his expression carrying the weight of the world. "But here's another poser for you. Wormser's not the only one that's skipped out; Sorrel's gone too."

"Surely not," exclaimed Dr. Evans. "I knew the man was undependable and indiscreet, but I didn't think he'd be so foolish as to do that. Are you sure that he has left the court's jurisdiction?"

"Yes," the Colonel was positive. "He's probably headed for the Okefenokee Swamp. I had thought a good deal about the way he lied to us, so I decided to drive by his house on my way out here. I found one of his brats in his yard; and when I questioned the youngster about his father, he naively spilled the beans.

"It seems that Will took the first southbound train after we left him yesterday. I asked the boy where he had gone. He said, 'I don't know. I reckon he's went down to Uncle Hezzie's.' Mrs. Sorrel then appeared in the doorway. She had evidently heard what the boy had said and tried to lie out of it. She contradicted herself worse than Will had, then, finally confessed that he was gone, but claimed that she had no idea where."

"That's a pretty kettle of fish!" Dr. Evans was pulling at his Vandyke. "Let me see . . . Hezzie Sorrel . . . He lives in Charlton County. We should call up the authorities there right away."

"We'd better get in touch with all the swamp counties, for Hezzie will try to hide Will out no telling where."

They rang Sheriff Satterfield and had him put in the calls. Returning to the veranda, they were beginning to discuss the bearing that this new move of Sorrel's might have on the case when Allen came up, his reddish face redder than usual.

Confronted with the fact that he had been seen coming from the old Lawson grounds about the time of Bob's murder, he had an explanation ready.

"I do not deny having gone over there from the garage as soon as the storm was over that night," he said. "I wanted to talk with Bob privately about an important matter. I knew that he was to be over there about that time and had decided that might be my best chance.

"I found him there, but he had been murdered already. In fact, I almost stumbled over his body."

"Mr. Harvey, will you tell us what this important matter you wanted to talk with Bob about was?" Colonel Livingston asked.

"Do I *have* to tell you that?"

"We cannot force you to tell it now," the Colonel said, "but it seems far wiser that you lay all your cards on the table. We'll never mention what you say if it doesn't become necessary. But, I must warn you, that whatever you say may be used as evidence against you if it does become necessary."

After a moment's hesitation, Allen said: "I consider that a gentleman's agreement. I had decided to have it out with Bob about Mrs. Harvey."

"Just what do you mean by 'have it out'?" the Colonel questioned.

"Perhaps that was an unfortunate way to put it. I certainly did not mean to imply any more than a frank face-to-face talk. Bob and I were the best of friends, but I disliked the embarrassment and annoyance of her enthusiasm for Bob and his ideas. I meant to talk with him as dispassionately as I could about the matter and request him as a friend to be more discreet in the future."

"Mr. Harvey, why had you not told us this before?" Dr. Evans inquired.

"Because I knew that I had not killed Bob Lawson, and I knew that if this unfortunate move of mine became known, it would lend weight to the unjust suspicion already existing against me."

"Thank you, Mr. Harvey. John, have you any further questions you would like to ask?"

"Not now, Doctor."

When Allen had gone, Colonel Livingston said, "At least we're sure of a few things: The healer committed the robbery; he may have committed the murder and he may not. Sorrel and Wormser have skipped out. And Harvey's in one hell of a mess. I'm going to Sylvania now, and Joe and I are going to put that healer on the grill for proper. He's very emotional and he may break down. Then too, I have hopes we may soon get hold of Wormser or Sorrel—or both. As to Harvey, I'm not quite sure whether we should really turn the heat on him; I want to consider that further."

XXIV
Confessions

Wednesday night

Late in the evening of the same day a tense group was seated in the living room at Linger-long—Prudence, Lester, the guests, the doctor, the Colonel, the sheriff, and Taft. Priscilla sat close to Allen. Sheriff Satterfield, his six-shooter protruding from its holster, sat next to Colonel Livingston and seemed to be eyeing all the others at once. Wormser, whom the officers had brought in with them, sat next to the sheriff.

Only three or four of those present knew exactly why the meeting had been arranged. Among the others there was much speculation. Were they now to learn the full truth about the murders? Or were they to be put through another inquisition? They knew that the healer had been caught, but had he confessed? Had Sorrel been found, and had he confessed? Or was it Hendrix? Or was one of their own number ready to confess? Or was one of them to be put on the spot, confronted with new and damning evidence? If so, who would it be and what would be his—or her—reaction? Here was Wormser again. Why had he run away, and how had he been rounded up so quickly?

Colonel Livingston cleared his throat and fumbled with his watch chain, as if wondering how to begin. There was a moment of tense silence.

"Mr. Wormser," Colonel Livingston's steely eyes were inscrutably directed at him and Wormser's eyes were equally inscrutable, "I believe you have a confession to make."

"Yes." There was no shadow of change in Wormser's impassive expression. "I've realized all along that my presence here has been something of a mystery. Mr. Lawson and I have kept it that way purposely. Mr. Lawson knew me well enough, had known me for years.. The only one present who knew me before I came here is Mr. Tyler. He and I had come to know each other rather casually through Mr. Lawson. I learned that he and Mrs. Tyler were coming down here at the same time I was last week; so I invited them to come in my car. That's the first time I had seen Mrs. Tyler. So far as I am aware, they knew nothing of my affairs, or why I was invited here. Perhaps you do not know, although I told the authorities on Monday morning, that I am a social psychologist. I also deal in statistical analyses; I'm an actuary."

"What in God's name is all that?" the sheriff groaned.

"Well, Mr. Lawson called it 'ground work,'" Wormser explained patiently. "I studied the territory that Georgia Life covered—its wealth, health, education, unexplored possibilities, and so on. He and I worked on approaches suitable to each agent's field. Perhaps you would be interested to know that Mr. Lawson planned to establish insurance seminars for his agents, instructing them in such social, psychological and statistical background as I have mentioned, and acquainting them with their relationship to insurance at large."

"Bob and his ideas!" Colonel Livingston said.

Gordon took his handkerchief and wiped his brow.

"As you can readily see," Wormser continued, "I have observed all classes. I have even spent hours listening to trials of criminal cases, occasionally doing a little sleuthing myself just from natural interest, and, of course, looking into company affairs.

"But, to get on with the story. When I came down here, I was to mix a little business with pleasure. Mr. Lawson and I had always agreed to keep my connection with the business between us two. On this trip I was to observe reactions to Georgia Life, but mostly I was to enjoy 'God's Country'. Of course, Mr. Lawson couldn't have had the least notion that anything violent was about to occur. Then this horrible thing happened. Since I was already employed by Mr. Lawson, even though I was handicapped by not having a private investigator's license, I naturally felt a responsibility in the investigation.

"The discovery of Mr. Lawson's death on Sunday completely bewildered me. There seemed to be no clues that pointed with any certainty to any particular person. And all the tangled mass of circumstantial evidence only made the case more confusing. What seemed to be the most promising lead on Sunday pointed toward the healer, and Taft undertook to follow that up. I overheard most of his conversation with Prudence on Sunday, and knew that he was the man for that particular job. And you all probably know by now how well he lived up to the confidence placed in him."

"We certainly do," Colonel Livingston said. "Taft," he called.

"Yes sir, Colonel Livingston." Taft stood tall near the door opening into the living room. His expression was a blending of pride and modesty.

"We're mighty proud of you, Taft. No one could have done a better job than you did. Ezra Starkes is still in custody, and it was Taft who found him," the Colonel commended.

"Thank you, Colonel, thank you, sir." Taft bowed several times as all those present cheered.

"Then it must have been Ezra Starkes who did it," Allen volunteered.

Colonel Livingston nodded to Wormser, who continued his account: "Well, it was Starkes who committed the robbery. But, he wasn't the murderer."

"Do you mean we're still looking for the murderer?" Allen asked.

"Let me finish my explanation," Wormser cautioned. "From evidence that I discovered on Monday, I became pretty well convinced that, while the healer might have been the robber, he was not the killer.

"It was in the second killing the criminal made his fatal blunder. If it hadn't been for this, the mystery of Mr. Lawson's death might have gone unsolved. I had taken sweepings, of course, from Mr. Lawson's body, but I hadn't found anything that seemed of consequence when I examined them."

"How on Earth," Lester inquired dubiously, "did you get a chance to gather such stuff from Uncle Bob without it being known?"

"Well, the fact is that I discovered Mr. Lawson's body and had examined it just a little while before Taft found it. I didn't report the killing right away because I wanted to look the place over well first. Then, Taft found the body before I got a chance.

"Later, when I discovered Jake's body and examined it closely, I found some evidence that required further investigation. I observed on his clothes tiny particles of fiber which evidently came from the coarse baggings known as tow sacks; also, I noted short strands of reddish brown animal hair clinging to Jake's skin.

"These particles in themselves might have been of little or no assistance, but you all remember there was no blood on the grass where Jake lay. That meant that he had been killed elsewhere and brought here. So, I was led to hope that sweepings from his body might yield telltale evidence. I took the animal hair and some of the fibers, and I wiped onto my handkerchief from Jake's hands some sticky substance which I couldn't identify. On examining these under my small microscope I found other particles that pointed toward clues that might be conclusive. For example, there was something which looked like pollen, but I wasn't sure.

"On Monday morning I made up my mind to go to Washington and take such evidence as I had gathered for a more thorough examination in the Department of Justice. But, I wanted to write some letters and gather some further information before leaving. I'll tell you more about that later. Anyway, on Monday afternoon, I drove down to Savannah and took a train to Washington. I had requested permission of the authorities Monday morning to do this, but they asked me to wait until they could investigate other leads. I understood their fear of turning me loose, but I realized I had no way of proving my sincerity." Wormser turned to Dr. Evans and Colonel Livingston: "Your reasoning was logical, gentlemen.

"Under laboratory tests, the sweepings that I had gathered from Bob on Sunday revealed nothing of importance; but those found on Jake revealed much. The hair proved to be that of an ox; at least it had come from a bovine, which was used as a draft animal. Under a powerful microscope some strands that were quite short showed that they had been worn down by the scrubbing back and forth of a collar or yoke. I had suspected this when I had examined the hair here on Monday, but I couldn't be certain whether it had come from a horse, a mule, or an ox. What I had taken to be pollen turned out to be pollen from the tobacco plant. And the substance from Jake's hands was tobacco gum."

"Holloman!" The name sprang from Priscilla involuntarily.

"Exactly, Mrs. Harvey. And it was he whom I came to suspect after I had examined the sweepings as best I could here on Monday morning. From the shade of color and the texture I thought the hair was that of an ox. I had heard it said that Holloman was the only person for miles around that worked an ox. Then, when I found this pollen with which I wasn't familiar—I don't know much about plants—I was reminded that the one exotic plant that I had heard of in this locality was the tobacco that Holloman grew for his own use, and it could have come from that."

"Oh-h!" Priscilla clenched her fists and sighed in agony, "I just now remember! The very morning I came here I heard Mr. Holloman's loud voice as we were going to Sylvania. Bob told me he was preaching to a snake in his well. I should have known then that the man was crazy and might be dangerous."

"Woman's hindsight," Lester whispered audibly.

"Not necessarily dangerous," Mr. Wormser said to Priscilla. "Such people are generally thought of as merely queer or cranky, but harmless. Though my suspicion of him wasn't positive, I was pretty sure by Monday that he was our man. From his peculiarities, I had already thought of him from the first as a possible suspect. It was my opinion that he was a victim of a mild case of dementia praecox of the paranoid variety. This is a mental illness that is unpredictable. People with this illness may never harm anyone; on the other hand they may sometimes suddenly go haywire, and with some real or fancied provocation become dangerous criminals. In such cases they may even turn violently upon their own loved ones or most valued friends.

"So on Monday morning I paid Holloman a visit, pretending to be an agent taking orders for a new edition of the Bible. I had found such a book in Bob's library. When offered one of these—you know how it is—almost anyone will take it and thumb through it, if only to look at the pictures. Though Holloman insisted that he didn't need another Bible, he did take the book in his hands and thumb through the pages. I went away with good specimens of his fingerprints. I came back to my room here; and, since I am accustomed to developing fingerprints of the employees of Georgia Life, I brought these prints out and made photographic copies of them.

"Then, before I left here on Monday, I wrote letters to every insane asylum in the bright tobacco belt. I described Holloman carefully, enclosed copies of the fingerprints, and inquired whether such a person had ever been known in that institution, and if so what type of insanity he had been diagnosed as having. I asked for a reply only in case such identification could be made. I sent all the letters special delivery, and requested an immediate reply to be sent to Dover, general delivery.

"This afternoon, when I got to Sylvania, I tried to get in touch with Colonel Livingston, but he wasn't in at the time. Then, I went to Sheriff Satterfield, showed him what I had discovered, and asked him to go with me to Holloman's place. The sheriff and I drove first to Dover to get such mail as might be there for me. I found a letter postmarked Raleigh, North Carolina. It was from the insane asylum there.

"Here it is!" Wormser drew a letter form his pocket. "I'll read it to you: 'The man identified by your description and fingerprints escaped from here fifteen years ago. The diagnosis of him indicated a mild case of dementia praecox. He had never shown any signs of violence and was the sort who might never have been dangerous. Yet, because there is always some risk of allowing his kind to run at large, we were holding him pending further developments. He was highly intolerant of any sort of confinement and that, no doubt, is why he escaped from here. We were never able to trace him although we kept his file open for years.

"'Your letter is the first we have heard of him since. We feel that he should be returned here for re-evaluation. Please hold him until we can send a guard to bring him back here. Thank you for your help.'

"After reading this, Mr. Satterfield and I went straight to Holloman's house. Confronted with the evidence, he denied both killings. He insisted someone was 'out to get him,' as such men normally do. We had enough evidence to take him in for questioning. The sheriff handcuffed him, and we dragged him, still protesting his innocence, to my car.

"On the way to jail we pumped a disconnected story out of him.

"Jake Martin had tormented the life out of the man—stealing his fruit and tobacco. Early Saturday morning, before the tragedy, Holloman had caught the boy stripping leaves from his tobacco plants. He had driven him off angrily, warning him never to come back. I was out for my morning walk and heard the confrontation. About all I could make out was Jake's voice saying, 'You act like you own the world, but Bob Lawson's back here now, and you'll see who's boss.' I asked Bob about this on the way to Savannah later that morning. Bob told me that the Lawsons and the Coopers had founded Cooperville. 'I guess that adds respect to the Lawson name,' Bob had said, 'but I doubt that I have any special influence.'

"However, Holloman must have taken Jake's words seriously. Here he had lived freely in God's great out-of-doors for all these years and had molested no one. Ever since Mr. Lawson had come back here to live, Holloman had been afraid that some of the many people he kept bringing here might identify him. He had grown more and more paranoid. He said he felt like they all were watching him. And now, he was afraid Bob Lawson, himself, would take away his liberty and have him shut up in an asylum.

" 'I was afraid this was going to happen,' he kept saying over and over again.

"Sheriff Satterfield grew impatient and asked him, 'Where the heck were you Saturday?'

"He said that after his encounter with Jake on Saturday, he spent part of the day wandering about his house 'in a fuddlement,' as he put it. The idea of confinement haunted him until he was unable to think of anything else. He couldn't bear being cooped up, even in his own house. He had to get out. He had to get out where it was wide. So, he gathered his fishing tackle as best he could, and went down to the river. Even fishing in his favorite spot, he felt he was being watched; so, he wandered along the river bank looking for a better place. Finally he settled down to fish again. He was afraid to go home. He had visions of Bob Lawson and some of the men from Atlanta waiting there to get him. At sundown, he cleaned some fish and cooked them over an open fire in a small iron skillet he carried with his fishing supplies. He ate by moonlight and then lay back to rest; looking up at the sky. He couldn't remember how long he stayed there; but when he saw the clouds begin to rise, he gathered the rest of his catch and headed for home. It was a long walk; and he said he had a feeling he was being followed, probably a symptom of his illness. He began to run. The thunderstorm began about the time he approached the old Lawson yard. He claims he ran across the yard and on over to his shack."

"So Holloman was at the old Lawson place when Bob was murdered," Allen broke in.

"Exactly, Mr. Harvey," Wormser confirmed. "Holloman still insists he did not kill Bob Lawson, but the evidence is conclusive.

"Now, about Jake, maybe Jake knew who killed Bob Lawson, and maybe he didn't. However, Holloman heard Jake had said that he knew who killed Bob Lawson. That made it necessary to silence Jake. He caught Jake and slit his throat."

"Jake must have been running from him and stumbled and fell," Dr. Evans confirmed. "The autopsy showed that his knees and elbows were freshly skinned."

"No doubt, Dr. Evans," Wormser continued. "Then, from some peculiar urge—perhaps to return to the scene of his first crime, perhaps to mislead the officers—the man arranged to take Jake to the same spot where Mr. Lawson had lain the night before. The boy was small for his age, so he just stuck him in tow sacks, packed in enough corn shucks to round out the bundle, and after dark he took the grim burden on his ox to the place under the Ghoat Oak. There, he removed the bag and packing and left the body where we found it. It was the shreds of evidence left on Jake's body when it was moved that confirmed to me that Holloman was our man.

"After we got him to the jail in Sylvania, we were able to reach Colonel Livingston, and he came right over. We confronted Holloman with the evidence that he had killed Jake. In spite of all the evidence, he still denied killing him. Then I read him the letter from the asylum in North Carolina. Holloman's face grew red and angry. 'They'll never shut me up again,' he protested. 'I ain't killed nobody.' He lashed out at Sheriff Satterfield with his free hand and became so violent that we had to lock him up.

"'Jail is too good for you,' Satterfield said as he dragged Holloman to a cell and locked him up.

"With Holloman locked up, we decided to go search his shack. We still had not found the murder weapon. In his fishing tackle box we found a sharp knife. It had been cleaned, but we found traces of blood in the crevices where the blade joins the wooden handle. That clinched his guilt."

Dr. Evans spoke up. "When we talked to Holloman on Sunday he seemed so calm and reasonable. Even on Tuesday when he came to me, he seemed like he was trying to be helpful. It's hard to believe a man like that, so peaceful and inoffensive for all these years—"

"Incredible as it seems, Dr. Evans, as I explained before, that's just the way a man of his mental type may act," Wormser replied. "As a matter of fact, Holloman still claims he didn't kill anyone. But, we have the letter attesting to his insanity, and the evidence is unmistakable."

Colonel Livingston had never once taken his eyes off Wormser from the time he began his story; and as he spoke now one could not be sure whether he was talking to himself, the group, or Mr. Wormser: "I see now. But I never would have thought it. Somehow we have all taken Holloman so completely for granted. He has always seemed so self-contained and so harmless." The Colonel stared pensively for a moment. "I'm wondering as to his psychology in trying to sic us onto Will Sorrel?"

"I asked him about that," the sheriff volunteered. "He said he did hear a mule, or a horse, gallopin' by his place just as he got to his house that night. He allowed it might of been Sorrel. I kind of suspected it was Sorrel. And I think Sorrel must have known what had happened before he left the old Lawson place that night."

The telephone rang. It was for Colonel Livingston.... "Poor fellow, he's better off!" the group heard him say. He returned presently to the room and announced: "Holloman's dead!"

"Dead?"

"Yes—poor fellow! He couldn't bear the confinement. He managed to conceal a knife from his supper things, sharpened it on the masonry of his cell, and slashed his own throat."

There was a momentary silence in the group. Then, they began moving around, talking to each other and congratulating Wormser, Colonel Livingston, Sheriff Satterfield, Dr. Evans, and Taft. One by one they later left the room.

Alone in his room after all the congratulations, Wormser locked the door and took a sealed envelope from his breast pocket. He opened it and counted the ten one-thousand dollar bills that Gordon Tyler had given him to kill Bob Lawson.